# A LOST LEADER

## E. PHILLIPS OPPENHEIM

1st WORLD
LIBRARY
Literary Society

# A Lost Leader

## E. Phillips Oppenheim

© 1st World Library, 2007
PO Box 2211
Fairfield, IA 52556
www.1stworldlibrary.com
First Edition

LCCN: 2007927786

Softcover ISBN: 978-1-4218-4520-3
Hardcover ISBN: 978-1-4218-4436-7
eBook ISBN: 978-1-4218-4604-0

Purchase *"A Lost Leader"*
as a traditional bound book at:
www.1stWorldLibrary.com/purchase.asp?ISBN=978-1-4218-4520-3

1st World Library is a literary, educational organization
dedicated to:

- Creating a free internet library of downloadable ebooks

- Hosting writing competitions and offering book publishing
scholarships.

Interested in more 1st World Library books? contact:
literacy@1stworldlibrary.com
Check us out at: www.1stworldlibrary.com

# 1ˢᵗ World Library Literary Society

## Giving Back to the World

"If you want to work on the core problem, it's early school literacy."

**- James Barksdale, former CEO of Netscape**

"No skill is more crucial to the future of a child, or to a democratic and prosperous society, than literacy."

**- Los Angeles Times**

"Literacy... means far more than learning how to read and write... The aim is to transmit... knowledge and promote social participation."

**- UNESCO**

"Literacy is not a luxury, it is a right and a responsibility. If our world is to meet the challenges of the twenty-first century we must harness the energy and creativity of all our citizens."

**- President Bill Clinton**

"Parents should be encouraged to read to their children, and teachers should be equipped with all available techniques for teaching literacy, so the varying needs and capacities of individual kids can be taken into account."

**- Hugh Mackay**

# CONTENTS

## BOOK III

## BOOK IV

# BOOK I

## CHAPTER I

### RECONSTRUCTION

The two men stood upon the top of a bank bordering the rough road which led to the sea. They were listening to the lark, which had risen fluttering from their feet a moment or so ago, and was circling now above their heads. Mannering, with a quiet smile, pointed upwards.

"There, my friend!" he exclaimed. "You can listen now to arguments more eloquent than any which I could ever frame. That little creature is singing the true, uncorrupted song of life. He sings of the sunshine, the buoyant air; the pure and simple joy of existence is beating in his little heart. The things which lie behind the hills will never sadden him. His kingdom is here, and he is content."

Borrowdean's smile was a little cynical. He was essentially of that order of men who are dwellers in cities, and even the sting of the salt breeze blowing across the marshes—marshes riven everywhere with long arms of the sea—could bring no colour to his pale cheeks.

"Your little bird—a lark, I think you called it," he  remarked, "may be a very eloquent prophet for the whole kingdom of his species, but the song of life for a bird and that for a man are surely different things!"

"Not so very different after all," Mannering answered, still watching the bird. "The longer one lives, the more clearly one recognizes the absolute universality of life."

Borrowdean shrugged his shoulders, with a little gesture of impatience. He had left London at a moment when he could ill be spared, and had not travelled to this out-of-the-way corner of the kingdom to exchange purposeless platitudes with a man whose present attitude towards life at any rate he heartily despised. He seated himself upon a half-broken rail, and lit a cigarette.

"Mannering," he said, "I did not come here to simper cheap philosophies with you like a couple of schoolgirls. I have a real live errand. I want to speak to you of great things."

Mannering moved a little uneasily. He had a very shrewd idea as to the nature of that errand.

"Of great things," he repeated slowly. "Are you in earnest, Borrowdean?"

"Why not?"

"Because," Mannering continued, "I have left the world of great things, as you and I used to regard them, very far behind. I am glad to see you here, of course, but I cannot think of any serious subject which it would be useful or profitable for us to discuss. You understand me, Borrowdean, I am sure!"

Borrowdean closely eyed this man who once had been

his friend.

"The old sore still rankles, then, Mannering," he said. "Has time done nothing to heal it?"

Mannering laughed easily.

"How can you think me such a child?" he exclaimed. "If Rochester himself were to come to see me he would be as welcome as you are. In fact," he continued, more seriously, "if you could only realize, my friend, how peaceful and happy life here may be, amongst the quiet places, you would believe me at once when I assure you that I can feel nothing but gratitude towards those people and those circumstances which impelled me to seek it."

"What should you think, then," Borrowdean asked, watching his friend through half-closed eyes, "of those who sought to drag you from it?"

Mannering's laugh was as free and natural as the wind itself. He had bared his head, and had turned directly seawards.

"Hatred, my dear Borrowdean," he declared, "if I thought that they had a single chance of success. As it is— indifference."

Borrowdean's eyebrows were raised. He held his cigarette between his fingers, and looked at it for several moments.

"Yet I am here," he said slowly, "for no other purpose."

Mannering turned and faced his friend.

"All I can say is that I am sorry to hear it," he declared. "I know the sort of man you are, Borrowdean, and I know very well that if you have come down here with something to say to me you will say it. Therefore go on. Let us have it over."

Borrowdean stood up. His tone acquired a new earnestness. He became at once more of a man. The cynical curve of his lips had vanished.

"We are on the eve of great opportunities, Mannering," he said. "Six months ago the result of the next General Election seemed assured. We appeared to be as far off any chance of office as a political party could be. To-day the whole thing is changed. We are on the eve of a general reconstruction. It is our one great chance of this generation. I come to you as a patriot. Rochester asks you to forget."

Mannering held up his hand.

"Stop one moment, Borrowdean," he said. "I want you to understand this once and for all. I have no grievance against Rochester. The old wound, if it ever amounted to that, is healed. If Rochester were here at this moment I would take his hand cheerfully. But—"

"Ah! There is a but, then," Borrowdean interrupted.

"There is a but," Mannering assented. "You may find it hard to understand, but here is the truth. I have lost all taste for public life. The whole thing is rotten, Borrowdean, rotten from beginning to end. I have had enough of it to last me all my days. Party policy must come before principle. A man's individuality, his whole character, is assailed and suborned on every side. There is but one life, one measure of days, that you or I know anything of. It doesn't last very long. The months and years have a knack of slipping away emptily enough unless we are always standing to attention. Therefore I think that it becomes our duty to consider very carefully, almost religiously, how best to use them. Come here for a moment, Borrowdean. I want to show you something."

The two men stood side by side upon the grassy bank, Mannering broad-shouldered and vigorous, his clean, hard-cut features tanned with wind and sun, his eyes bright and vigorous with health; Leslie Borrowdean, once his greatest friend, a man of almost similar physique, but with the bent frame and listless pallor of a dweller in the crowded places of life. Without enthusiasm his tired eyes followed the sweep of Mannering's arm.

"You see those yellow sandhills beyond the marshes there? Behind them is the sea. Do you catch that breath of wind? Take off your hat, man, and get it into your lungs. It comes from the North Sea, salt and fresh and sweet. I think that it is the purest thing on earth. You can walk here for miles and miles in the open, and the wind is like God's own music. Borrowdean, I am going to say things to you which one says but once or twice in his life. I came to this country a soured man, cynical, a pessimist, a materialist by training and environment. To-day I speak of a God with bowed head, for I believe that somewhere behind all these beautiful things their prototype must exist. Don't think I've turned ranter. I've never spoken like this to any one else before, and I don't suppose I ever shall again. Here is Nature, man, the greatest force on earth, the mother, the mistress, beneficent, wonderful! You are a creature of cities. Stay with me here for a day or two, and the joy of all these things will steal into your blood. You, too, will know what peace is."

Borrowdean, as though unconsciously, straightened himself. If no colour came to his cheeks, the light of battle was at least in his eyes. This man was speaking heresies. The words sprang to his lips.

"Peace!" he exclaimed, scornfully. "Peace is for the dead. The last reward perhaps of a breaking heart. The life effective, militant, is the only possible existence for men. Pull yourself together, Mannering, for Heaven's sake. Yours is the *faineant* spirit of the decadent, masquerading in the garb of a sham primitivism. Were you born into the world, do you think, to loiter through life an idle worshipper at the altar of beauty? Who are you to dare to skulk in the quiet places, whilst the battle of life is fought by others?"

Another lark had risen almost from their feet, and, circling its way upwards, was breaking into song. And below, the full spring tide was filling the pools and creeks with the softly flowing, glimmering sea-water. The fishing boats, high and dry an hour ago, were passing now seaward along the silvery way. All these things Mannering was watching with rapt eyes, even whilst he listened to his companion.

"Dear friend," he said, "the world can get on very well without me, and I have no need of the world. The battle that you speak of—well, I have been in the fray, as you know. The memory of it is still a nightmare to me."

Borrowdean had the appearance of a man who sought to put a restraint upon his words. He was silent for a moment, and then he spoke very deliberately.

"Mannering," he said, "do not think me wholly unsympathetic. There is a side of me which sympathises deeply with every word which you have said. And there is another which forces me to remind you again, and again, that we men were never born to linger in the lotos lands of the world. You do not stand for yourself alone. You exist as a unit of humanity. Think of your responsibilities. You have found for yourself a beautiful corner of the world. That is all very well for you, but how about the rest? How about the millions who are chained to the cities that they may earn their living pittance, whose wives and children fill the churchyards, the echoes of whose weary, never-ceasing cry must reach you even here? They are the people, the sufferers, fellow-links with you in the chain of humanity. You may stand aloof as you will, but you can never cut yourself wholly away from the great family of your fellows. You may hide from your responsibilities, but the burden of them will lie heavy upon your conscience, the poison will penetrate sometimes into your most jealously guarded paradise. We are of the people's party, you and I, Mannering, and I tell you that the tocsin has sounded. We need you!"

A shadow had fallen upon Mannering's face. Borrowdean was in earnest, and his appeal was scarcely one to be treated lightly. Nevertheless, Mannering showed no sign of faltering, though his tone was certainly graver.

"Leslie," he said, "you speak like a prophet, but believe me, my mind is made up. I have taken root here. Such work as I can do from my study is, as it always has been, at your service. But I myself have finished with actual political life. Don't press me too hard. I must seem churlish and ungrateful, but if I listened to you for hours the result would be the same. I have finished with actual political life."

Borrowdean shrugged his shoulders despairingly. Such a man was hard to deal with.

"Mannering," he protested, "you must not, you really must not, send me away like this. You speak of your written work. Don't think that I underestimate it because I have not alluded to it before. I myself honestly believe that it was those wonderful articles of yours in the *Nineteenth Century* which brought back to a reasonable frame of mind thousands who were half led away by the glamour of this new campaign.

You kindled the torch, my friend, and you must bear it to victory. You bring me to my last resource. If you will not serve under Rochester, come back—and Rochester will serve under you when the time comes."

Mannering shook his head slowly.

"I wish I could convince you," he said, "once and for all, that my refusal springs from no such reasons as you seem to imagine. I would sooner sit here, with a volume of Pater or Meredith, and this west wind blowing in my face, than I would hear myself acclaimed Prime Minister of England. Let us abandon this discussion once and for all, Borrowdean. We have arrived at a cul-de-sac, and I have spoken my last word."

Borrowdean threw his half-finished cigarette into the ever-widening creek below. It was characteristic of the man that his face showed no sign of disappointment. Only for several moments he kept silence.

"Come," Mannering said at last. "Let us make our way back to the house. If you are resolved to get back to town to-night, we ought to be thinking about luncheon."

"Thank you," Borrowdean said. "I must return."

They started to walk inland, but they had taken only a few steps when they both, as though by a common impulse, stopped. An unfamiliar sound had broken in upon the deep silence of this quiet land. Borrowdean, who was a few paces ahead, pointed to the bend in the road below, and turned towards his companion with a little gesture of cynical amusement.

"Behold," he exclaimed, "the invasion of modernity. Even

your time-forgotten paradise, Mannering, has its civilizations, then. What an anachronism!"

With a cloud of dust behind, and with the sun flashing upon its polished metal parts, a motor car swung into sight, and came rushing towards them. Borrowdean, always a keen observer of trifles, noticed the change in Mannering's face.

"It is a neighbour of mine," he remarked. "She is on her way to the golf links."

"Golf links!" Borrowdean exclaimed.

Mannering nodded.

"Behind the sandhills there," he remarked.

There was a grinding of brakes. The car came to a standstill below. A woman, who sat alone in the back seat, raised her veil and looked upwards.

"Am I late?" she asked. "Clara has gone on—they told me!"

She had addressed Mannering, but her eyes seemed suddenly drawn to Borrowdean. As though dazzled by the sun, she dropped her veil. Borrowdean was standing as though turned to stone, perfectly rigid and motionless. His face was like a still, white mask.

"I am so sorry," Mannering said, "but I have had a most unexpected visit from an old friend. May I introduce Sir Leslie Borrowdean—Mrs. Handsell!"

The lady in the car bent her head, and Borrowdean performed an automatic salute. Mannering continued:

"I am afraid that I must throw myself upon your mercy! Sir Leslie insists upon returning this afternoon, and I am taking him back for an early luncheon. You will find Clara and Lindsay at the golf club. May we have our foursome to-morrow?"

"Certainly! I will not keep you for a moment. I must hurry now, or the tide will be over the road."

She motioned the driver to proceed, but Borrowdean interposed.

"Mannering," he said, "I am afraid that the poison of your lotos land is beginning to work already. May I stay until to-morrow and walk round with you whilst you play your foursome? I should enjoy it immensely."

Mannering looked at his friend for a moment in amazement. Then he laughed heartily.

"By all means!" he answered. "Our foursome stands, then, Mrs. Handsell. This way, Borrowdean!"

The two men turned once more seaward, walking in single file along the top of the grassy bank. The woman in the car inclined her head, and motioned the driver to proceed.

# CHAPTER II

## THE WOMAN WITH AN ALIAS

Borrowdean seemed after all to take but little interest in the game. He walked generally, some distance away from the players, on the top of the low bank of sandhills which fringed the sea. He was one of those men whom solitude never wearies, a weaver of carefully thought-out schemes, no single detail of which was ever left to chance or impulse. Such moments as these were valuable to him. He bared his head to the breeze, stopped to listen to the larks, watched the sea-gulls float low over the lapping waters, without paying the slightest attention to any one of them. The instinctive cunning which never deserted him led him without any conscious effort to assume a pleasure in these things which, as a matter of fact, he found entirely meaningless. It led him, too, to choose a retired spot for those periods of intensely close observation to which he every now and then subjected his host and the woman who was now his partner in the game. What he saw entirely satisfied him. Yet the way was scarcely clear.

They caught him up near one of the greens, and he stood with his hands behind him, and his eyeglass securely fixed, gravely watching them approach and put for the hole. To him the whole performance seemed absolutely idiotic, but he showed no sign of anything save a mild and genial interest. Clara, Mannering's niece, who was immensely impressed with him, lingered behind.

"Don't you really care for any games at all, Sir Leslie?" she asked.

He shook his head.

"I know that you think me a barbarian," he remarked, smiling.

"On the contrary," she declared, "that is probably what you think us. I suppose they are really a waste of time when one has other things to do! Only down here, you see, there is nothing else to do."

He looked at her thoughtfully. He had never yet in his life spoken half a dozen words with man, woman or child without wondering whether they might not somehow or other contribute towards his scheme of life. Clara Mannering was pretty, and no doubt foolish. She lived alone with her uncle, and possibly had some influence over him. It was certainly worth while.

"I do not know you nearly well enough, Miss Mannering," he said, smiling, "to tell you what I really think. But I can assure you that you don't seem a barbarian to me at all."

She was suddenly grave. It was her turn to play a stroke. She examined the ball, carefully selected a club from her bag, and with a long, easy swing sent it flying towards the hole.

"Wonderful!" he murmured.

She looked up at him and laughed.

"Tell me what you are thinking," she insisted.

"That if I played golf," he answered, "I should like to be able to play like that."

"But you must have played games sometimes," she insisted.

"When I was at Eton—" he murmured.

Mannering looked back, smiling.

"He was in the Eton Eleven, Clara, and stroked his boat at college. Don't you believe all he tells you."

"I shall not believe another word," she declared.

"I hope you don't mean it," he protested, "or I must remain dumb."

"You want to go off and tramp along the ridges by yourself," she declared. "Confess!"

"On the contrary," he answered, "I should like to carry that bag for you and hand out the—er—implements."

She unslung it at once from her shoulder.

"You have rushed upon your fate," she said. "Now let me fasten it for you."

"Is there any remuneration?" he inquired, anxiously.

"You mercenary person! Stand still now, I am going to play. Well, what do you expect?"

"I am not acquainted with the usual charges," he answered,

"but to judge from the weight of the clubs—"

"Give me them back, then," she cried.

"Nothing," he declared, firmly, "would induce me to relinquish them. I will leave the matter of remuneration entirely in your hands. I am convinced that you have a generous disposition."

"The usual charge," she remarked, "is tenpence, and twopence for lunch."

"I will take it in kind!" he said.

She laughed gaily.

"Give me a mashie, please."

He peered into the bag.

"Which of these clubs now," he asked, "rejoices in that weird name?"

She helped herself, and played her shot.

"I couldn't think," she said, firmly, "of paying the full price to a caddie who doesn't know what a mashie is."

"I will be thankful," he murmured, "for whatever you may give me—even if it should be that carnation you are wearing."

She shook her head.

"It is worth more than tenpence," she said.

"Perhaps by extra diligence," he suggested, "I might deserve a little extra. By the bye, why does your partner, Mr. Lindsay, isn't it, walk by himself all the time?"

"He probably thinks," she answered, demurely, "that I am too familiar with my caddie."

"You will understand," he said, earnestly, "that if my behaviour is not strictly correct it is entirely owing to ignorance. I have no idea as to the exact position a caddie should take up."

"What a pity you are going away so soon," she said. "I might have given you lessons."

"Don't tempt me," he begged. "I can assure you that without me the constitution of this country would collapse within a week."

She looked at him—properly awed.

"What a wonderful person you are!"

"I am glad," he said, meekly, "that you are beginning to appreciate me."

"As a caddie," she remarked, "you are not, I must confess, wholly perfect. For instance, your attention should be entirely devoted to the person whose clubs you are carrying, instead of which you talk to me and watch Mrs. Handsell."

He was almost taken aback. For a pretty girl she was really not so much of a fool as he had thought her.

"I deny it *in toto*!" he declared.

"Ah, but I know you," she answered. "You are a politician, and you would deny anything. Don't you think her very handsome?"

Borrowdean gravely considered the matter, which was in itself a somewhat humorous thing. Slim and erect, with a long, graceful neck, and a carriage of the head which some-how suggested the environment of a court, Mrs. Handsell was distinctly, even from a distance, a pleasant person to look upon. He nodded approvingly.

"Yes, she is good-looking," he admitted. "Is she a neighbour of yours?"

"She has taken a house within a hundred yards of ours," Clara Mannering answered. "We all think that she is delightful."

"Is she a widow?" Borrowdean asked.

"I imagine so," she answered. "I have never heard her speak of her husband. She has beautiful dresses and things. I should think she must be very rich. Stand quite still, please. I must take great pains over this stroke."

A wild shot from Clara's partner a few minutes later resulted in a scattering of the little party, searching for the ball. For the first time Borrowdean found himself near Mrs. Handsell.

"I must have a few words with you before I go back," he said, nonchalantly.

"Say that you would like to try my motor car," she answered. "What do you want here?"

"I came to see Mannering."

E. Phillips Oppenheim

"Poor Mannering!"

"It would be," he remarked, smoothly, "a mistake to quarrel."

They separated, and immediately afterwards the ball was found. A little later on the round was finished. Clara attributed her success to the excellence of her caddie. Mrs. Handsell deplored a headache, which had put her off her putting. Lindsay, who was in a bad temper, declined an invitation to lunch, and rode off on his bicycle. The rest of the little party gathered round the motor car, and Borrowdean asked preposterous questions about the gears and the speeds.

"If you are really interested," Mrs. Handsell said, languidly, "I will take you home. I have only room for one, unfortunately, with all these clubs and things."

"I should be delighted," Borrowdean answered, "but perhaps Miss Mannering—"

"Clara will look after me," Mannering interrupted, smiling. "Try to make an enthusiast of him, Mrs. Handsell. He needs a hobby badly."

They started off. She leaned back in her seat and pulled her veil down.

"Do not talk to me here," she said. "We shall have a quarter of an hour before they can arrive."

Borrowdean assented silently. He was glad of the respite, for he wanted to think. A few minutes' swift rush through the air, and the car pulled up before a queer, old-fashioned dwelling house in the middle of the village. A smart maid-servant came hurrying out to assist her mistress. Borrowdean was ushered into a long, low drawing-room, with open windows leading out on to a trim lawn. Beyond was a walled garden bordering the churchyard.

Mrs. Handsell came back almost immediately. Borrowdean, turning his head as she entered, found himself studying her with a new curiosity. Yes, she was a beautiful woman. She had lost nothing. Her complexion—a little tanned, perhaps—was as fresh and soft as a girl's, her smile as delightfully full of humour as ever. Not a speck of grey in her black hair, not a shadow of embarrassment. A wonderful woman!

"The one thing which we have no time to do is to stand and look at one another," she declared. "However, since you have tried to stare me out of countenance, what do you find?"

"I find you unchanged," he answered, gravely.

"Naturally! I have found a panacea for all the woes of life. Now what do you want down here?"

"Mannering!"

"Of course. But you won't get him. He declares that he has finished with politics, and I never knew a man so thoroughly in earnest."

Borrowdean smiled.

"No man has ever finished with politics!"

"A platitude," she declared. "As for Mannering, well, for the first few weeks I felt about him as I suppose you do now. I know him better now, and I have changed my mind. He is unique, absolutely unique! Do you think that I could have existed here for nearly two months without him?"

E. Phillips Oppenheim

"May I inquire," Borrowdean asked, blandly, "how much longer you intend to exist here with him?"

She shrugged her shoulders.

"All my days—perhaps! He and this place together are an anchorage. Look at me! Am I not a different woman? I know you too well, my dear Leslie, to attempt your conversion, but I can assure you that I am—very nearly in earnest!"

"You interest me amazingly," he remarked, smiling. "May I ask, does Mannering know you as Mrs. Handsell only?"

"Of course!"

"This," he continued, "is not the Garden of Eden. I may be the first, but others will come who will surely recognize you."

"I must risk it," she answered.

Borrowdean swung his eyeglass backwards and forwards. All the time he was thinking intensely.

"How long have you been here?" he asked.

"Very nearly two months," she answered. "Imagine it!"

"Quite long enough for your little idyll," he said. "Come, you know what the end of it must be. We need Mannering! Help us!"

"Not I," she answered, coolly. "You must do without him for the present."

"You are our natural ally," he protested. "We need your help now. You know very well that with a slip of the tongue I could change the whole situation."

"Somehow," she said, "I do not think that you are likely to make that slip."

"Why not?" he protested. "I begin to understand Mannering's firmness now. You are one of the ropes which hold him to this petty life—to this philandering amongst the flower-pots. You are one of the ropes I want to cut. Why not, indeed? I think that I could do it."

"Do you want a bribe?"

"I want Mannering."

"So do I!"

"He can belong to you none the less for belonging to us politically."

"Possibly! But I prefer him here. As a recluse he is adorable. I do not want him to go through the mill."

"You don't understand his importance to us," Borrowdean declared. "This is really no light affair. Rochester and Mellors both believe in him. There is no limit to what he might not ask."

"He has told me a dozen times," she said, "that he never means to sit in Parliament again."

"There is no reason why he should not change his mind," Borrowdean answered. "Between us, I think that we could induce him."

"Perhaps," she answered. "Only I do not mean to try."

"I wish I could make you understand," he said impatiently, "that I am in deadly earnest."

"You threaten?"

"Don't call it that."

"Very well, then," she declared, "I will tell him the truth myself."

"That," he answered, "is all that I should dare to ask. He would come to us to-morrow."

"You used not to underrate me," she murmured, with a glance towards the mirror.

"There is no other man like Mannering," he said. "He abhors any form of deceit. He would forgive a murderer, but never a liar."

"My dear Leslie," she said, "as a friend—and a relative—"

"Neither counts," he interrupted. "I am a politician."

She sat quite still, looking away from him. The peaceful noises from the village street found their way into the room. A few cows were making their leisurely mid-day journey towards the pasturage, a baker's cart came rattling round the corner. The west wind was rustling in the elms, bending the shrubs upon the lawn almost to the ground. She watched them idly, already a little shrivelled and tarnished with their endless struggle for life.

"I do not wish to be melodramatic," she said, slowly, "but you are forcing me into a corner. You know that I am rich. You know the people with whom I have influence. I want to purchase Lawrence Mannering's immunity from your schemes. Can you name no price which I could pay? You and I know one another fairly well. You are an egoist, pure and simple. Politics are nothing to you save a personal affair. You play the game of life in the first person singular. Let me pay his quittance."

Borrowdean regarded her thoughtfully.

"You are a strange woman," he said. "In a few months' time, when you are back in the thick of it all, you will be as anxious to have him there as we are. You will not be able to understand how you could ever have wished differently. This is rank sentiment, you know, which you have been talking. Mannering here is a wasted power. His life is an unnatural one."

"He is happy," she objected.

"How do you know? Will he be as happy, I wonder, when you have gone, when there is no longer a Mrs. Handsell? I think not! You are one of the first to whom I should have looked for help in this matter. You owe it to us. We have a right to demand it. For myself personally I have no life now outside the life political. I am tired of being in opposition. I want to hold office. One mounts the ladder very slowly. I see my way in a few months to going up two rungs at a time. We want Mannering. We must have him. Don't force me to make that slip of the tongue."

The sound of a gong came through the open window. She rose to her feet.

E. Phillips Oppenheim

"We are keeping them waiting for luncheon," she remarked. "I will think over what you have said."

# CHAPTER III

## WANTED—A POLITICIAN

Sir Leslie carefully closed the iron gate behind him, and looked around.

"But where," he asked, "are the roses?"

Clara laughed outright.

"You may be a great politician, Sir Leslie," she declared, "but you are no gardener. Roses don't bloom out of doors in May—not in these parts at any rate."

"I understand," he assented, humbly. "This is where the roses will be."

She nodded.

"That wall, you see," she explained, "keeps off the north winds, and the chestnut grove the east. There is sun here all the day long. You should come to Blakely in two months' time, Sir Leslie. Everything is so different then."

He sighed.

E. Phillips Oppenheim

"You forget, my dear child," he murmured, "that you are speaking to a slave."

"A slave!" she repeated. "How absurd! You are a Cabinet Minister, are you not, Sir Leslie?"

He shrugged his shoulders.

"I was once," he answered, "until an ungrateful country grew weary of the monotony of perfect government and installed our opponents in our places. Just now we are in opposition."

"In opposition," she repeated, a little vaguely.

"Meaning," he explained, "that we get all the fun, no responsibility, and, alas, no pay."

"How fascinating," she exclaimed. "Do sit down here, and tell me all about it. But I forgot. You are not used to sitting down out of doors. Perhaps you will catch cold."

Sir Leslie smiled.

"I am inclined to run the risk," he said gravely, "if you will share it. Seriously, though, these rustic seats are rather a delusion, aren't they, from the point of view of comfort?"

"There shall be cushions," she declared, "for the next time you come."

He sighed.

"Ah, the next time! I dare not look forward to it. So you are interested in politics, Miss Mannering?"

"Well, I believe I am," she answered, a little doubtfully. "To tell you the truth, Sir Leslie, I am shockingly ignorant. You must live in London to be a politician, mustn't you?"

"It is necessary," he assented, "to spend some part of your time there, if you want to come into touch with the real thing."

"Then I am very interested in politics," she declared. "Please go on."

He shook his head.

"I would rather you talked to me about the roses. You should ask your uncle to tell you all about politics. He knows far more than I do."

"More than you! But you have been a Cabinet Minister!" she exclaimed.

"So was your uncle once," he answered. "So he could be again whenever he chose."

She looked at him incredulously.

"You don't really mean that, Sir Leslie?"

"Indeed I do!" he asserted. "There was never a man within my recollection or knowledge who in so short a time made for himself a position so brilliant as your uncle. There is no man to-day whose written word carries so much weight with the people."

She sighed a little doubtfully.

"Then if that is so," she said, "I cannot imagine why we live down here, hundreds of miles away from everywhere. Why did he give it up? Why is he not in Parliament now?"

"It is to ask him that question, Miss Mannering," Borrowdean said, "that I am here. No wonder it seems surprising to you. It is surprising to all of us."

She looked at him eagerly.

"You mean, then, that you—that his party want him to go back?" she asked.

"Assuredly!"

"You have told him this?"

"Of course! It was my mission!"

"Sir Leslie, you must tell me what he said."

Borrowdean sighed.

"My dear young lady," he said, "it is rather a painful subject with me just now. Yet since you insist, I will tell you. Something has come over your uncle which I do not understand. His party—no, it is his country that needs him. He prefers to stay here, and watch his roses blossom."

"It is wicked of him!" she declared, energetically.

"It is inexplicable," he agreed. "Yet I have used every argument which can well be urged."

"Oh, you must think of others," she begged. "If you knew how weary one gets of this place—a man, too, like my uncle! How can he be content? The monotony here is enough to drive even a dull person like myself mad. To choose such a life, actually to choose it, is insanity!"

Borrowdean raised his head. He had heard the click of the garden gate.

"They are coming," he said. "I wish you would talk to your uncle like this."

"I only wish," she answered, passionately, "that I could make him feel as I do."

They entered the garden, Mannering, bareheaded, following his guest. Borrowdean watched them closely as they approached. The woman's expression was purely negative. There was nothing to be learned from the languid smile with which she recognized their presence. Upon Mannering, however, the cloud seemed already to have fallen. His eyebrows were set in a frown. He had the appearance of a man in some manner perplexed. He carried two telegrams, which he handed over to Borrowdean.

"A boy on a bicycle," he remarked, "is waiting for answers. Two telegrams at once is a thing wholly unheard of here, Borrowdean. You really ought not to have disturbed our postal service to such an extent."

Borrowdean smiled as he tore them open.

"I think," he said, "that I can guess their contents. Yes, I thought so. Can you send me to the station, Mannering?"

"I can—if it is necessary," Mannering answered. "Must you really go?"

Borrowdean nodded.

E. Phillips Oppenheim

"I must be in the House to-night," he said, a little wearily. "Rochester is going for them again."

"You didn't take a pair?" Mannering asked.

"It isn't altogether that," Borrowdean answered, "though Heaven knows we can't spare a single vote just now. Rochester wants me to speak. We are a used-up lot, and no mistake. We want new blood, Mannering!"

"I trust that the next election," Mannering said, "may supply you with it. Will you walk round to the stables with me? I must order a cart for you."

"I shall be glad to," Borrowdean answered.

They walked side by side through the chestnut grove. Borrowdean laid his hand upon his friend's arm.

"Mannering," he said, slowly, "am I to take it that you have spoken your last word? I am to write my mission down a failure?"

"A failure without doubt, so far as regards its immediate object," Mannering assented. "For the rest, it has been very pleasant to see you again, and I only wish that you could spare us a few more days."

Borrowdean shook his head.

"We are better apart just now, Mannering," he said, "for I tell you frankly that I do not understand your present attitude towards life—your entire absence of all sense of moral responsibility. Are you indeed willing to be written down in history as a philanderer in great things, to loiter in your flower gardens, whilst other men fight the battle of life for you and your fellows? Persist in your refusal to help us, if you will, Mannering, but before I go you shall at least hear the truth."

Mannering smiled.

"Be precise, my dear friend. I shall hear your view of the truth!"

"I do not accept the correction," Borrowdean answered, quickly. "There are times when a man can make no mistake, and this is one of them. You shall hear the truth from me this afternoon, and when your days here have been spun out to their limit—your days of sybaritic idleness—you shall hear it again, only it will be too late. You are fighting against Nature, Mannering. You were born to rule, to be master over men. You have that nameless gift of genius—power—the gift of swaying the minds and hearts of your fellow men. Once you accepted your destiny. Your feet were firmly planted upon the great ladder. You could have climbed—where you would."

A curious quietness seemed to have crept over Mannering. When he answered, his voice seemed to rise scarcely above a whisper.

"My friend," he said, "it was not worth while!"

Borrowdean was almost angry.

"Not worth while," he repeated, contemptuously. "Is it worth while, then, to play golf, to linger in your flower gardens, to become a dilettante student, to dream away your days in the idleness of a purely enervating culture? What is it that I heard you yourself say once—that life apart from one's fellows must always lack robustness. You have the instincts of the creator, Mannering. You cannot stifle them. Some day the cry of the world to its own children will find its echo in your heart, and it may be too late. For sooner or later, my friend, the place of all men on earth is filled."

For a moment that somewhat cynical restraint which seemed to divest of enthusiasm Borrowdean's most earnest words, and which militated somewhat against his reputation as a public speaker, seemed to have fallen from him. Mannering, recognizing it, answered him gravely enough, though with no less decision.

"If you are right, Borrowdean," he said, "the suffering will be mine. Come, your time is short now. Perhaps you had better make your adieux to my niece and Mrs. Handsell."

They all came out into the drive to see him start. A curious change had come over the bright spring day. A grey sea-fog had drifted inland, the sunlight was obscured, the larks were silent. Borrowdean shivered a little as he turned up his coat-collar.

"So Nature has her little caprices, even—in paradise!" he remarked.

"It will blow over in an hour," Mannering said. "A breath of wind, and the whole thing is gone."

Borrowdean's farewells were of the briefest. He made no further allusion to the object of his visit. He departed as one who had been paying an afternoon call more or less agreeable. Clara waved her hand until he was out of sight, then she turned somewhat abruptly round and entered the house. Mannering and Mrs. Handsell remained for a few moments in the avenue, looking along the road. The sound of the horse's feet could still be heard, but the trap itself was long since invisible.

"The passing of your friend," she remarked, quietly, "is almost allegorical. He has gone into the land of ghosts—or are we the ghosts, I wonder, who loiter here?"

Mannering answered her without a touch of levity. He, too, was unusually serious.

"We have the better part," he said. "Yet Borrowdean is one of those men who know very well how to play upon the heartstrings. A human being is like a musical instrument to him. He knows how to find out the harmonies or strike the discords."

She turned away.

"I am superstitious," she murmured, with a little shiver. "I suppose that it is this ghostly mist, and the silence which has come with it. Yet I wish that your friend had stayed away from Blakely!"

* * * * *

Upstairs from her window Clara also was gazing along the road where Borrowdean had disappeared. And Borrowdean himself was puzzling over a third telegram which Mannering had carelessly passed on to him with his own, and which, although it was clearly addressed to Mannering, he had, after a few minutes' hesitation, opened. It had been handed in at the Strand Post-office.

"I must see you this week.—Blanche."

A few hours later, on his arrival in London, Borrowdean repeated this message to Mannering from the same post-office, and quietly tearing up the original went down to the House.

"I cannot tell," he reported to his chief, "whether we have succeeded or not. In a fortnight or less we shall know."

# CHAPTER IV

## THE DUCHESS ASKS A QUESTION

Clara stepped through the high French window, and with skirts a little raised crossed the lawn. Lindsay, who was following her, stopped to light a cigarette.

"We're getting frightfully modern," she remarked, turning and waiting for him. "Mrs. Handsell and I ought to have come out here, and you and uncle ought to have stayed and yawned at one another over the dinner-table."

"You have an excellent preceptress—in modernity," he remarked. "May I?"

"If you mean smoke, of course you may," she answered. "But you may not say or think horrid things about my best friend. She's a dear, wonderful woman, and I'm sure uncle has not been like the same man since she came."

"I'm glad you appreciate that," he answered. "Do you honestly think he's any the better for it?"

"I think he's immensely improved," she answered. "He doesn't grub about by himself nearly so much, and he's had his hair cut. I'm sure he looks years younger."

"Do you think that he seems quite as contented?"

"Contented!" she repeated, scornfully. "That's just like you, Richard. He hasn't any right to be contented. No one has. It is the one absolutely fatal state."

He stretched himself out upon, the seat, and frowned.

"You're picking up some strange ideas, Clara," he remarked.

"Well, if I am, that's better than being contented to all eternity with the old ones," she replied. "Mrs. Handsell is doing us all no end of good. She makes us think! We all ought to think, Richard."

"What on earth for?"

"You are really hopeless," she murmured. "So bucolic—"

"Thanks," he interrupted. "I seem to recognize the inspiration. I hate that woman."

"My dear Richard!" she exclaimed.

"Well, I do!" he persisted. "When she first came she was all right. That fellow Borrowdean seems to have done all the mischief."

"Poor Sir Leslie!" she exclaimed, demurely. "I thought him so delightful."

"Obviously," he replied. "I didn't. I hate a fellow who doesn't do things himself, and has a way of looking on which makes you feel a perfect idiot. Neither Mr. Mannering nor Mrs. Handsell—nor you—have been the same since he was here."

"I gather," she said, softly, "that you do not find us improved."

"I do not," he answered, stolidly. "Mrs. Handsell has begun to talk to you now about London, of the theatres, the dressmakers, Hurlingham, Ranelagh, race meetings, society, and all that sort of rot. She talks of them very cleverly. She knows how to make the tinsel sparkle like real gold."

She laughed softly.

"You are positively eloquent, Richard," she declared. "Do go on!"

"Then she goes for your uncle," he continued, without heeding her interruption. "She speaks of Parliament, of great causes, of ambition, until his eyes are on fire. She describes new pleasures to you, and you sit at her feet, a mute worshipper! I can't think why she ever came here. She's absolutely the wrong sort of woman for a quiet country place like this. I wish I'd never let her the place."

"You are a very foolish person," she answered. "She came here simply because she was weary of cities and wanted to get as far away from them as possible. Only last night she said that she would be content never to breathe the air of a town again."

Lindsay tossed his cigarette away impatiently.

"Oh, I know exactly her way of saying that sort of thing!" he exclaimed. "A moment later she would be describing very cleverly, and a little regretfully, some wonderful sight or other only to be found in London."

"Really," she declared, "I am getting afraid of you. You are more observant than I thought."

"There is one gift, at least," he answered, "which we country folk are supposed to possess. We know truth when we see it. But I am saying more than I have any right to. I don't want to make you angry, Clara!"

She shook her head.

"You won't do that," she said. "But I don't think you quite understand. Let me tell you something. You know that I am an orphan, don't you? I do not remember my father at all, and I can only just remember my mother. I was brought up at a pleasant but very dreary boarding-school. I had very few friends, and no one came to see me except my uncle, who was always very kind, but always in a desperate hurry. I stayed there until I was seventeen. Then my uncle came and fetched me, and brought me straight here. Now that is exactly what my life has been. What do you think of it?"

"Very dull indeed," he answered, frankly.

She nodded.

"I have never been in London at all," she continued. "I really only know what men and women are like from books, or the one or two types I have met around here. Now, do you think that that is enough to satisfy one? Of course it is very beautiful here, I know, and sometimes when the sun is shining and the birds singing and the sea comes up into the creeks, well, one almost feels content. But the sun doesn't always shine, Richard, and there are times when I am right down bored, and I feel as though I'd love to draw my allowance from uncle, pack my trunk, and go up to London, on my own!"

He laughed. Somehow all that she had said had sounded so natural that some part of his uneasiness was already passing away.

"Yours," he admitted, "is an extreme case. I really don't know why your uncle has never taken you up for a month or so in the season."

"We have lived here for four years," she said, "and he has never once suggested it. He goes himself, of course, sometimes, but I am quite sure that he doesn't enjoy it. For days before he fidgets about and looks perfectly miserable, and when he comes back he always goes off for a long walk by himself. I am perfectly certain that for some reason or other he hates going. Yet he seems to have been everywhere, to know every one. To hear him talk with Mrs. Handsell is like a new Arabian Nights to me."

He nodded.

"Your uncle was a very distinguished man," he said. "I was only at college then, but I remember what a fuss there was in all the papers when he resigned his seat."

"What did they say was the reason?" she asked, eagerly.

"A slight disagreement with Lord Rochester, and ill-health."

"Absurd!" she exclaimed. "Uncle is as strong as a horse."

"Would you like him," he asked, "to go back into political life?"

Her eyes sparkled.

"Of course I should."

"You may have your wish," he said, a little sadly. "I don't fancy he has been quite the same man since Sir Leslie Borrowdean was here, and Mrs. Handsell never leaves him alone for a moment."

She laughed.

"You talk as though they were conspirators!" she exclaimed.

"That is precisely what I believe them to be," he answered, grimly.

"Richard!"

"Can't help it," he declared. "I will tell you something that I have no right to tell you. Mrs. Handsell is not your friend's real name."

"Richard, how exciting!" she exclaimed. "Do tell me how you know."

"Her solicitors told mine so when she took the farm."

"Not her real name? But—I wonder they let it to her."

"Oh, her references were all right," he answered. "My people saw to that. I do not mean to insinuate for a moment that she had any improper reasons for calling herself Mrs. Handsell, or anything else she liked. The explanations given were quite satisfactory. But she has become very friendly with you and with your uncle, and I think that she ought to have told you both about it."

"Do you know her real name?"

"No! It is not my affair. My solicitors knew, and they were

satisfied. Perhaps I ought not to have told you this, but—"

"Hush!" she said. "They are coming out. If you like you can take me down to the orchard wall, and we will watch the tide come in—"

Mannering came out alone and looked around. The full moon was creeping into the sky. The breath of wind which shook the leaves of the tall elm trees that shut in his little demesne from the village, was soft, and, for the time of year, wonderfully mild. Below, through the orchard trees, were faint visions of the marshland, riven with creeks of silvery sea. He turned back towards the room, where red-shaded lamps still stood upon the white tablecloth, a curiously artificial daub of color after the splendour of the moonlit land.

"The night is perfect," he exclaimed. "Do you need a wrap, or are you sufficiently acclimatized?"

She came out to him, tall and slender in her black dinner gown, the figure of a girl, the pale, passionate face of a woman, to whom every moment of life had its own special and individual meaning. Her eyes were strangely bright. There was a tenseness about her manner, a restraint in her tone, which seemed to speak of some emotional crisis. She passed out into the quiet garden, in itself so exquisitely in accordance with this sleeping land, and even Mannering was at once conscious of some alien note in these old-world surroundings which had long ago soothed his ruffled nerves into the luxury of repose.

"A wrap!" she murmured. "How absurd! Come and let us sit under the cedar tree. Those young people seem to have wandered off, and I want to talk to you."

"I am content to listen," he answered. "It is a night for listeners, this!"

"I want to talk," she continued, "and yet—the words seem difficult. These wonderful days! How quickly they seem to have passed."

"There are others to follow," he answered, smiling. "That is one of the joys of life here. One can count on things!"

"Others for you!" she murmured. "You have pitched your tent. I came here only as a wanderer."

"But scarcely a month ago," he exclaimed, "you too—"

"Don't!" she interrupted. "A month ago it seemed to me possible that I might live here always. I felt myself growing young again. I believed that I had severed all the ties which bound me to the days which have gone before. I was wrong. It was the sort of folly which comes to one sometimes, the sort of folly for which one pays."

His face was almost white in the moonlight. His deep-set grey eyes were fixed upon her.

"You were content—a month ago," he said. "You have been in London for two days, and you have come back a changed woman. Why must you think of leaving this place? Why need you go at all?"

"My friend," she said, softly, "I think that you know why. It is very beautiful here, and I have never been happier in all my life. But one may not linger all one's days in the pleasant places. One sleeps through the nights and is rested, but the days—ah, they are different."

"I cannot reason with you," he said. "You are too vague. Yet—you say that you have been contented here."

"I have been happy," she murmured.

"Then you must speak more plainly," he insisted, a note of passion throbbing in his hoarse tones. "I ask you again—why do you talk of going back, like a city slave whose days of holiday are over? What is there in the world more beautiful than the gifts the gods shower on us here? We have the sun, and the sea, and the wind by day and by night—this! It is the flower garden of life. Stay and pluck the roses with me."

"Ah, my friend," she murmured, "if that were possible!"

She sank down into the seat under the cedar tree. Her hands were clasped nervously together, her head was downcast.

"Your words," she continued, her voice sinking almost to a whisper, yet lacking nothing in distinctness, "are like wine. They mount to the head, they intoxicate, they tempt! And yet all the time one knows that it is not possible. Surely you yourself—in your heart—must know it!"

"Not I!" he answered, fiercely. "The world would have claimed me if it could, but I laughed at it. Our destinies are our own. With our own fingers we mould and shape them."

"There is the little voice," she said, "the little voice, which rings even through our dreams. Life—actual, militant life, I mean—may have its vulgarities, its weariness and its disappointments, but it is, after all, the only place for men and women. The battle may be sordid, and the prizes tinsel— yet it is only the cowards who linger without."

"Then let you and me be cowards," he  answered. "We  shall

at least be happy."

She shook her head a little sadly.

"I doubt it," she answered. "Happiness is a gift, not a prize. It comes seldom enough to those who seek it."

He laughed scornfully.

"I am not a seeker," he cried. "I possess. It seems to me that all the beautiful things of life are here to-night. Listen! Do you hear the sea, the full tide sweeping softly up into the land, a long drawn out undernote of breathless harmonies, the rustling of leaves there in the elm trees, the faint night wind, like the murmuring of angels? Lift your head! Was there anything ever sweeter than the perfume from that hedge of honeysuckle? What can a man want more than these things—and—"

"Go on!"

"And the woman he loves! There, I have said it. Useless words enough! You know very well that I love you. I meant to have said nothing just yet, but who could help it—on such a night as this! Don't talk of going away, Berenice. I want you here always."

She held herself away from him. Her face was deathly white now. Her eyes questioned him fiercely.

"Before I answer you. You were in London last week?"

"Yes."

"Why?"

"I had business."

"In Chelsea, in Merton Street?"

He gave a little gasp.

"What do you know about that?" he asked, almost roughly.

"You were seen there, not for the first time. The person whom you visited—I have heard about. She is somewhat notorious, is she not?"

He was very quiet, pale to the lips. A strange, hunted expression had crept into his eyes.

"I want to know what took you there. Am I asking too much? Remember that you have asked me a good deal."

"Has Borrowdean anything to do with this?" he demanded.

"I have known Sir Leslie Borrowdean for many years," she answered, "and it is quite true that we have discussed certain matters—concerning you."

"You have known Sir Leslie Borrowdean for many years," he repeated. "Yet you met here as strangers."

"Sir Leslie divined my wishes," she answered. "He knew that it was my wish to spend several months away from everybody, and, if possible, unrecognized. Perhaps I had better make my confession at once. My name is not Mrs. Handsell. I am the Duchess of Lenchester."

Mannering stood as though turned to stone. The woman watched him eagerly. She waited for him to speak—in vain.

E. Phillips Oppenheim

A sudden mist of tears blinded her. She closed her eyes. When she opened them Mannering was gone.

# CHAPTER V

## THE HESITATION OF MR. MANNERING

The peculiar atmosphere of the room, heavy with the newest perfume from the Burlington Arcade, and the scent of exotic flowers, at no time pleasing to him, seemed more than usually oppressive to Mannering as he fidgetted about waiting for the woman whom he had come to see. He was conscious of a restless longing to open wide the windows, take the flowers from their vases, throw them into the street, and poke out the fire. The little room, with all its associations, its almost pathetic attempts at refinement, its furniture which reeked of the Tottenham Court Road, was suddenly hateful to him. He detested his presence there, and its object. He was already in a state of nervous displeasure when the door opened.

The girl who entered seemed in a sense as ill in accord with such surroundings as himself. She was plainly dressed in black, her hair brushed back, her complexion pale, her eyes brilliant with a not altogether natural light. She regarded him with a curious mixture of fear and welcome. The latter, however, triumphed easily. She came towards him with outstretched hand and a delightful smile.

"You;—so soon again!" she exclaimed. "Were there—so

many mistakes?"

Mannering's face softened. He was half ashamed of his irritation. He answered her kindly.

"Scarcely any, Hester," he answered. "Your typing is always excellent."

Her anxiety was only half allayed.

"There is nothing else wrong?" she demanded, breathlessly.

"Nothing whatever," he assured her. "Where is your mother?"

She sat down. The light died out of her face.

"Out!" she answered. "Gone to Brighton for the day. What do you want with her?"

"Nothing," he answered, gravely. "I only wanted to know whether we were likely to be interrupted."

"She will not be in for some time," the girl answered. "She is almost certain to stay down there and dine."

He nodded.

"Hester," he asked, "do you know any one—a man named Borrowdean? Sir Leslie Borrowdean?"

She shook her head a little doubtfully.

"I have heard mother speak of him," she said.

"He is a friend of hers, then?"

"She met him at a supper party at the Savoy a few weeks ago," she answered.

"And since?"

"I believe so! She talks about him a great deal. Why do you ask me this?"

"I cannot tell you, Hester," he said, gravely. "By the bye, do you think that she is likely to have mentioned my name to him?"

The girl flushed up to her eyebrows.

"I—I don't know! I am sorry," she faltered. "You know what mother is. If any one asked her questions she would be more than likely to answer them. I do hope that she has not been making mischief."

He left her anxiety unrelieved. For some few moments he did not speak at all. Already he fancied that he could see the whole pitiful little incident—Borrowdean, diplomatic, genial, persistent, the woman a fool, fashioned to his own making; himself the sacrifice. Yet the meaning of it all was dark to him.

She moved over to his side. Her eyes and tone were full of appeal. She sat close to him, her long white fingers nervously interlocked.

"I am afraid of you. More afraid than ever to-day," she murmured. "You look stern, and I don't understand why you have come."

"To see you, Hester," he answered, with a sudden impulse of kindness.

"Ah, no!" she interrupted, choking back a little sob. "We both know so well that it is not that. It is pity which brings you, pity and nothing else. You know very well what a difference it makes to me. If I have your work to do, and a letter sometimes, and see you now and then, I can bear everything. But it is not easy. It is never easy!"

"Of course it is not," he assented. "Hester, have you thought over what I said to you last time I was here?"

She shook her head.

"What is the use of thinking?" she asked, quietly. "I could not leave her."

"You mean that she would not let you go?" Mannering asked.

"No! It is not that," the girl answered. "Sometimes I think that she would be glad. It is not that."

He nodded gravely.

"I understand. But—"

"If you understand, please do not say any more."

"But I must, Hester," he persisted. "There is no one else to give you advice. I know all that you can tell me, and I say that this is no fitting home for you. Your mother's friends are not fit friends for you. She has chosen her way in life, and she will not brook any interference. You can do no good by remaining with her. On the contrary, you are doing yourself a great deal of harm. I am old enough to be your father, child. Wise enough, I hope, to be your adviser. You shall be my secretary, and come and live at Blakely."

A faint flush stole into her anaemic. One realized then that under different conditions she might have been pretty. Her face was no longer expressionless.

"You are so kind," she said, softly. "I shall always like to think of this. And yet—it is impossible."

"Why?"

She hesitated.

"It is difficult to explain," she said. "But my being here makes a difference. I found it out once when I went away for a week. Some of—of mother's friends came to the house then whom she will not have when I am here. If I were away altogether—oh, I can't explain, but I would not dare to go."

Mannering seemed to have much to say—and said nothing. This queer, pale-faced girl, with her earnest eyes and few simple words, had silenced him. She was right—right at least from her own point of view. A certain sense of shame suddenly oppressed him. He was acutely conscious of his only half-admitted reason for this visit. He had argued for himself. It was his own passionate desire to free himself from associations that were little short of loathsome which had prompted this visit. And then what he had dreaded most of all happened. As they sat facing one another in the silent, half-darkened room, Mannering trying to bring himself into accord with half-admitted but repugnant convictions, she watching him hopelessly, the tinkle of a hansom bell sounded outside. The sudden stopping of a horse, the rattle of a latchkey, and she was in the room. Mannering rose to his feet with a little exclamation.

The woman stood and looked in upon them. She wore a pink cloth gown, a flower-garlanded hat, a white coaching veil, beneath which her features were indistinguishable. She brought with her a waft of strong perfume. Her figure was a living suggestion of the struggle between maturity and the corsetiere. Before she spoke she laughed—not altogether pleasantly.

"You here again!" she exclaimed to Mannering. "Upon my word! I'm not a ghost! Hester, go and see about some tea, and a brandy and soda. Billy Foa brought me up on his motor, and I'm half choked with dust."

The girl rose obediently and quitted the room. The woman untwisted her veil, drew out the pins from her hat, and threw both upon the sofa. Then she turned suddenly upon Mannering.

"Look here," she said, "the last twice you've been here you seem to have carefully chosen times when I am out. I don't understand it. It can't be that you want to see that chit of a girl of mine. Why don't you come when I ask you? Why do you act as though I were something to be avoided?"

Mannering rose to his feet.

"I came to-day without knowing where you were," he answered, "but I will admit that I wished to see Hester."

"What for?"

"I have asked her to come and live at Blakely with my niece and myself. She is an excellent typist, and I require a secretary."

The woman looked at him angrily. Without her veil she displayed features not in themselves unattractive, but a complexion somewhat impaired by the use of cosmetics. The powder upon her cheeks was even then visible.

"What about me?" she asked, sharply.

Mannering looked her steadily in the face.

"I do not think," he said, "that such a life would suit you."

She was an angry woman, and she did not become angry gracefully.

"You mean that I'm not good enough for you and your friends in the country. That's what you mean, isn't it? And I should like to know, if I'm not, whose fault it is. Tell me that, will you?"

Mannering flinched, though almost imperceptibly.

"I meant simply what I said," he said. "Blakely would not suit you at all. We have few friends there, and our simple life would not attract you in the slightest. With Hester it is different. She would have her work, in which she takes some interest, and I believe the change would be in every way good for her."

"Well, she shan't come," the woman said, throwing herself into a chair, and regarding him insolently. "I'm not going to live all alone—and be talked about. Don't stare at me like that, Lawrence. I'm the child's mother, am I not?"

"It is because you are her mother," he said, quietly, "that I thought you might be glad to find a suitable home for her."

"What's good enough for me ought to be good enough for her," she answered, doggedly.

Mannering was silent for a moment. This woman seemed to belong to a different world from that with whose denizens he was in any way familiar. Years of isolation, and a certain epicureanism of taste, from which necessity had never taken the fine edge, had made him a little intolerant. He could see nothing that was not absolutely repulsive in this woman, whose fine eyes were seeking even now to attract his admiration. She was making the best of herself. She had chosen the darkest corner of the room, and her pose was not ungraceful. Her skirts were skilfully raised to show just as much as possible of her long, slender foot, with the patent shoes and silver buckles. She knew that her ankles were above reproach, and her dress becoming. A dozen men had paid her compliments during the day, yet she knew that every admiring glance, every whispered word which had come to her to-day, or for many days past, would count for nothing if only she could pierce for a single moment the unchanging coldness of the man who sat watching her now with the face of a Sphynx. A slow tide of passion welled up in her heart. Was not he a man and free, and was not she a woman? It was not much she asked from him, no pledge, no bondage. His kindness only, she told herself, was all she craved. She wanted him to look at her as other men looked at her. Who was he that he should set himself on a pedestal? Perhaps he had grown shy from the rust of his country life, the slow drifting apart from the world of men and women. Perhaps—she rose swiftly to her feet and crossed the room.

# CHAPTER VI

## SACRIFICE

She leaned over him, one hand on the back of his chair, the other seeking in vain for his.

"Lawrence," she said, "you grow colder and more unkind every day. What have I done to change you so? I am a foolish woman, I know, but there are things which I cannot forget."

He rose at once to his feet, and stood apart from her.

"I thought," he said, "I believed that we understood one another."

She laughed softly.

"I am very sure that I do not understand you," she said. "And as for you—I do not believe that you have ever understood any woman. There was a time, Lawrence—"

His impassivity was gone. He threw out his hands.

"Remember," he said, "there is a promise between us. Don't break it. Don't dare to break it!"

She looked at him curiously. A new idea concerning this man and his avoidance of her crept into her mind. It was at least consoling to her vanity, and it left her a chance. She had roused him too, at last, and that was worth something.

"Why not?" she asked, moving a step towards him. "It was a foolish promise. It has done neither of us any good. It has spoilt a part of my life. Why should I keep silence, and let it go on to the end? Do you know what it has made of me, this promise?"

He shrank back.

"Don't! I have done all I could!"

"All you could!" she repeated, scornfully. "You drew a diagram of your duty, and you have moved like a machine along the lines. You talk like a Pharisee, Lawrence! Come! You knew me years ago! Do you find me changed? Tell me the truth."

"Yes," he admitted, "you are changed."

She nodded.

"You admit that. Perhaps, perhaps," she continued more slowly, "there are things about me now of which you don't approve. My friends are a little fast, I go out alone, I daresay people have said things. There, you see I am very frank. I mean to be! I mean you to know that whatever I am, the fault is yours."

"You are as God or the Devil made you," he answered, hardly. "You are what you would have become, in any case."

"Lawrence!"

Already he hated the memory of his words. True or not, they were spoken to a woman who was cowering under them as under a lash. He was at a disadvantage now. If she had met him with anger they might have cried quits. But he had seen her wince, seen her sudden pallor, and it was not a pleasant sight.

"Forgive me," he said. "I do not know quite what I am saying. You have broken a compact which I had hoped might have lasted all our days. Let us be better friends, if you will, but let us keep that promise which we made to one another."

"It was so many years ago," she said, in a low tone. "I am afraid to think how many. It makes me lonely, Lawrence, to look ahead. I am afraid of growing old!"

He looked at her steadily. Yes, the signs were there. She was a good-looking woman to-day, a handsome woman in some lights, but she had reached the limit. It was a matter of a few years at most, and then—He stood with his hands behind his back.

"It is a fear which we must all share," he said, quietly. "The only antidote is work."

"Work!" she repeated, scornfully. "That is the man's resource. What about us? What about me?"

"It is no matter of sex," he declared. "We all make our own choice. We are what we make of ourselves."

"It is not true," she answered, bluntly. "Not with us, at any rate. We are what our menkind make of us. Oh, what cowards you all are."

"Cowards?"

"Yes. You do what mischief you choose, and then soothe your conscience with platitudes. You will take hold of pleasure with both hands, but your shoulders are not broad enough for the pack of responsibility. Don't look at me as though I were a mile off, Lawrence, as though this were simply an impersonal discussion. I am speaking to you—of you. You avoid me whenever you can. I don't often get a chance of speaking to you. You shall listen now. You live the life of a poet and a scholar, they tell me. You live in a beautiful home, you take care that nothing ugly or disturbing shall come near you. You are pleased with it, aren't you? You think yourself better than other men. Well, you are making a big mistake. A man doesn't have to answer for his own life only. He has to carry the burden of the lives his influence has wrecked and spoilt. I know just what you think of me. I am a middle-aged woman, clinging to my youth and pleasures—the sort of pleasures for which you have a vast contempt. There isn't an hour of my days of which you wouldn't disapprove. I'm not your sort of woman at all. And yet I was all right once, Lawrence, and what I am now—" she paused, "what I am now—"

Hester came in, followed by a maid with the tea-tray. She looked from one to the other a little anxiously. The atmosphere of the room seemed charged with electricity. Mannering's face was grey. Her mother was nervously crumpling into a ball her tiny lace handkerchief. Mrs. Phillimore rose abruptly from her seat.

"Have you got the brandy and soda, Hester?" she asked.

"I'm afraid I forgot it, mother," the girl answered. "Mayn't I make you some Russian tea? I've had the lemon sliced."

The woman laughed, a little unnaturally.

"What a dutiful daughter," she exclaimed. "That's right! I want looking after, don't I? I'll have the tea, Hester, but send it up to my room. I'm going to lie down. That wretched motoring has given me a headache, and I'm dining out to-night. Good-bye, Mr. Mannering, if I don't see you again."

She nodded, without glancing in his direction, and left the room. The maid arranged the tea-tray and departed. Hester showed no signs of being aware that anything unusual had happened. She made a little desultory conversation. Mannering answered in monosyllables.

When at last he put his cup down he rose to go.

"You are quite sure, Hester," he said. "You have made up your mind?"

She, too, rose, and came over to him.

"You know that I am right," she answered, quietly. "The life you offer me would be paradise, but I dare not even think of it. I may not do any good here, perhaps I don't, but I can't come away."

"You are a true daughter of your sex," he said, smiling. "The keynote of your life must be sacrifice."

"Perhaps we are not so unwise, after all," she answered, "for I think that there are more happy women in the world than men."

"There are more, I think, who deserve to be, dear," he answered, holding her hand for a moment. "Good-bye!"

Mannering walked in somewhat abstracted fashion to the

corner of the street, and signalled for a hansom. With his foot upon the step he hesitated.

# CHAPTER VII

## THE DUCHESS'S "AT HOME"

"The perfect man," the Duchess murmured, as she stirred her tea, "does not exist. I know a dozen perfect women, dear, dull creatures, and plenty of men who know how to cover up the flaw. But there is something in the composition of the male sex which keeps them always a little below the highest pinnacle."

"It is purely a matter of concealment," her friend declared. "Women are cleverer humbugs than men."

Borrowdean shrugged his shoulders.

"I know your perfect woman!" he remarked, softly. "You search for her through the best years of your life, and when you have found her you avoid her. That," he added, handing his empty cup to a footman, "is why I am a bachelor."

The Duchess regarded him complacently.

"My dear Sir Leslie," she said, "I am afraid you will have to find a better reason for your miserable state. The perfect woman would certainly have nothing to do with you if you found her."

"On the contrary," he declared, confidently, "I am convinced that she would find me attractive."

The Duchess shook her head.

"Your theory," she declared, "is antiquated. Like and unlike do not attract. We seek in others the qualities which we strive most zealously to develop in ourselves. I know a case in point."

"Good!" Sir Leslie remarked. "I like examples. The logic of them appeals to me."

The Duchess half closed her eyes. For a moment she was silent. She seemed to be listening to something a long way off. Through the open windows of her softly shaded drawing-rooms, odourous with flowers, came the rippling of water falling from a fountain in the conservatory, the lazy hum of a mowing machine on the lawn, the distant tinkling of a hansom bell in the Square. But these were not the sounds which for a moment had changed her face.

"I myself," she murmured, "am an example!"

A woman who had risen to go sat down again.

"Do go on, Duchess!" she exclaimed. "Anything in the nature of a personal confession is so fascinating, and you know you are such an enigma to all of us."

"Am I?" she answered, smiling. "Then I am likely to remain so."

"A perfectly obvious person like myself," the woman remarked, "is always fascinated by the unusual. But if you are really not going to give yourself away, Duchess, I am afraid I must move on. One hates to leave your beautifully cool rooms. Shall I see you to-night, I wonder, at Esholt House?"

"Perhaps!"

There were still many people in the room. Some fresh arrivals occupied his hostess's attention, and Borrowdean, with a resigned shrug of the shoulders, prepared to depart. He had come, hoping for an opportunity to be alone for a few minutes with the Duchess, and himself a skilful tactician in such small matters, he could not but admire the way she had kept him at arm's length. And then the opportunity for a master stroke came. A servant sought him out with a card. A man of method, he seldom left his rooms without instructions as to where he was to be found.

"The gentleman begged you to excuse his coming here, sir," the man whispered, confidentially, "but he is returning to the country this evening, and was anxious to see you. He is quite ready to wait your convenience."

Borrowdean held the card in his hand, scrutinizing it with impassive face. Was this a piece of unparalleled good fortune, or simply a trick of the fates to tempt him on to catastrophe? With that wonderful swiftness of thought which was part of his mental equipment he balanced the chances— and took his risk.

"I should be glad," he said, looking the servant in the face, "if you would show the gentleman up here as an ordinary visitor. I should like to find you down stairs when I come out. You understand?"

"Perfectly, sir," the man answered, and withdrew.

E. Phillips Oppenheim

Mannering had no idea whose house he was in. The address Borrowdean's servant had given him had been simply 81, Grosvenor Square. Nevertheless, he was conscious of a little annoyance as he followed the servant up the broad stairs. He would much have preferred waiting until Borrowdean had concluded his call. He remembered his grey travelling clothes, and all his natural distaste for social amenities returned with unabated force as he neared the reception-rooms and heard the softly modulated rise and fall of feminine voices, the swishing of silks and muslin, the faint perfume of flowers and scents which seemed to fill the air. At the last moment he would have withdrawn, but his guide seemed deaf. His words passed unheeded. His name, very softly but very distinctly, had been announced. He had no option but to pass into the room and play the cards which fate and his friend had dealt him.

Borrowdean rose to greet his friend. Mannering, not knowing who his hostess might be, and feeling absolutely no curiosity concerning her, confined his attention wholly to the man whom he had come to seek.

"I did not wish to disturb you here, Borrowdean," he said, quickly, "but if your call is over, could you come away for a few minutes? I have a matter to discuss with you."

Borrowdean smiled slightly, and laid his hand upon the other's shoulder.

"By all means, Mannering," he answered. "But since you have discovered our little secret, don't you think that you had better speak to our hostess?"

Mannering was puzzled, but his eyes followed Borrowdean's slight gesture. Berenice, who at the sound of his voice had suddenly abandoned her conversation and risen to her feet, was within a few feet of him. A sudden light swept into Mannering's face.

"You!" he exclaimed softly.

Her hands went out towards him. Borrowdean, with an almost imperceptible movement, checked his advance.

"So you see we are found out, after all, Duchess," he said, turning to her. "You have known Mrs. Handsell, Mannering, let me present you now to her other self. Duchess, you see that our recluse has come to his senses at last. I must really introduce you formally: Mr. Mannering—the Duchess of Lenchester."

Berenice, arrested in her forward movement, watched Mannering's face eagerly. So carefully modulated had been Borrowdean's voice that no word of his had reached beyond their own immediate circle. It was as though a silent tableau were being played out between the three, and Mannering, to whom repression had become a habit, gave little indication of anything he might have felt. Borrowdean's fixed smile betokened nothing but an ordinary interest in the intro-duction of two friends, and the Duchess's back was turned towards her friends. They both waited for Mannering to speak.

"This," he said, slowly, "is a surprise! I had no idea when I called to see Borrowdean here, of the pleasure which was in store for me."

Borrowdean dropped his eyeglass.

"Are you serious, my dear Mannering?" he exclaimed. "Do you mean to say that you came here—"

"Only to see you," Mannering interrupted. "That you should know perfectly well. I am sorry to hurry you out, but the few minutes' conversation which I desired with you is of some importance, and my train leaves in an hour. I hope that you will pardon me," he added, looking steadily at Berenice, "if I hurry away one of your guests."

She laughed quite in her natural manner.

"I will forgive anything," she said, "except that you should hurry away yourself so unceremoniously. Come and sit down near me. I want to talk to you about Blakeley."

She swept her gown on one side, disclosing a vacant place on the settee where she had been sitting. For a second her eyes said more to him than her courteous but half-careless words of invitation. Mannering made no movement forward.

"I am sorry," he said, "but it is impossible for me to stay!"

She seemed to dismiss him and the whole subject with a careless little shrug of the shoulders, which was all the farewell she vouchsafed to either of them. A woman who had just entered seemed to absorb her whole attention. The two men passed out.

Mannering spoke no word until they stood upon the pavement. Then he turned almost savagely upon his companion.

"This is a trick of yours, I suppose!" he exclaimed. "Damn you and your meddling, Borrowdean. Why can't you leave me and my affairs alone? No, I am not going your way. Let us separate here!"

Borrowdean shook his head.

"You are unreasonable, Mannering," he said. "I have done only what I believe you were on your way to ask me to do. I have brought you and Berenice together again. It was for both your sakes. If there has been any misunderstanding between you, it would be better cleared up."

Mannering gripped his arm.

"Let us go to your rooms, Borrowdean," he said. "It is time we understood one another."

"Willingly!" Borrowdean said. "But your train?"

"Let my train go," Mannering answered. "There are some things I have to say to you."

Borrowdean called a hansom. The two men drove off together.

# CHAPTER VIII

## THE MANNERING MYSTERY

Borrowdean was curter than usual, even abrupt. The calm geniality of his manner had departed. He spoke in short, terse sentences, and he had the air of a man struggling to subdue a fit of perfectly reasonable and justifiable anger. It was a carefully cultivated pose. He even refrained from his customary cigarette.

"Look here, Mannering," he said, "there are times when a few plain words are worth an hour's conversation. Will you have them from me?"

"Yes!"

"This thing was started six months ago, soon after those two bye-elections in Yorkshire. Even the most despondent of us then saw that the Government could scarcely last its time. We had a meeting and we attempted to form on paper a trial cabinet. You know our weakness. We have to try to form a National party out of a number of men who, although they call themselves broadly Liberals, are as far apart as the very poles of thought. It was as much as they could do to sit in the same room together. From the opening of the meeting until its close, there was but one subject upon which every one was unanimous. That was the absolute necessity of getting you to come back to our aid."

"You flatter me," Mannering said, with fine irony.

"You yourself," Borrowdean continued, without heeding the interruption, "encouraged us. From the first pronouncement of this wonderful new policy you sprang into the arena. We were none of us ready. You were! It is true that your weapon was the pen, but you reached a great public. The country to-day considers you the champion of Free Trade."

"Pass on," Mannering interrupted, brusquely. "All this is wasted time!"

"A smaller meeting," Borrowdean continued, "was held with a view of discussing the means whereby you could be persuaded to rejoin us. At that meeting the Duchess of Lenchester was present."

Mannering, who had been pacing the room, stopped short. He grasped the back of a chair, and turning round faced Borrowdean.

"Well?"

"You know what place the Duchess has held in the councils of our party since the Duke's death," Borrowdean continued. "She has the political instinct. If she were a man she would be a leader. All the great ladies are on the other side, but the Duchess is more than equal to them all. She entertains magnificently, and with tact. She never makes a mistake. She is part and parcel of the Liberal Party. It was she who volunteered to make the first effort to bring you back."

Mannering turned his head. Apparently he was looking out

of the window.

"Her methods," Borrowdean continued, "did not commend themselves to us, but beggars must not be choosers. Besides, the Duchess was in love with her own scheme. Such objections as we made were at once overruled."

He paused, but Mannering said nothing. He was still looking out of the window, though his eyes saw nothing of the street below, or the great club buildings opposite. A scent of roses, lost now and then in the salter fragrance of the night breeze sweeping over the marshes, the magic of a wonderful, white-clad presence, the low words, the sense of a world apart, a world of speechless beauty.... What empty dreams! A palace built in a poet's fancy upon a quicksand.

"The Duchess," Borrowdean continued, "undertook to discover from you what prospects there were, if any, of your return to political life. She took none of us into her confidence. We none of us knew what means she meant to employ. She disappeared. She communicated with none of us. We none of us had the least idea what had become of her. Time went on, and we began to get a little uneasy. We had a meeting and it was arranged that I should come down and see you. I came, I saw you, I saw the Duchess! The situation very soon became clear to me. Instead of the Duchess converting you, you had very nearly converted the Duchess."

"I can assure you—" Mannering began.

"Let me finish," Borrowdean pleaded. "I realized the situation at a glance. Your attitude I was not so much surprised at, but the attitude of the Duchess, I must confess, amazed me. I came to the conclusion that I had found my way into a forgotten corner of the world, where the lotos flowers still blossomed, and the sooner I was out of it the better. Now I think that brings us, Mannering, up to the present time."

Mannering turned from the window, out of which he had been steadfastly gazing. There was a strained look under his eyes, and little trace of the tan upon his, cheeks. He had the air of a jaded and a weary man.

"That is all, then," he remarked. "I can still catch my train."

Borrowdean held out his hand.

"No," he said. "It is not all. This explanation I have made for your sake, Mannering, and it has been a truthful and full one. Now it is my turn. I have a few words to say to you on my own account."

Mannering paused. There was a note of something unusual in Borrowdean's voice, a portent of things behind. Mannering involuntarily straightened himself. Something was awakened in him which had lain dormant for many years—dormant since those old days of battle, of swift attack, of ambushed defence and the clamour of brilliant tongues. Some of the old light flashed in his eyes.

"Say it then—quickly!"

"We speak of great things," Borrowdean continued, "and the catching of a train is a trifle. My wardrobe and house are at your service. Don't hurry me!"

Mannering smiled.

"Go on!" he said.

"The men who count in this world," Borrowdean declared,

E. Phillips Oppenheim

calmly lighting a cigarette, "are either thinkers of great thoughts or doers of great deeds. To the former belong the poets and the sentimentalists; to the latter the statesmen and the soldiers."

"What have I done," Mannering murmured, "that I should be sent back to kindergarten? Platitudes such as this bore me. Let me catch my train."

"In a moment. To all my arguments and appeals, to all my entreaties to you to realize yourself, to do your duty to us, to history and to posterity, you have replied in one manner only. You have spoken from the mushroom pedestal of the sentimentalist. Not a single word that has fallen from your lips has rung true. You have spoken as though your eyes were blind all the time to the letters of fire which truth has spelled out before you. Any further argument with you is useless, because you are not honest. You conceal your true position, and you adopt a false defence. Therefore, I relinquish my task. You can go and grow your roses, and think your poetry, and call it life if you will. But before you go I should like you to know that I, at least, am not deceived. I do not believe in you, Mannering. I ask you a question, and I challenge you to answer it. What is your true reason for making a scrap-heap of your career?"

"Are you my friend," Mannering asked, quietly, "that you wish to pry behind the curtain of my life? If I have other reasons they concern myself alone."

Borrowdean shook his head. He had scored, but he took care to show no sign of triumph.

"The issue is too great," he said, "to be tried by the ordinary rules which govern social life. Will you presume that I am your friend, and let us consider the whole matter afresh together?"

"I will not," Mannering answered. "But I will do this. I will answer your question. There is another reason which makes my reappearance in public life impossible. Not even your subtlety, Borrowdean, could remove it. I do not even wish it removed. I mean to live my own life, and not to be pitchforked back into politics to suit the convenience of a few adventurous office-seekers, and the Duchess of Lenchester!"

"Mannering!"

But Mannering had gone.

*　*　*　*　*

Borrowdean felt that this was a trying day. After a battle with Mannering he was face to face with an angry woman, to whose presence an imperious little note had just summoned him. Berenice was dressed for a royal dinner party, and she had only a few minutes to spare. Nevertheless she contrived to make them very unpleasant ones for Borrowdean.

"The affair was entirely an accident," he pleaded.

"It was nothing of the sort," she answered, bluntly. "I know you too well for that. Your bringing him here without warning was an unwarrantable interference with my affairs."

Borrowdean could hold his own with men, but Berenice in her own room, a wonderful little paradise of soft colourings and luxury so perfectly chosen that it was rather felt than seen; Berenice, in her marvellous gown, with the necklace upon her bosom and the tiara flashing in her dark hair, was an overwhelming opponent. Borrowdean was helpless. He could not understand the attack itself. He failed altogether to appreciate its tenour.

"Forgive me," he protested, "but I did not know that you had any plans. All that you told us on your return from Blakely was that you had failed. So far as you were concerned the matter seemed to me to be over, and with it, I imagined, your interest in Mannering. I brought him here—"

"Well?"

"Because I wished him to know who you were. I wished him to understand the improbability of your ever again returning to Blakely."

"You are telling the truth now, at any rate," she remarked, curtly, "or what sounds like the truth. Why did you trouble in the matter at all? Where I have failed you are not likely to succeed."

Borrowdean smiled for the first time.

"I have still some hopes of doing so," he admitted.

The Duchess glanced at the little Louis Seize time-piece, and hesitated.

"You had better abandon them," she said. "Lawrence Mannering may be wrong, or he may be right, but he believes in his choice. He has no ambition. You have no motive left to work upon."

Borrowdean shook his head.

"You are wrong, Duchess," he remarked, simply. "I never believed in Mannering's sentimentality. To-day, with his own lips, he has confessed to me that another, an unbroached reason, stands behind his refusal!"

"And he never told me," the Duchess murmured, involuntarily.

"Duchess," Borrowdean answered, with a faint, cynical parting of the lips, "there are matters which a man does not mention to the woman in whose high opinion he aims at holding an exalted place."

There was a knock at the door. The Duchess's maid entered, carrying a long cloak of glimmering lace and satin.

The Duchess nodded.

"I come at once, Hortense," she said, in French. "Sir Leslie," she added, turning towards him, "you are making a great mistake, and I advise you to be careful. You are one of those who think ill of all men. Such men as Lawrence Mannering belong to a race of human beings of whom you know nothing. I listened to you once, and I was a fool. You could as soon teach me to believe that you were a saint, as that Mannering had anything in his past or present life of which he was ashamed. Now, Hortense."

Borrowdean walked off, still smiling. How simple half the world was.

# CHAPTER IX

## THE PUMPING OF MRS. PHILLIMORE

Hester sprang to her feet eagerly as she heard the front door close, and standing behind the curtain she watched the man, who was already upon the pavement looking up and down the street for a hansom. His erect, distinguished figure was perfectly familiar to her. It was Sir Leslie Borrowdean again.

She resumed her seat in front of the typewriter, and touched the keys idly. In a few moments what she had been expecting happened. Her mother entered the room.

Of her advent there were the usual notifications. An immense rustling of silken skirts, and an overwhelming odour of the latest Bond Street perfume. She flung herself into a chair, and regarded her daughter with a complacent smile.

"That delightful man has been to see me again," she exclaimed. "I could scarcely believe it when Mary brought me his card. By the bye, where is Mary? I want her to try to take that stain out of my pink silk skirt. I shall have to wear it to-night."

"I will ring for her directly," the girl answered. "So that was

Sir Leslie Borrowdean, mother! Why did he come to see you again so soon?"

"I haven't the least idea," Mrs. Phillimore announced, "but I thought it was very sweet of him. It seems all the more remarkable when one considers the sort of man he is. He's very ambitious, you know, and devoted to politics."

"Where did you meet him first?" Hester asked.

"It was at the Metropole at Bexhill," Mrs. Phillimore answered. "We motored down there one day, and Lena Roberts told me that she heard him inquiring who I was directly we came into the room. He joined our party at luncheon. Billy knew him slightly, so I made him go over and ask him."

Hester nodded, and seemed to be absorbed in some trifling defect of one of the keys of her typewriter.

"Does he still ask you many questions about Mr. Mannering, mother?" she asked, quietly.

"About Mr. Mannering!" Mrs. Phillimore repeated, with raised eyebrows. "Why, he scarcely ever mentions his name."

She took up a small mirror from the table by her side, and critically touched her hair.

"About Mr. Mannering, indeed," she repeated. "Why do you ask me such a question?"

The girl hesitated.

"Do you really want to know, mother?" she asked.

"Of course!"

"When Mr. Mannering was here last," Hester said, "he asked me whether Sir Leslie Borrowdean was a friend of yours. I fancy that they are political acquaintances, but I don't think that they are on very good terms."

Mrs. Phillimore laid down the mirror and yawned.

"Well, there's nothing very strange about that," she declared. "Lawrence isn't the sort to get on with many people, especially since he went and buried himself in the country. How pale you are looking, child. Why don't you go and take a walk, instead of hammering away at that old typewriter? Any one would think that you had to do it for a living!"

"I prefer to earn my own living," the girl answered, "and I am not in the least tired. Tell me, are you going to see Sir Leslie Borrowdean again, mother?"

The woman on the couch smoothed her hair once more, with a smile of gratification.

"Sir Leslie has asked me to join a small party of friends for dinner at the Carlton this evening," she announced. "Why on earth are you looking at me like that, child? You're always grumbling that my friends are a fast lot, and don't suit you. You can't say anything against Sir Leslie."

The girl had risen to her feet. The trouble in her face was manifest.

"Mother," she said, slowly, "I wish that you were not going. I wish that you would have nothing whatever to do with Sir Leslie Borrowdean."

"Good Heavens!—and why not?" the woman exclaimed, suddenly sitting up.

"I believe that he only asked you because he has an idea that you can tell him—something he wants to know about Mr. Mannering," the girl answered, steadily. "I don't think that you ought to go!"

"Rubbish!" her mother answered, crossly. "I don't believe that he has such an idea in his head. As though he couldn't ask me for the sake of my company. And if he does ask me questions, I'm not obliged to answer them, am I? Do you think that I'm to be turned inside out like a schoolgirl?"

"Sir Leslie is very clever, and he is very unscrupulous," the girl answered. "I wish you weren't going! I believe that he wants to find out things."

Mrs. Phillimore frowned uneasily.

"I'm not a fool!" she said. "He's welcome to all he can get to know through me. I don't know what you want to try to make me uncomfortable for, Hester, I'm sure. Sir Leslie has never betrayed the least curiosity about Mr. Mannering, and I don't believe that he's any such idea in his head. Upon my word I don't see why you should think it impossible that Sir Leslie should come here just for the sake of improving an acquaintance which he found pleasant. That's what he gave me to understand, and he put it very nicely too!"

"I do not think that Sir Leslie is that sort of man, mother."

"And I don't see how you know anything about it," was the sharp response. "Ring the bell, please. I want to speak to Mary about my skirt."

"You mean to dine with him then, mother?" she asked, crossing the room towards the bell.

"Of course! I've accepted. To-night and as often as he chooses to ask me. Now don't upset me, please. I want to look my best to-night, and if I get angry my hair goes all out of curl."

The girl went back to her typewriter. She unfolded a sheet of copy, and placed it on the stand before her.

"If you have made up your mind, mother, I suppose you will go," she said. "Still—I wish you wouldn't."

Mrs. Phillimore shrugged her shoulders.

"If I did what you wished all the time," she remarked, pettishly, "I might as well drown myself at once. Can't you understand, Hester?" she added, with a sudden change of manner, "that I must do something to help me to forget? You don't want to see me go mad, do you?"

The girl turned half round in her chair. She was fronting a mirror. She caught a momentary impression of herself— pallid, hollow-eyed, weary. She sighed.

"There are other ways of forgetting," she murmured. "There is work."

Her mother laughed scornfully.

"You have chosen your way," she said, "let me choose mine. Turn round, Hester."

The girl obeyed her languidly. Her mother eyed her with an attention she seldom vouchsafed to anything. Her plain black frock was ill-fitting and worn. She wore no ribbon or jewellery or adornment of any sort. Negatively her face was not ill-pleasing, but her figure was angular, and her complexion almost anaemic. The woman on the couch represented other things. She was tastefully, though somewhat elaborately dressed. She wore chains and trinkets about her neck, rings upon her fingers, and in her face had begun in earnest the tragic struggle between an actual forty and presumptive twenty. She laughed again, a little hardly.

"And you are my daughter," she exclaimed. "You are one of the freaks of heredity. I'm perfectly certain you don't belong to me, and as for him—"

"Stop!" the girl cried.

The woman nodded.

"Quite right," she said. "I didn't mean to mention him. I won't again. But we are different, aren't we? I wonder why you stay with me. I wonder you don't go and make a home for yourself somewhere. I know that you hate all the things I do, and care for, and all my friends. Why don't you go away? It would be more comfortable for both of us!"

"I have no wish to go away," the girl said, softly, "and I don't think that we interfere with one another very much, do we? This is the first time I have ever made a remark about any— of your friends. To-night I cannot help it. Sir Leslie Borrowdean is Mr. Mannering's enemy. I am sure of it! That is why I do not like the idea of your going out with him. It doesn't seem to be right—and I am afraid."

"Afraid! You little idiot!"

"Sir Leslie Borrowdean is a very clever man," the girl said.

"He is a very clever man, and he has been a lawyer. That sort of person knows how to ask questions—to—find out things."

"Rubbish!" the woman remarked, sitting up on the couch. "Why do you try to make me so uncomfortable, Hester? Sir Leslie may be very clever, but I am not exactly a fool myself."

She spoke confidently, but under the delicate coating of rouge her cheeks had whitened.

"Besides," she continued, "Sir Leslie has never even mentioned Mr. Mannering's name in anything except the most casual way. You don't understand everything, Hester. Of course Lena and Billy Aswell and Rothe and all of them are all right, but they are just a little—well, you would call it fast, and it does one good to be seen with a different set sometimes. Sir Leslie Borrowdean and his friends are altogether different, of course."

The girl bent over her work.

"No doubt, mother," she answered, "There's Mary stamping on the floor. I expect she has your bath ready."

An hour or so later Mrs. Phillimore departed in a hired brougham. Her hair had been carefully arranged by a local expert who had an establishment in the next street, her pink silk gown had come through the ordeal of cleansing with remarkable success, and the heels on her new evening shoes resembled more than anything else, miniature stilts. Her face was wreathed in smiles, and she possessed the good conscience and light heart of a woman who feels that she has made a successful toilette. All the vague misgivings of a short while ago had vanished. She gave her hair a final touch in the side window of the carriage as she drove off, and quite forgot to wave her hand to Hester, who was standing at the window to see her go. If any misgivings remained at all between the two, they were not with her. She settled herself back amongst the cushions with a little sigh of content. Sir Leslie was a most charming person, and evidently not at all insensible to her charms. She was sure that she was going to have a delightful evening.

* * * * *

Borrowdean, if he possessed no conscience, was not altogether free from some kindred eccentricity. He was reminded sharply enough of the fact about one o'clock the next morning, when the door of the little house on Merton Street was suddenly opened before he could touch the bell. Framed in a little slanting gleam of light, Hester, still wearing her plain black gown, stood and looked at him. His careless words of explanation died away upon his lips. The fire which flashed from her hollow eyes seemed to wither up the very sources of speech within him. The half lights were kind to her. He saw nothing of the hollow cheeks. The weariness of her pose and manner had passed like magic away. She stood there, erect as a dart, her head thrown back, a curious mixture of scorn, of loathing, and of fear in her expression. She looked at him steadily, and he felt his cheeks burn. He was ashamed—ashamed of himself, ashamed of his errand.

"Your mother," he said, struggling to look away from her, "is—a little unwell. The heat of the room—"

She swept down the steps and passed him. Before he could reach her side she was tugging at the handle of the carriage door.

"Mother," she cried, through the window, "undo the door!"

But Mrs. Phillimore made no answer. When at last the door was opened she was discovered half asleep in a corner. Her hair was in some disorder, and her cheeks no longer preserved that even colouring which is a result of the artistic use of the rouge-pot. Her head was thrown back, and she was apparently asleep. Hester stifled a sob. She took her mother by the arm, and shook her.

Mrs. Phillimore sat up and smiled a sleepy smile. She made a few incoherent remarks. They helped her into the house and into an easy-chair, where she promptly turned her face towards the cushions and resumed her slumber. Sir Leslie moved towards the door, then hesitated.

"Miss Phillimore," he said, "I cannot tell you how sorry I am that this should have happened."

She was on her knees before her mother. She turned and rose slowly to her feet. Sir Leslie never quite forgot her gesture as she motioned him towards the door. It was one of the most uncomfortable moments of his life.

"I am afraid—"

She did not speak a word, yet Sir Leslie obeyed what seemed to him more eloquent than words. He turned and left the room and the house. Without any change in her tense expression she waited until she heard him go. Then she sank upon her knees on the hearthrug, and hid her face in her hands.

# CHAPTER X

## THE MAN WITH A MOTIVE

Mannering sat alone in the shade of his cedar tree. He had walked in his rose-garden amongst a wilderness of drooping blossoms, for the season of roses was gone. He had crossed the marshland seawards, only to find a little crowd of holiday-makers in possession of the golf links and the green tufted stretch of sandy shore. The day had been long, almost irksome. A fit of restlessness had driven him from his study. He seemed to have lost all power of concentration. For once his brain had failed him. The shadowy companions who stood ever between him and solitude remained uninvoked. His cigar had burnt out between his fingers. He threw it impatiently away. These were the days, the hours he dreaded.

Clara came down the garden from the house, and seeing him, crossed the lawn and sat down beside him.

"Why, my dear uncle," she exclaimed, "you look almost as dull as I feel! Let us be miserable together!"

"With all my heart," he answered. "Whilst we are about it, can we invent a cause?"

E. Phillips Oppenheim

"Invent!" she repeated. "I do not think we need either of us look very far. Every one seems to have gone away whose presence made this place endurable. Uncle, do you know when Mrs. Handsell is coming back? She promised to write, and I have never heard a word!"

Mannering turned his head. A little rustling wind had stolen in from seaward. Above their heads flights of sea-gulls were floating out towards the creeks. He watched them idly until they dropped down.

"I do not think that she will come back at all," he said, quietly. "I heard to-day that the place was to let again."

"And Sir Leslie Borrowdean?"

"I think you may take it for granted," Mannering remarked, dryly, "that we shall see no more of him."

The girl leaned back and sighed.

"Uncle, what is it that makes you such a hermit?" she asked.

"Age, perhaps, and experience," he answered, lightly. "There are not many people in the world, Clara, who are worth while!"

"Mrs. Handsell was worth while," she murmured.

Mannering did not reply.

"And Sir Leslie Borrowdean," she continued, "was more than just worth while. I think that he was delightful."

"Very young ladies, and very old ones," Mannering remarked, grimly, "generally like Borrowdean."

"And what about Mrs. Handsell?" she asked, with a spice of malice in her tone.

"Mrs. Handsell," Mannering answered, coolly, "was a very charming woman. Since both these people have passed out of our lives, Clara, I scarcely see why we need discuss them."

"One must talk about something," she answered. "At least I must talk, and you must pretend to listen. I positively cannot exist in the house by myself any longer."

"Where is Richard?" Mannering asked.

"Gone into Norwich to dine at the barracks with some stupid men. Not that I mind his going," she added, hastily. "I wish he'd stay away for a month. Of course he's a very good sort, and all that, but he's deadly monotonous. Uncle, really, as a matter of curiosity, before I get to be an old woman I should like to see one other young man."

"Plenty on the links just now!"

"I know it. I sat out near the ninth hole all this morning. There are some Cambridge boys who looked quite nice. One of them was really delightful when I showed him where his ball was, but I can't consider that an introduction, can I? Heavens, who's this?"

Behind the trim maid-servant already crossing the lawn, and within a few yards of them, came a strange, almost tragical, figure. Her plain black clothes and hat were powdered with dust, there were deep lines under her eyes, she swayed a little when she walked, as though with fatigue. She seemed to bring with her into the cool, quiet garden, with its country odours and general air of peace, an alien note. One almost heard the deep undercry from a far-away world of suffering—the great, ever-moving wheels seemed to have caught her up and thrown her down in this most incongruous of places. Clara, in her cool white dress, her fresh complexion, her general air of health and girlish vigour, seemed, as she rose to her feet, a creature of another sex, almost of another world. The two girls exchanged for a moment wondering glances. Then Mannering intervened.

"Hester!" he exclaimed. "Why—is there anything wrong?"

"Nothing—very serious," she answered. "But I had to see you. I thought that I had better come."

He held out his hands.

"You have had a tiring journey," he said. "You must come into the house and let them find you something to eat. Clara, this is Hester Phillimore, the daughter of an old friend of mine. Will you see about a room for her, and lend her anything she requires?"

"Of course," Clara answered. "Won't you come into the house with me?" she added pleasantly to the girl. "You must be horribly tired travelling this hot weather, and this is such an out-of-the-way corner of the world!"

Hester lingered for a moment, glancing nervously at Mannering.

"I must go back to-night," she said. "I only came because I thought that it would be quicker than writing."

"To-night?" he exclaimed. "But, my dear girl, that is impossible. There are no trains, and you are tired out already. Go into the house with my niece, and we will have a talk afterwards."

He walked across the lawn with them, talking pleasantly to Hester, as though her visit were in no sense of the word unpleasant, or an extraordinary event. But when he returned to his seat under the cedar tree his whole expression was changed. The lines about his face had insensibly deepened. He leaned a little forward, looking with weary, unseeing eyes into the tangled shrubbery. Had all men, he wondered, this secret chapter in their lives—the one sore place so impossible to forget, the cupboard of shadows never wholly closed, shadows which at any moment might steal out and encompass his darkening life? He sat there motionless, and his thoughts travelled backwards. There were many things in his life which he had forgotten, but never this. Every word that had been spoken, every detail in that tragic little scene seemed to glide into his memory with a distinctness and amplitude which time had never for one second dimmed. So it must be until the end. He forgot the girl and her errand. He forgot the carefully cultivated philosophy which for so many years had helped him towards forgetfulness. So he sat until the sound of their voices upon the lawn recalled him to the present.

"I will leave you to have your talk with uncle," Clara said. "Afterwards I will come back to you. There he is, sitting under the cedar tree."

The girl came swiftly over to his side. For a moment the compassion which he had always felt for her swept away the memory of his own sorrow. Her pallid, colourless face had lost everything except expression. If the weariness, which seemed to have found a home in her eyes, was just now absent, it was because a worse thing was shining out of them—a fear, of which there were traces even in her hurried walk and tone. He rose at once and held out his hands.

"Come and sit down, Hester," he said, "and don't look so frightened."

She obeyed him at once.

"I am frightened," she said, "because I feel that I ought not to have come here, and yet I thought that you ought to know at once what has happened. Sir Leslie Borrowdean has been coming to see mother. Last night he took her out to dinner. She came home—late—she was not quite herself. This morning she was frightened and hysterical. She said—that she had been talking."

"To Sir Leslie Borrowdean?"

"Yes."

Mannering showed no signs of dismay. He took the girl's thin white hand in his, and held it almost affectionately.

"I am very glad to know this at once, dear," he said, "and you did what was right and kind when you came to see me. But Sir Leslie Borrowdean has no reason to make himself my enemy. On the contrary, just now he seems particularly anxious to cultivate my friendship."

"Then why," the girl asked, "has he gone out of his way to—to—"

Mannering stopped her.

"He had a motive, of course. Borrowdean is one of those men who do nothing without a motive. I believe that I can even guess what it is. Don't let this thing distress you too much, Hester. I do not think that we have anything to worry about."

"But he knows!"

"I could not imagine a man," Mannering answered, "better able to keep a secret."

The girl sat silent for a moment.

"I suppose I have been an idiot," she remarked.

"You have been nothing of the sort," Mannering asserted, firmly. "You have done just what is kind, and what will help me to save the situation. I must confess that I should not like to have been taken by surprise. You have saved me from that. Now let us put the whole subject away for a time. How I wish that you could stay here for a few days."

The girl smiled a little piteously.

"I ought not to have left her even for so long as this," she said. "I must go back to-morrow morning by the first train."

He nodded. He felt that it was useless to combat her resolution.

"You and I," he said, gravely, "have both our burdens to carry. Only it seems a little unfair that Providence should have made my back so much the broader. Listen, Hester!"

The full murmur of the sea growing louder and louder as the salt water flowed up into the creeks betokened the change of tide. Faint wreaths of mist were rising up from over the shadowy marshland. Above them were the stars. He laid his hand upon her shoulder.

"Dear child!" he said, "I think that you understand how it is that the burden, after all, is easier for me. A man may forget his troubles here, for all the while there is this eternal background of peaceful things."

Her hand stole into his.

"Yes," she murmured, "I understand. Don't let them ever bring you away."

# CHAPTER XI

## MANNERING'S ALTERNATIVE

Once again Mannering found himself in the over-scented, overheated room, which was perhaps of all places in the world the one he hated the most. Fresh from the wind-swept places of his country home, he found the atmosphere intolerable. After a few minutes' waiting he threw open the windows and leaned out. Hester was walking in the Square somewhere. He had a shrewd idea that she had been sent out of the way. With a restless impatience of her absence he awaited the interview which he dreaded.

Her mother's coming took him a little by surprise. She seemed to have laid aside all her usual customs. She entered the room quietly. She greeted him almost nervously. She was dressed, without at any rate any obvious attempt to attract, in a plain black gown, and with none of the extravagances in which she sometimes delighted. Her usual boisterous confidence of manner seemed to have deserted her. Her face, without its skilful touches of rouge, looked thin, and almost peaked.

"I am so glad that you came, Lawrence," she said. "It was very good of you."

She glanced towards the opened windows, and he closed them at once.

"I am afraid," he said, "that you have not been well!"

There was a touch of her old self in the hardness of her low laugh.

"It is remorse!" she declared. "I think that for once in my life I have permitted myself to think! It is a great mistake. One loses confidence when one realizes what a beast one is."

He waited in silence. It seemed to him the best thing. She sat down a little wearily. He remained standing a few feet away.

"I have given you away, Lawrence," she said, quietly.

"So," he remarked, "I understand."

"Hester has told you, of course. I am not blaming her. She did quite right. Only I should have told you myself. I wanted to be the first to assure you of this. Our secret is quite safe. The man—with whom I made a fool of myself—has given me his word of honour."

"Sir Leslie Borrowdean's—word of honour!" Mannering remarked, with slow scorn. "Do you know the man, I wonder?"

"I know that he wishes to be your friend, and not your enemy," she said.

"He chooses his friends for what they are worth to him," Mannering answered. "It is all a matter of self-interest. He has some idea of making me the stepping-stone to his advancement. I have a place just now in his scheme of life.

But as for friendship! Borrowdean does not know the meaning of the word."

"You speak bitterly," she remarked.

"I know the man," he answered.

"Will you tell me," she asked, "what it is that he wants of you?"

He shrugged his shoulders.

"Is this worth discussing between us?" he asked.

"Yes."

"Very well, then, you shall know. He wants me to re-enter political life, to be the jackal to pull the chestnuts out of the fire for him."

"To re-enter political life! And why don't you?"

Mannering turned abruptly round and looked her in the face. He had been gazing out of the window, wondering how long it would be before Hester returned.

"Why don't I!" he repeated, a little vaguely. "How can you ask me such a question as that?"

She was undisturbed. Again he marvelled at the change in her.

"Is it so very extraordinary a question?" she said. "I have often wondered whether you meant to content yourself with your present life always. It is scarcely worthy of you, is it? You were born to other things than to live the life of a country gentleman. You dabble in literature, they say, and poke your stick into politics through the pages of the reviews. Why don't you take your coat off and play the game?"

Mannering was silent for several moments. He was, however, meditating his own reply less than studying his questioner. Her attitude was amazing to him. She watched him all the time, frowning.

"You are not usually so tongue-tied," she remarked, irritably. "Have you nothing to say to me?"

"I am wondering," he said, quietly, "what has given birth to this sudden interest in my proceedings. What does it matter to you how my days are spent, or what manner of use I make of them?"

"There was a time—" she began.

"A time irretrievably past," he interrupted, shortly.

"I am not so sure!" she declared, doubtfully.

"What has Borrowdean to do with this?" he asked her, abruptly.

"Borrowdean?"

"Surely! Some one has been putting notions into your head."

"Why take that for granted?" she asked, equably. "The pity of the whole thing is obvious enough, isn't it? Sometimes I think that we were a pair of fools. We played into the hands of fate. We were brought face to face with a terrible situation. Instead of meeting it bravely we played the coward. Why don't you forget, Lawrence, as I have done? Take up your work again. Set a seal upon—that memory."

"I have outgrown my ambitions," he answered. "Life was hot enough in my veins then. Desire grows cold with the years. I am content."

"But I," she answered, "am not."

"We each chose our life," he reminded her.

"Perhaps. I am not satisfied with my choice. You may be with yours."

"I am."

She leaned over towards him.

"Once," she said, "you offered me what you called—atonement. I refused it. Just then it seemed horrible. Now that feeling has passed away. I am lonely, Lawrence, and I am weary of the sort of life I have been living. Supposing I asked you to make me that offer again?"

Mannering turned slowly towards her. He was not a man who easily showed emotion, but there were traces of it now in his face. The hand which rested on the back of his chair shook. There was in his eyes the look of a man who sees evil things.

"It is too late, Blanche," he said. "You cannot be in earnest?"

"Why not?" she murmured, dropping her eyes. "I am tired of my life. What you owed me then you owe me now. Why should it be too late? I am not an old woman yet, nor are you an old man, and I am weary of being alone."

Mannering walked to the window. His hand went to his forehead. It was damp and cold. He was afraid! If she were in earnest! And she spoke like a woman who knew her mind. She was always, he remembered, a creature of caprice. If she were really in earnest!

"We have drifted too far apart, Blanche," he said, making an effort to face the situation. "Years ago this might have been possible. To-day it would be a dismal failure. My ways are not yours. The life I lead would bore you to death."

"There is no reason why you should not alter it," she answered, calmly. "In fact, I should wish you to. Blakely all the year round would be an impossibility. You could come and live in London."

He looked at her fixedly.

"Have you forgotten?" he asked.

She covered her face with her hands for a moment. If indeed she really felt any emotion it passed quickly away, for when she looked up again there were no traces left.

"I have forgotten nothing," she declared, defiantly. "Only the horror and fear of it all has passed away. I don't see why I should suffer all my life. In fact, I don't mean to. I don't want to be a miserable, lonely old woman. I want a home, something different from this."

Mannering faced her gravely.

"Blanche," he said, "you are proposing something which would most surely ruin the rest of our lives. What we might have been to one another if things had been different it is hard to say. But this much is very certain. We belong now to different worlds. We have drifted apart with the years. Even the little we see of one another now is far from a pleasure to either of us. What you are suggesting would be simply suicidal."

She was silent. He watched her anxiously. As a rule her face was easy enough to read. To-day it was impenetrable. He could not tell what was passing behind that still, almost stony, look. Her silence forced him again into speech.

"You agree with me, surely, Blanche? You must agree with me?"

She raised her head.

"I am not sure that I do," she answered. "But at least I understand you. That is something! You want to go on as you are—apart from me. That is true, isn't it?"

"Yes!"

She nodded.

"At least you are candid. You want your liberty—unfettered. What are you willing to pay for it?"

He looked at her incredulously.

"I do not quite understand!" he said.

She laughed, and the laugh belonged to her old self.

"Indeed! I thought that I was explicit enough, brutally explicit, even. What have you to offer me in place of your name and yourself? What sacrifice are you prepared to make?"

E. Phillips Oppenheim

He looked at her furtively, as though even then he doubted the significance of her words.

"You have already half my income," he said, slowly.

She shrugged her shoulders.

"A thousand a year! What can one do on that? To live decently in town one needs much more."

"It is as much as I can offer," he remarked, stiffly.

"Then you should earn money," she declared. "It's easy enough for men with brains. Go back into politics instead of idling your time away down in Blakely. I mean it! I've no patience with men who have a right to a place in the world which they won't fill."

"Surely," he remonstrated, "I may be allowed to choose the manner of my life!"

"If you can afford to—yes," she answered. "But I want one of two things. The first seems to scare you to death even to think of. The second is more money—a good deal more money."

"But," he protested, "even if I did as you suggested, and went back into politics, it would be some time, if ever, before I should be any better off."

"I will wait until that time comes," she answered, "provided that when it does, you share with me."

Then Mannering understood.

"Upon my word," he exclaimed, "you are an apt conspirator

indeed. All this time you have been fooling me. I even fancied—bah! How much is Borrowdean giving you for this?"

"Nothing at all," she answered, coolly. "It is my own sincere desire for your welfare which has prompted all that I have said to you. I am ambitious for you, Lawrence. I should like to see you Prime Minister. I am sure you could be if you tried. You are letting your talents rust, and I don't approve of it!"

The faint note of mockery in her tone was clearly apparent. Mannering found it hard to answer her calmly.

"Come," he said, "put it into plain words. What does it mean? What do you want?"

"Sir Leslie tells me," she said, raising her eyes and looking him in the face, "that his party is prepared to find you a safe seat to-morrow. I want you to give up your hermit's life and accept it."

"And the alternative?"

"You have it already before you. Your reception of it was not, I must admit, altogether flattering."

"I am allowed," he said, "some short space of time for consideration?"

"Until to-morrow, if you wish," she answered. "I imagine you know pretty well what you mean to do."

He picked up his hat and turned towards the door.

"Yes," he said, "I suppose I do!"

# BOOK II

## CHAPTER I

### BORROWDEAN MAKES A BARGAIN

Borrowdean sank into the chair which Berenice had indicated, with a little sigh of relief.

"These all-night sittings," he remarked, "get less of a joke as one advances in years. You read the reports this morning?"

She nodded.

"And Mannering's speech?"

"Every word of it."

"Our little conspiracy," he continued, "is bearing fruit. Honestly, Mannering is a surprise, even to me. After these years of rust I scarcely expected him to step back at once into all his former brilliancy. His speech last night was wonderful."

"I heard it," she said. "You are quite right. It was wonderful."

"You were in the House?" he asked, looking up quickly.

"I was there till midnight," she answered.

Borrowdean was thoughtful for a moment.

"His speech," he remarked, "sounded even better than it read."

"I thought so," she admitted. "He has all the smaller tricks of the orator, as well as the gift of eloquence. One can always listen to him with pleasure."

"Will you pardon me," Borrowdean asked, "if I make a remark which may sound a little impertinent? You and Mannering were great friends at Blakely. On my first visit there you will remember that you did not attempt to conceal that there was more than an ordinary intimacy between you. Yet to-day I notice that there are indications on both your parts of a desire to avoid one another as much as possible. It seems to me a pity that you two should not be friends. Is there any small misunderstanding which a common friend— such as I trust I may call myself—might help to smooth away?"

Berenice regarded him thoughtfully.

"It is strange," she said, "that you should talk to me like this, you who are certainly responsible for any estrangement there may be between Mr. Mannering and myself. Please answer me this question. Why do you wish us to be friends?"

Borrowdean shrugged his shoulders.

"You and he and myself, with about a dozen others," he answered, "form the backbone of a political party. As time goes on we shall in all probability be drawn closer and closer together. It seems to me best that our alliance should be as real a thing as possible."

Berenice smiled.

"Rather a sentimental attitude for you, Sir Leslie," she remarked. "Have you ever considered the fact that any coolness there may be between Lawrence Mannering and myself is entirely due to you?"

"To me!" he exclaimed.

"Exactly! At Blakely we were on terms of the most intimate friendship. I had grown to like and respect him more than any man I had ever met. I don't know exactly why I should take you so far into my confidence, but I am inclined to do so. Our friendship seemed likely to develop into—other things."

"My dear Duchess—"

"Don't interrupt me! I have an idea that you were perfectly aware of it. Perhaps it did not suit your plans. At any rate, you made statements to me concerning him which, as you very well knew, were likely to alter my entire opinion of him. I had an idea that there was some code of honour between men which kept them from discussing the private life of their friends with a woman. You seem to have been troubled with no such scruples. You told me things about Lawrence Mannering which made it absolutely necessary that I should hear them confirmed or denied from his own lips."

"You would rather have remained in ignorance, then?" he asked.

"I would rather have remained in ignorance," she repeated,

calmly. "Don't flatter yourself, Sir Leslie, that a woman ever has any real gratitude in her heart for the person who, out of friendship, or some other motive, destroys her ideals. I should have married Lawrence Mannering if you had not spoken."

Borrowdean was silent. In his heart he was thinking how nearly one of the most cherished schemes of his life had gone awry.

"I am afraid, then," he said, "that even at the risk of your further displeasure I have no regrets to offer you."

"I do not desire your regrets," she answered, scornfully. "You did what it suited you to do, and I presume you are satisfied. As for the rest, I can assure you that the relations between Mr. Mannering and myself are such that the balance of your political apple-cart is not likely to be disturbed. Now let us talk of something else. I have said all that I have to say on this matter—"

Sir Leslie was not entirely satisfied with the result of his afternoon call. He walked slowly from Grosvenor Square to a small house in Sloane Gardens, in front of which a well-appointed victoria was waiting. He looked around at the well-filled window-boxes, thick with geraniums and marguerites, at the coachman's new livery, at the evidences of luxury which met him the moment the door was opened, and his lips parted in a faint, unpleasant smile.

"Poor Mannering," he murmured to himself. "What a millstone!"

Mrs. Phillimore was at home. She would certainly see Sir Leslie, the trim parlour-maid thought, with a smile. She left him alone in a flower-scented drawing-room, crowded with rococo furniture and many knick-knacks, where he waited more or less impatiently for nearly twenty minutes. Then Mrs. Phillimore swept into the room, elaborately gowned for her drive in the park, dispersing perfumes in all directions and bestowing a dazzling smile upon him.

"I felt very much inclined not to see you at all," she declared. "How dared you keep away from me all this time? You haven't been near me since I moved in here. What do you think of my little house?"

"Charming!" he declared.

"Every one likes it," she remarked. "Such a time I had choosing the furniture. Hester wouldn't help with a single thing. You know that she has left me?"

"I understood that she had gone to Mr. Mannering as secretary," he answered. "She has done typing for him for some time, hasn't she?"

Mrs. Phillimore nodded.

"Worships him, the little fool!" she remarked. "I must admit I detest clever men. You are all so dull, and such scheming brutes, too."

Borrowdean smiled. A certain rough-and-ready humour about this woman always appealed to him. He looked around.

"You seem to have done very nicely with that little offering," he said.

"Oh, ready money goes a long way," she declared, carelessly.

"And when it is spent?" he asked. "Five thousand pounds is not an inexhaustible sum."

"By the time it is spent," she answered, "your party will be in, and I suppose you will make Lawrence something."

Borrowdean regarded the woman thoughtfully.

"Has it ever occurred to you," he asked, "that the time is likely to come when Mannering might want his money for himself? He might want to marry, for instance."

She laughed mirthlessly, but without a shade of uneasiness.

"You don't know Lawrence," she declared, scornfully. "He'd never do that whilst I was alive."

"I am not so sure," Borrowdean answered, calmly. "Between ourselves, I cannot see that your claim upon him amounts to very much."

"Then you're a fool!" she declared, brusquely.

"No, I'm not," Borrowdean assured her, blandly. "Now I fancy that I could tell you something which would surprise you very much."

"Has he been making love to any one?" she asked, quickly.

"Something of the sort," he admitted. "Mannering is quixotic, of course, and that hermit life of his down in Norfolk has made him more so. Now he has come back again into the world it is just possible that he may see things differently. I flatter myself that I am a man of common sense. I know how the whole affair seems to me, and I tell you frankly that I can see nothing from the point of view of honour to prevent Mannering marrying any woman he chooses. I think it very possible that he may readjust his whole point of view."

The woman looked around her, and outside, where her victoria was waiting. At last she had attained to an environment such as she had all her life desired. The very idea that at any moment it might be swept away sent a cold shiver through her. Borrowdean had a trick of speaking convincingly. And besides—

"Who is the woman?" she asked.

"I had been wondering," Borrowdean said, "whether it would not be better to tell you, so that you might be on your guard. The woman is the Duchess of Lenchester."

She stared at him.

"You're in earnest?"

"Absolutely!"

Her face hardened. Whatever other feelings she may have had for Mannering, she had lived so long with the thought that he belonged to her, at least as a wage-earning animal, a person whose province it was to make her ways smooth so far as his means permitted, that the thought of losing him stirred in her a dull, jealous anger.

"I'd stop it!" she declared. "I'd go and tell her everything."

"I am not sure," Borrowdean continued, smoothly, "that that would be the best course. Supposing that you were to tell her the story just as you told it to me. It is just possible that her point of view might be mine. She might regard Lawrence

Mannering as a quixotic person, and endeavour to persuade him that your claim was scarcely so binding as he seems to imagine. In any case, I do not think that your story would prevent her marrying him."

"Then all I can say is that she is a woman with a very queer sense of right and wrong," Mrs. Phillimore declared, angrily.

Borrowdean smiled.

"A woman," he said, "who is fond of a man is apt to have her judgment a little warped. The Duchess is a woman of fine perceptions and sound judgment. But she is attracted by Lawrence Mannering. She admires him. He is the sort of person who appeals to her imagination. These feelings might easily become, if they have not already developed into, something else. And I tell you again that I do not believe your story would stop her from marrying him."

She leaned a little towards him.

"What would?" she asked, earnestly.

He hesitated.

"Well," he said, "I think I could tell you that!"

She held up her hand.

"Stop, please," she said. "I want to ask you something else. Are you Lawrence's enemy?"

"I? Why, of course not!"

"Then where do you come in?" she asked, bluntly. "You couldn't persuade me that it is interest on my account which brings you here and makes you tell me these things. You don't care a button for me."

Borrowdean took her hand and leaned forward in his chair. She snatched it away.

"Oh, rot!" she exclaimed. "I may be a fool, but I'm not quite fool enough for that. I'm simply a useful person for the moment in some scheme of yours, and I just want to know what that scheme is. That's all! I'm not the sort of woman you'd waste a moment with, except for some purpose of your own. You've proved that. You wormed my story out of me very cleverly, but I haven't quite forgotten it yet, you know. And to tell you the truth," she continued, "you're not my sort, either. You and Lawrence Mannering are something of the same kidney after all, though he's worth a dozen of you. You've neither of you any time for play in the world, and that sort of man doesn't appeal to me. Now where do you come in?"

Borrowdean looked at her thoughtfully. He had the air of a man a trifle piqued. Perhaps for the first time he realized that Blanche Phillimore was not altogether an unattractive-looking woman. If she had desired to stir him from his indifference she could not have chosen any more effectual means.

"I am not going to argue with you," he said, quietly. "I have ambitions, it is true, and the world is not exactly a playground for me. Nevertheless, I am not an ascetic like Mannering. The world, the flesh and the devil are very much to me what they are to other men. But in a sense you have cornered me, and you shall have the truth. I want to marry the Duchess of Lenchester myself."

She nodded.

"That's right," she said. "Now we know where we are. You want to marry the Duchess, and therefore you don't want her to have Lawrence. You think that I can stop it, and as I don't want him married, either, you come to me. That is reasonable. Now how can I prevent it?"

"By a slight variation from your story," he answered. "In fact, words are not needed. A suggestion only would be enough, and circumstances," he added, glancing around, "are strongly in favour of that suggestion."

"You mean—"

He shrugged his shoulders.

"Mannering is security for your lease," he remarked. "You pay in his cheques to your bank every quarter. He occupies just that position which in a general way is capable of one explanation only."

"Well?"

"Let the Duchess believe him, or continue to believe him, to be an ordinary man—instead of a fool—and she will never marry him."

"And she will you?"

"I hope so!"

She leaned back in her chair. He could not altogether understand her silence. Surely she could have no scruples?

"It seems to me," she said at last, "that I am to play your game for nothing. I don't care so very much, after all, if he marries. He'd settle all he could on me. In fact, I should have just as much claim on him as I have now."

"I did not say that you should play it for nothing," he answered. "I want us to understand each other, because I have an idea that you may be seeing something of the Duchess at any moment. Let us put it this way. Suppose I promise to give you a diamond necklace of the value of, say five thousand pounds, the day I marry the Duchess!"

She rose and put pen and paper before him. He shook his head.

"I can't put an arrangement of that sort on paper," he protested. "You must rely upon my word of honour."

She held out the pen to him.

"On paper, or the whole thing is off absolutely," she declared.

"You won't trust me?"

She looked at him.

"There isn't much honour about an arrangement of this sort, is there?" she said. "It has to be on paper, or not at all."

A carriage stopped outside. They heard the bell.

"That," she remarked, "may be the Duchess of Lenchester."

He caught up the pen and wrote a few hurried lines. The smile with which he handed it to her was not altogether successful.

"After all, you know," he said, "there should be honour

amongst thieves."

"No doubt there is," she answered. "Only thieves are a cut above us, aren't they?"

"I don't believe," Borrowdean said to himself, as he reached the pavement, "that that woman is such a fool as she seems."

# CHAPTER II

## "CHERCHEZ LA FEMME"

Mannering hated dinner parties, but this one had been a necessity. Nevertheless, if he had known who his companion for the evening was fated to be he would most certainly have stayed away. Her first question showed him that she had no intention of ignoring memories which to him were charged with the most subtle pain.

He looked down the table, and back again into her face.

"You are quite right," he said. "This is different. We cannot compare. We can judge only by effect—the effect upon ourselves."

"Can you be analytical and yet remain within the orbit of my understanding?" she asked, with a faint smile. "If so, I should like to know exactly how you feel about it all."

He passed a course with a somewhat weary gesture of refusal, and leaned back in his chair.

"You are comprehensive—as usual," he remarked. "Just then I was wondering whether the perfume of these banks of hot-house flowers—I don't know what they are—was as sweet as the odour of the salt from the creeks, or my roses when the night wind touched them."

"You were wondering! And what have you decided?"

"Ah, I must not say. In any case you would not agree with me. Wasn't it you who once scoffed at my idyll in the wilderness?"

"I do not think that I believe in idylls, nowadays," she answered. "One risks so many disappointments when one believes in anything."

He raised his eyebrows.

"You did not talk like this at Blakely," he remarked.

"I am nearly a year older," she answered, "and a year wiser."

"You pain me," he answered, with a little sigh. "You are a person of intelligence, and you talk of growing wiser with the years. Don't you know that the only supreme wisdom is the wisdom of the child? Our inherent ignorance is fed and nourished by experience."

"You are hiding yourself," she remarked, "behind a fence of words—words that mean less than nothing! I don't suppose that even you would hesitate to admit that you have come into a larger world. You may have to pay for it. We all do. But at any rate it is an atmosphere which breeds men."

"And changes women," he murmured, under his breath.

She did not speak to him for several moments. Then the alteration in her tone and manner was almost marked.

"You mentioned Blakely a few minutes ago," she said. "I wonder whether you remember our discussion there upon precisely what has come to pass."

"Perfectly!"

"I remember that in those days," she continued, reflectively, "you were very firm indeed, or was it my poor arguments that were at fault? Your vegetable and sentimental existence was a part of yourself. Ambition! You had forgotten what it was. Duty! You spouted individualism by the hour. Gratify my curiosity, won't you? Tell me what made you change your mind?"

Mannering was silent for a moment. A close observer might have noticed a certain alteration in his face. A touch of the coming weariness was already there.

"I have never changed my mind," he answered, quietly. "My inclinations to-day are what they have always been."

She dropped her voice a little.

"You puzzle me," she said, softly. "Do you mean that it was your sense of duty which was awakened?"

"No, I do not mean that," he answered. "Forgive me—but I cannot tell you what I do mean. Circumstances brought me here against my will."

"You talk like a slave," she said, lightly enough. She, too, was brave. She drank wine to keep the colour in her cheeks, and she told herself that the pain at her heart was nothing. Nevertheless, some words of Borrowdean's were mocking her all the while.

"We are all slaves," he answered. "The folly of it all is when we stop to think. Then we realize it."

Their conversation was like a strangled thing. Neither made any serious effort to re-establish it. It was a great dinner party, chiefly political, and long drawn out. Afterwards came a reception, and Mannering was at once surrounded. It was nearly midnight when by chance they came face to face again. She touched him with her fan, and leaned aside from the little group by whom she was surrounded.

"Are you very much occupied, Mr. Mannering," she asked, lightly, "or could you spare me a moment?"

He stopped short. Whatever surprise he may have felt he concealed.

"I am entirely at your service, Duchess," he answered. "Mr. Harrison will excuse me, I am sure," he added, turning to his companion.

She rested her fingers upon his arm. The house belonged to a relative of hers, and she knew where to find a quiet spot. When they were alone she did not hesitate for a moment.

"Lawrence," she said, quietly, "will you imagine for a moment that we are back again at Blakely?"

"I would to God we were!" he answered, impulsively. "That is—if you wish it too!"

She did not answer at once. The sudden abnegation of his reserve took her by surprise. She had to readjust her words.

"At least," she said, "there are many things about Blakely which I regret all the time. You know, of course, the chief one, our own altered selves. I know, Lawrence, that I need to ask your forgiveness. I came there under an assumed name, and I will admit that my coming was part of a scheme between Ronalds, Rochester and myself. Well, I am ready to ask your forgiveness for that. I don't think you ought to refuse it me. It doesn't alter anything that happened. It doesn't even affect it. You must believe that!"

"I believe it, if you tell me so," he answered.

"I do tell you," she declared. "I can explain it all. I am longing to have it all off my mind. But first of all, there is just one thing which I want to ask you."

His face as he looked towards her gave her almost a shock. Very little was left of his healthy colouring. Already there were lines under his eyes, and he was certainly thinner. And there was something else which almost appalled her. There was fear in his manner. He sat like a man waiting for sentence, a man fore-doomed.

"I want to know," she said, "what has brought you—here. I want to know what manner of persuasion has prevailed—when mine was so ineffectual. Don't think that I am not glad that you decided as you did. I am glad—very. You are in your rightful place, and I am only too thankful to hear about you, and read—and watch. But—we are jealous creatures, we women, you know, and I want to know whose and what arguments prevailed, when mine were so very insufficient."

He answered her without hesitation, but his tone was dull and spiritless.

"I cannot tell you!"

There was a short silence. She gathered her skirts for a

moment in her hand as though about to rise, but apparently changed her mind. She waited for some time, and then she spoke again.

"Perhaps you think that I ought not to ask?"

He looked at her hopelessly.

"No, I don't think that. You have a right to ask. But it doesn't alter things, does it? I can't tell you."

"You asked me to marry you."

"It was at Blakely. We were so far out of the world—such a different world. I think that I had forgotten all that I wished to forget. Everything seemed possible there."

"You mean that you would have married me and told me nothing of circumstances in your life, so momentous that they have practically exercised in this matter of your return to politics a compelling influence over you?"

"I am sure," he said, "that I should not have told you!"

His unhappiness moved her. She still lingered. She drew a little breath, and she went a good deal further than she had meant to go.

"It has been suggested to me," she said, "that your reappearance was due to a woman's influence. Is this true?"

"A woman had something to do with it," he admitted.

"Who is she?"

"Her name," he answered, "is Blanche Phillimore. It was  the person to whom you yourself alluded."

The Duchess maintained her self-control. She was quite pale, however, and her tone was growing ominously harder.

"Is she a connection of yours?"

"No!"

"Is there anything which you could tell me about her?"

"No!"

"Yet at her bidding you have done—what you refused me."

"I had no choice! Borrowdean saw to that," he remarked, bitterly.

She rose to her feet. She was pale, and her lips were quivering, but she was splendidly handsome.

"What sort of a man are you, Lawrence Mannering?" she asked, steadily. "You play at idealism, you asked me to marry you. Yet all the time there was this background."

"It was madness," he admitted. "But remember it was Mrs. Handsell whom I asked to be my wife."

"What difference does that make? She was a woman, too, I suppose, to be honoured—or insulted—by your choice!"

"There was no question of insult, I think."

She looked at him steadfastly. Perhaps for a moment her thoughts travelled back to those unforgotten days in the rose-gardens at Blakely, to the man whose delicate but wholesome joy in the wind and the sun and the flowers, the sea-stained marshes and the windy knolls where they had so often stood together, she could not forget. His life had seemed to her then so beautiful a thing. The elementary purity of his thoughts and aspirations were unmistakable. She told herself passionately that there must be a way out.

"Lawrence," she said, "we are man and woman, not boy and girl. You asked me to marry you once, and I hesitated, only because of one thing. I do not wish to look into any hidden chambers of your life. I wish to know nothing, save of the present. What claim has this woman Blanche Phillimore upon you?"

"It is her secret," he answered, "not mine alone."

"She lives in your house—through her you are a poor man— through her you are back again, a worker in the world."

"Yes!"

"It must always be so?"

"Yes."

"And you have nothing more to say?"

"If I dared," he said, raising his eyes to hers, "I would say— trust me! I am not exactly—one of the beasts of the field."

"Will you not trust me, then? I am not a foolish girl. I am a woman. You may destroy an ideal, but there would be something left."

"I can tell you no more."

"Then it is to be good-bye?"

"If you say so!"

She turned slowly away. He watched her disappear. After-wards, with a curious sense of unreality, he remained quite still, his eyes still fixed upon the portiere through which she had passed.

# CHAPTER III

## ONE OF THE "SUFFERERS"

Mannering kept no carriage, and he left Downing Street on foot. The little house which he had taken furnished for the season was in the somewhat less pretentious neighborhood of Portland Crescent, and as there were no hansoms within hail he started to walk home. An attempt at a short cut landed him presently in a neighborhood which he failed to recognize. He paused, looking about him for some one from whom to inquire the way. Then he at once realized what he had already more than once suspected. He was being followed.

The footsteps ceased as he himself had halted. It was a wet night, and the street was ill-lit. Nevertheless, Mannering could distinguish the figure of a man standing in the shadows of the houses, apparently to escape observation. For a moment he hesitated. His follower could scarcely be an ordinary hooligan, for not more than fifty yards away were the lights of a great thoroughfare, and even in this street, quiet though it was, there were people passing to and fro. His curiosity prompted him to subterfuge. He took a cigarette from his case, and commenced in a leisurely manner the operation of striking a light. Instantly the figure of the man began to move cautiously towards him.

E. Phillips Oppenheim

Mannering's eyes and hearing, keenly developed by his country life, apprised him of every step the man took. He heard him pause whilst a couple of women passed on the other side of the way. Afterwards his approach became swifter and more stealthy. Barely in time to avoid, he scarcely knew what, Mannering turned sharply round.

"What do you want with me?" he demanded.

The man showed no signs of confusion. Mannering, as he looked sternly into his face, lost all fear of personal assault. He was neatly but shabbily dressed, pale, and with a slight red moustache. He had a somewhat broad forehead, eyes with more than an ordinary lustre, and, in somewhat striking contradiction to the rest of his features, a large sensitive mouth with a distinctly humorous curve. Even now its corners were receding into a smile, which had in it, however, other elements than mirth alone.

"You are Mr. Lawrence Mannering?"

"That is my name," Mannering answered, "but if you want to speak to me why don't you come up like a man, instead of dogging my footsteps? It looked as though you wanted to take me by surprise. What is that you are hiding up your sleeve?"

The man held it out, placed it even in Mannering's hand.

"A life preserver, steel, as you see, and with a beautiful spring. Deadly weapon, isn't it, sir? Even a half-hearted sort of blow might kill a man."

Mannering swung the weapon lightly in his hand. It cut the air with a soft, sickly swish.

"What were you doing following me, on tiptoe, with this in your hand?" he asked, sternly.

"Well," the man answered, as though forced to confess an unpleasant truth, "I am very much afraid that I was going to hit you with it."

Mannering looked up and down the street for a policeman.

"Indeed!" he said. "And may I ask why you changed your mind?"

"It was an inspiration," the man answered, easily. "To tell you the truth, the clumsiness of the whole thing grated very much upon me. Personally, I ran no risk, don't think it was that. My escape was very carefully provided for. But one thinks quickly in moments of excitement, and it seemed to me as I took those last few steps that I saw a better way."

"A better way," Mannering repeated, puzzled. "I am afraid I don't quite understand you. I presume that you meant to rob me. You would not have found it worth while, by the bye."

The man laughed softly.

"My dear sir," he exclaimed, "do I look like a robber? Rumour says that you are a poor man. I should think it very likely that, although I am not a rich one, I am at least as well off as you."

Mannering looked out no more for the policeman. He was getting interested.

"Come," he said, "I should like to understand what all this means. You were going to tap me on the head with this particularly unpleasant weapon, and your motive was not robbery. I am not aware of ever having seen you before. I am not aware of having an enemy in the world. Explain yourself."

"I should be charmed," the man answered. "I do not wish to keep you standing here, however. Will you allow me to walk with you towards your home? You can retain possession of that little trifle, if you like," he added, pointing to the weapon which was still in Mannering's hand. "I can assure you that I have nothing else of the sort in my possession. You can feel my pockets, if you like."

"I will take your word!" Mannering said. "I was on my way to Portland Crescent, but I fancy that I have taken a wrong turn."

"We can get there this way," the man answered. "Excuse me one second."

He paused, and lit a cigarette. Then with his hands behind his back he stepped out by Mannering's side.

"What was that you said just now?" he remarked, "that you were not aware of having an enemy in the world? My dear sir, there was never a more extraordinary delusion. I should seriously doubt whether in the whole of the United Kingdom there is a man who has more. I know myself of a million or so who would welcome the news of your death to-morrow. I know of a select few who have opened, and will open their newspapers to-morrow, and for the next few days, in the hope of seeing your obituary notice."

A light commenced to break in upon Mannering. He looked towards his companion incredulously.

"You mean political opponents!" he exclaimed. "Is that what

you are driving at all the time?"

The man laughed softly.

"My friend," he said—"excuse me, Mr. Mannering—you remind me irresistibly of *Punch's* cartoon last week—the ostrich politician with his head in the sand. You have thrust yours very deep down indeed, when you talk of political opponents. Do you know what they call you in the North, sir?"

"No!"

"The enemy of the people! It isn't a pleasant title, is it?"

"It is a false one!" Mannering declared, with a little note of passion quivering in his tone.

"It is as true and certain as the judgment of God!" his companion answered, with almost lightning-like rapidity.

There was a moment's silence. They passed a lamp-post, and Mannering, turning his head, scrutinized the other's features closely.

"I should like to know who you are," he said, "and what your name is."

"It is a reasonable curiosity," the man answered. "My name is Fardell, Richard Fardell, and I am a retired bookmaker."

"A bookmaker!" Mannering repeated, incredulously.

"Precisely. I should imagine from what I know of you, Mr. Mannering, that my occupation, or rather my late occupation, is not one which would appeal to you favourably. Very likely not! I don't see why it should myself. But at any rate, it taught me a lot about my fellow men. I did my business in shillings and half-crowns, you see. Did it with the working classes, the sort who used to go to a race-meeting for a jaunt, and just have a bit on for the sake of the sport. Took their missus generally, and made a holiday of it, and if they lost they'd grin and come and chaff me, and if they won they'd spend the money like lords. I made money, of course, bought houses, and made a lot more. Then business fell off. I didn't seem to meet with that cheerful holiday-making crew at any of the meetings up in the North, and I got sick of it. You see, I'd made sort of friends with them. They all knew Dicky Fardell, and I knew hundreds of 'em by sight. They'd come and mob me to stand 'em a drink when the wrong horse won, and I can tell you I never refused. They were always good-tempered, real sports to the backbone, and I tell you I was fond of 'em. And then they left off coming. I couldn't understand it at first. The one or two who came talked of bad trade, and when I asked after their pals they shook their heads. They betted in shillings instead of half-crowns, and I didn't like the look of their faces when they lost. I tell you, it got so at last that I used to watch for the horse they'd put their bit on to win, and feel kind o' sick when it didn't. You can imagine I couldn't stand that sort of thing long. I chucked it, and I went to look for my pals. I wanted to find out what had become of them."

Mannering looked at him curiously.

"You found, I hope," he said, drily, "that the British workman had discovered a better investment for his shillings and half-crowns than the race-course."

Mr. Richard Fardell smiled pleasantly, but tolerantly.

"It's clear," he said, "that you, meaning no offence, Mr.

Mannering, know nothing about the British workman. Whatever else he may be, he's a sportsman. He'll look after his wife and kids as well as the best of them, but he'll have his bit of sport so long as he's got a copper in his pocket. When he didn't come I put my kit on one side and went to look for him. I went, mind you, as his friend, and knowing a bit about him. And what I found has made a changed man of me."

Mannering nodded.

"I am afraid things are bad up in the North," he said. "You mustn't think that we people who are responsible for the laws of the country ignore this, Mr. Fardell. It is a very anxious time indeed with all of us. Still, I presume you study the monthly trade returns. Some industries seem prosperous enough."

"I'm no politician," Fardell answered, curtly. "Figures don't interest me. They're just the drugs some of your party use to keep your conscience quiet. Things I see and know of are what I go by. And what I've seen, and what I know of, are just about enough to tear the heart out of any man who cares a row of pins about his fellows. Now I'm going to talk plain English to you, Mr. Mannering. I bought that little article you have in your pocket seriously meaning to knock you on the head with it. And that may come yet."

Mannering looked at him in amazement.

"But my dear sir," he said, "what is your grievance against me? I have always considered myself a people's politician."

"Then the people may very well say 'save me from my friends'," Fardell answered, grimly. "Mind, I believe you're honest, or you'd be lying on your back now with a cracked skull. But you are using a great influence on the wrong side. You're standing between the people and the one reasonable scheme which has been brought forward which has a fair chance of changing their condition."

Then Mannering began to understand.

"I oppose the scheme you speak of," he answered, "simply because I don't believe in it. Every man has a right to his opinion. I don't believe for a moment that it would improve the present condition of things."

"Then what is your scheme?" Fardell asked.

"My scheme!" Mannering repeated. "I don't quite understand you!"

"Of course you don't," Fardell answered, vigourously. "You can weave academic arguments, you can make figures and statistics dance to any damned tune you please. If I tried to argue with you, you'd squash me flat. And what's it all come to? My pals must starve for the gratification of your intellectual vanity. You won't listen to Tariff Reform. Then what do you propose, to light the forges and fill the mills? Nothing! I say, unless you've got a counter scheme of your own, you ought to try ours."

"Come, Mr. Fardell," Mannering said, "I can assure you that all I have said and written is the outcome of honest thought. I—"

"Stop!" Fardell exclaimed. "Honest thought! Yes! Where? In your study. That's where you theorists do your mischief. You can't make laws for the people in your study. You can't tell the status of the workingman from the figures you read in your study. You're like half the smug people in the world who discuss this question in the railway carriages and in their clubs. I've heard 'em till I'd like to shove their self-opinionated arguments down their throats, strip their clothes off their backs, and send them down to live with my pals, or starve with them. Any little idiot who buys a penny paper and who's doing pretty well for himself, thinks he can lay down the law about Free Trade. You're all of one kidney, sir! You none of you realize this. There are men as good as any of you, whose wives and children are as dear to them as yours to you, who've got to see them get thinner and thinner, who don't know where to get a day's work or lay their hands upon a copper, and all the while their kids come crying to them for something to eat. Put yourself in their place, sir, and try and realize the torture of it. I've been amongst 'em. I've spent half of what I made, and a good many thousands it was, buying food for them. Can you wonder that my fingers have itched for the throats of these smug, prosperous pigs, who spurt platitudes and think things are very well as they are because they're making their little bit? What right have you—any of you—to hesitate for a second to try any means to help those poor devils, unless you've got a better scheme of your own? Will you tell me that, sir?"

They had reached Mannering's house, and he threw open the gate.

"You must come in with me and talk about these things," Mannering said, gravely. "You seem to be the sort of person I've been wanting to meet for a long time."

# CHAPTER IV

## DEBTS OF HONOUR

Berenice found the following morning a note from Borrowdean, which caused her some perplexity.

"If you really care," he said, "to do Mannering a good turn, look his niece up now and then. I am afraid that young woman has rather lost her head since she came to London, and she is making friends who will do her no particular good."

Berenice ordered her carriage early, and drove round to Portland Crescent.

"My dear child," she exclaimed, as Clara came into the room, "what have you been doing with yourself? You look ghastly!"

Clara shrugged her shoulders, and looked at herself in a mirror.

"I do look chippy, don't I?" she remarked. "I've been spending the week-end down at Bristow."

"At Bristow?" Berenice repeated. Her voice spoke volumes.

Clara looked up a little defiantly.

"Yes! We had an awful spree! I like it there immensely, only—"

Berenice looked up.

"I notice," she remarked, "that there is generally an 'only' about people who have spent week-ends at Bristow. They play cards there, don't they, until daylight? Some one once told me that they kept a professional croupier for roulette!"

"That horrid game!" Clara exclaimed. "Please don't mention it. I've scarcely slept a wink all night for thinking of it."

Berenice looked at her in surprise.

"Do you mean to say," she inquired, deliberately, "that they allowed you to play—and lose?"

"It wasn't their fault I lost," Clara answered. "Oh, what a fool I was. Bobby Bristow showed me a system. It seemed so easy. I didn't think I could possibly lose. It worked beautifully at first. I thought that I was going to pay all my bills, and have lots of money to spend. Then I doubled the stakes—I wanted to win a lot—and everything went wrong!"

"How much did you lose?" Berenice asked. Clara shivered.

"Don't ask me!" she cried. "Sir Leslie Borrowdean gave his own cheques for all my I.O.U.'s. He is coming to see me some time to-day. I don't know what I shall say to him."

"Do you mean to go on playing?" Berenice asked, quietly, "or is this experience enough for you?"

"I shall never sit at a roulette table again as long as I live," she declared. "I hate the very thought of it."

"Then you can just ask Sir Leslie the amount of the I.O.U.'s, and tell him that he shall have a cheque in the morning," Berenice said. "I will lend you the money."

Clara gave a little gasp.

"You are too kind," she exclaimed, "but I don't know when I shall be able to repay you. It is—nearly three hundred pounds!"

"So long as you keep your word," Berenice answered, "and do not play again, you need never let that trouble you. You shall have the cheque before two o'clock. No, please don't thank me. If you take my advice you won't spend another week-end at Bristow. It is not a fit house for young girls. How is your uncle?"

"I haven't seen him this morning," Clara answered. "Perkins told me that he came home after midnight with a man whom he seemed to have picked up in the street, and they were in the study talking till nearly five this morning."

Berenice rose.

"I came to see if you would care to drive down to Ranelagh with me this morning," she said, "but you are evidently fit for nothing except to go back to bed again. I won't forget the cheque, and remember me to your uncle. By the bye, where's that nice young man who used to be always with you down in the country?"

"You must mean Mr. Lindsay," Clara answered. "I have no idea. At Blakely, I suppose."

"If I were you," Berenice said, as she rose, "I should write to him to come up and look after you. You need it!"

She nodded pleasantly and took her leave. Clara threw herself into a chair and rang the bell.

"Perkins," she said, "I have had no sleep and no breakfast. What should you recommend?"

"An egg beaten up in milk, miss," the man suggested, "same as I've just taken Mr. Mannering."

"Is my uncle up?" Clara asked.

"Not yet, miss," the man answered; "He is just dressing."

Clara nodded.

"Very well. Please get me what you said, and if Sir Leslie Borrowdean calls I want to see him at once."

"Sir Leslie is in the study now, miss," the man answered. "I showed him in there because I thought he would want to see Mr. Mannering, but he asked for you."

"Will you say that I shall be there in three minutes," Clara said.

The three minutes became rather a long quarter of an hour, but Clara had used the time well. When she entered the library she had changed her dress, rearranged her hair, and by some means or another had lost her unnatural pallor. Sir Leslie greeted her a little gravely,

"Glad to see you looking so fit," he remarked. "They did us a bit too well down at Bristow, I thought. It's all very well for you children," he continued, with a smile, "but when a man gets to my time of life he misses a night's rest."

She smiled.

"You don't call yourself old, Sir Leslie!" she remarked.

"Well, I'm not young, although I like to think I am," he answered. "I'm afraid there's pretty nearly a generation between us, Miss Clara. By the bye, where's your uncle this morning?"

"Getting up," she answered. "He did not go to bed until after five, Perkins tells me. He brought some one home with him from Dorchester's reception, or some one he picked up afterwards, and they seem to have sat up talking all night."

Borrowdean was interested.

"You have no idea who it was, I suppose?" he asked.

She shook her head.

"None at all. Perkins had never seen him before. When do you poor creatures get your holiday, Sir Leslie?"

He smiled.

"The session will be over in about three weeks," he answered, "unless we defeat the Government before then. Your uncle has been hitting them very hard lately. I think before long we shall be in office."

"Politics," she said, "seems to be rather a greedy sort of business. You are always trying to turn the other side out, aren't you?"

"You must remember," he answered, "that politics is rather a one-sided sort of affair. The party which is in makes a very comfortable living out of it, and we who are out have to scrape along as best we can. Rather hard upon people like your uncle and myself, who are, comparatively speaking, poor men. That reminds me," he said, bringing out his pocket-book, "I thought that I had better bring you these little documents."

"Those horrid I.O.U.'s," she remarked.

"Yes," he answered. "I am sorry that you were so unlucky. I bought these from the bank, Miss Clara, as I thought you would not feel comfortable if you had to leave Bristow owing this money to strangers."

"It was very thoughtful of you," she murmured. He changed his seat and came over to her side on the sofa.

"Have you any idea how much they come to?" he asked, smoothing them out upon his knee.

"I am afraid to nearly three hundred pounds," she answered.

He shook his head gravely.

"I am sorry to say that they come to a good deal more than that," he said. "I hope you do not forget that I took the liberty of advising you more than once to stop. You had the most abominable luck."

"More than three hundred?" she gasped. "How much more?"

"They seem to add up to five hundred and eighty five pounds," he declared. "I must confess that I was surprised myself."

"There—I think there must be some mistake," Clara faltered.

He handed them to her.

"You had better look them through," he said. "They seem all right."

She took them in her hand, and looked at them helplessly. There was one there for fifty pounds which she tried in vain to remember—and how shaky her handwriting was. A sudden flood of recollection brought the colour into her cheeks. She remembered the long table, the men all smoking, the women most of them a little hard, a little too much in earnest—the soft click of the ball, the silent, sickening moments of suspense. Others had won or lost as much as she, but perhaps because she had been so much in earnest, her ill-luck had attracted some attention. She remembered Major Bristow's whispered offer, or rather suggestion, of help. Even now her cheeks burned at something in his tone or look.

"I suppose it's all right," she said, dolefully, "only it's a lot more than I thought. I shall have three hundred pounds in the morning, but I've no idea where to get the rest."

"You are sure about the three hundred?" Sir Leslie asked, quietly.

"Quite."

"Then I think that you had better let me lend you the rest, for the present," he suggested. "I am afraid your uncle would be rather annoyed to know that you had been gambling to such an extent. You may be able to think of some way of paying me back later on."

She looked up at him hesitatingly. There was nothing in his manner which suggested in the least what Major Bristow had almost pronounced. She drew a little breath of relief. He was so much older, and after all, he was her uncle's friend.

"Can you really spare it, Sir Leslie?" she asked. "I can't tell you how grateful I should be."

He looked down at her with a faint smile.

"I can spare it for the present," he answered. "Only if you see any chance of paying me back before long, do so."

"You will pardon my interference," said an ominously quiet voice from the doorway, "but may I inquire into the nature of this transaction between you and my niece, Sir Leslie? Perhaps you had better explain it, Clara!"

They both turned quickly round. Mannering was standing upon the threshold, the morning paper in his hand. Clara sank into a chair and covered her face with her hands. Sir Leslie shrugged his shoulders.

He was congratulating himself upon the discretion with which he had conducted the interview. He had for a few moments entertained other ideas.

"Perhaps you will allow me to explain—" he began.

"I should prefer to hear my niece," Mannering answered, coldly.

Clara looked up. She was pale and frightened, and she had hard work to choke down the sobs.

"Sir Leslie was down at Bristow, where I was staying—this

E. Phillips Oppenheim

last week-end," she explained. "I lost a good deal of money there at roulette. He very kindly took up my I.O.U.'s for me, and was offering when you came in to let it stand for a little time."

"What is the amount?" Mannering asked.

Clara did not answer. Her head sank again. Her uncle repeated his inquiry. There was no note of anger in his tone. He might have been speaking of an altogether indifferent matter.

"I am afraid I shall have to trouble you to tell me the exact amount," he said. "Perhaps, Borrowdean, you would be so good as to inform me, as my niece seems a little overcome."

"The amount of the I.O.U.'s for which I gave my cheque," Borrowdean said, "was five hundred and eighty-seven pounds. I have the papers here."

There was a dead silence for a moment or two. Clara looked up furtively, but she could learn nothing from her uncle's face. It was some time before he spoke. When at last he did, his voice was certainly a little lower and less distinct than usual.

"Did I understand you to say—five hundred and eighty-seven pounds?"

"That is the amount," Borrowdean admitted. "I trust that you do not consider my interference in any way officious, Mannering. I thought it best to settle the claims of perfect strangers against Miss Mannering."

"May I ask," Mannering continued, "in whose house my niece was permitted to lose this sum?"

"It was at the Bristows'," Clara answered.

"And under whose chaperonage were you?" Mannering asked.

"Lady Bristow's! She called for me here, and took me down last Friday."

"Are these people who are generally accounted respectable?" Mannering asked.

"I don't think that Bristow is much better or worse than half of our country houses," Borrowdean answered. "People who are at all in the swim must have excitement nowadays, you know. Bristow himself isn't very popular, but people go to the house."

Mannering made no further remark.

"If you will come into the study, Borrowdean," he said, "I will settle this matter with you."

Borrowdean hesitated.

"Your niece said something about having three hundred pounds," he remarked.

Mannering glanced towards her.

"I think," he said, "that that must be a mistake. My niece has no such sum at her command."

Clara rose to her feet.

"You may as well know everything," she said. "The Duchess of Lenchester came in and found me very unhappy this morning. I told her everything, and she offered to lend me the money. I told her then that it was only three hundred pounds. I thought that was all I owed."

"Have you made any other confidants?" Mannering asked.

"No!"

"You will return the Duchess's cheque," Mannering said. "Borrowdean, will you come this way?"

# CHAPTER V

## LOVE *versus* POLITICS

Berenice was a little annoyed. It was the hour before dressing for dinner which she always devoted to repose—the hour saved from the stress of the day which had helped towards keeping her the young woman she certainly was. Yet Borrowdean's message was too urgent to ignore. She suffered her maid to wrap some sort of loose gown about her, and received him in her own study.

"My dear Sir Leslie," she said, a little reproachfully, "was this really necessary? You know that after half-past six I am practically a person not existing—until dinner time!"

"I should not have ventured to intrude upon you," Borrowdean said, quickly, "if the circumstances had not been altogether exceptional. I know your habits too well. I have just come from Mannering."

"From Mannering—yes!"

"Duchess," Borrowdean said, "have you—forgive a blunt question—but have you any influence over him?"

Berenice was silent for several moments.

"You ask me rather a hard question," she said. "A few months ago I think that I should have said yes. To-day—I am not sure. What has happened? Is anything wrong with him?"

"Nothing, except that he seems to have gone mad," Borrowdean said, bitterly. "I went to him to-day to get him to fix the dates for his meetings at Glasgow and Leeds. What do you think his answer was?"

"Don't tell me that he wants to back out!" Berenice exclaimed. "Don't tell me that!"

"Almost as bad! He told me quite coolly that he was not prepared finally to set out his views upon the question until he had completed a course of personal investigation in some of the Northern centres of trade, to which he had committed himself."

Berenice looked bewildered.

"But what on earth does he mean?" she exclaimed. "Surely he knows all that there is to be known. His mastery of statistics is something wonderful."

"What he means no man save himself can even surmise," Borrowdean answered. "He told me that he had had information of a state of distress in some of our Northern towns—Newcastle and Hull he mentioned, and some of the Lancashire places—which had simply appalled him. He was determined to verify it personally, and to commit himself to nothing further until he had done so. And he even asked me if I could not find him a pair until the end of the session, so that he could get away at once. I was simply dumbfounded. A pair for Mannering!"

Berenice rose to her feet. She walked up and down the little room restlessly.

"Sir Leslie," she said at last, "I am not sure whether I have what you would call any influence over Mr. Mannering now or not. I might have had but for you!"

"For me?" Borrowdean exclaimed.

"Yes. It was you who told me of—of—that woman," she said, haughtily, but with the colour rising almost to her temples. "After that, of course things were different between us. We are scarcely upon such terms at present as would justify my interference."

Borrowdean dropped his eyeglass, and swung it deliberately by its black ribbon. He looked steadily at Berenice, but his eyes seemed to travel past her.

"My dear Duchess," he said, quietly, "the game of life is a great one to play, and we who would keep our hands upon the board must of necessity make sacrifices. It is your duty to disregard in this instance your feelings towards Mannering. You must consider only his feelings towards you. They are such, I believe, as to give you a hold over him. You must make use of that hold for the sake of a great cause."

Berenice raised her eyebrows.

"Indeed! You seem to forget, Sir Leslie, that my share in this game, as you call it, must always be a passive one. I have no office to gain, no rewards to reap. Why should I commit myself to an unpleasant task for the sake of you and your friends?"

"It is your party," he protested. "Your party as much as ours."

"Granted," she answered. "Yet who are the responsible members of it? You know my opinion of Mannering as a politician. I would sooner follow him blindfold than all the others with my eyes open. Whatever he may lack, he is the most honest and right-seeing politician who ever entered the House."

"He lacks but one thing," Borrowdean said, "the mechanical adjustment of the born politician to party matters. There was never a time when absolute unity and absolute force were so necessary. If he is going to play the intelligent inquirer, if he falters for one moment in his wholesale condemnation of this scheme, he loses the day for himself and for us. The one thing which the political public never forgives is the man who stops to think."

"What do you want me to do?" Berenice asked.

"To go to him and find out what he means, what influences have been at work, what is underneath it all. Warn him of the danger of even appearing doubtful, or for a moment lukewarm. The one person whom the public will not have in politics is the trifler. Think how many there have been, brilliant men, too, who have lost their places through a single false step, a single year, a month of dilettantism. Remind him of them. The man who moves in a great cause may move slowly, if you will, but he must move all the time. Remind him, too, that he is risking the one great chance of his life!"

"He is to be Premier, then?" she asked.

"Yes! There is no alternative!"

"Very well, then," she said, "I will go. I make no promises, mind. I will listen to what he has to say. I will put our view of the situation before him. But I make no promises. It is possible, even, that I shall come to his point of view, whatever it may be."

Borrowdean smiled.

"I have no fear of that," he declared, "but at least it would be something to know what this point of view is. You will find him in a queer mood. That little fool of a niece of his has been getting in with a fast set, and making the money fly. You have heard of her last escapade at Bristow?"

Berenice nodded.

"Yes," she said. "I went there this morning directly I had your note. I feel rather self-reproachful about Clara Mannering. I meant to have looked after her more. She is rather an uninteresting young woman, though, and I am afraid I have let her drift away."

"She will be all right with a little looking after," Borrowdean said. "Forgive me, but it is getting late."

"I will go at once," she said.

\*   \*   \*   \*   \*

Afterwards she wondered often at that strange, uncertain fluttering of the heart, the rush and glow of feelings warmer than any which had lately stirred her, which seemed in those first few minutes of their being together, to make an altered woman of her. Mannering, as he entered the room, pale and listless, was conscious at once of a foreign element in it, something which stirred his somewhat slow-beating pulse, too, which seemed to bring back to him a flood of delicious memories, the perfume of his rose-gardens at evening, the soft night music of his wind-stirred cedars. She had thrown aside her opera cloak. The delicate lines of her bust seemed to have expanded with the unusual rise and fall of her bosom. A faint rose-tint flush of streaming colour had stained the ivory whiteness of her skin—her eyes as they sought his were soft, almost liquid. They met so seldom alone—and she was alone now with him in the room which was so characteristically his own, a room with many indications of his constant presence, which one by one she had been realizing with curiously quickened pulses during the few minutes of waiting. On her way here, driving in an open victoria, through the soft summer evening, she had seemed to be pursued everywhere by a new world of sensuous suggestions. Of the many carriages which she had passed, hers alone seemed to savour of loneliness. She was the only beautiful woman who sat alone and companionless. In a momentary block she had seen a man in a neighbouring hansom slip his hand, a strong, brown, well-looking hand, under the apron, to hold for a moment the fingers of the woman who sat by his side—Berenice had caught the answering smile, she had seen him lean forward and whisper something which had brought a deeper flush into her own cheeks and a look into her eyes, half amused, half tender. These were rare moments with her, these moments of sentiment—perhaps for that reason all the more dangerous. She forgot almost the cause of her coming. She remembered only that she was alone with the one man whose voice had the power to thrill her, whose touch would call up into life the great hidden forces of her own passionate nature. The memory of all other things passed away from her like a cloud gone from the face of the sun. She leaned towards him. His face was full of wonder—wonder, and the coming joy.

"Berenice!" he exclaimed.

She let herself drift down the surging tide of this suddenly awakened passion. She held out her arms and pressed her lips on his as he caught her.

*   *   *   *   *

Presently she pushed him gently away—held him there at arm's length.

"This is too absurd," she murmured, and drew him once more towards her with a choking little laugh. "I came for something quite different!"

"What does it matter what you came for, so long as you stay," he answered. "Say that you came to bring a glimpse of paradise to a lonely man!"

She disengaged herself, and her long white fingers strayed mechanically to her tumbled hair. The elegant precision of her toilette had given place to a most distracting disarray. She felt her cheeks burning still, and the lace at her bosom was all crushed.

"And I was on my way to a dinner party," she whispered, with humorously uplifted eyebrows. "I must drive back home, and—and—"

"And what?" he demanded.

"And send an excuse," she declared, demurely. "I am not equal to a family dinner party."

"And afterwards?"

She smiled.

"Would you like," she asked, "to take me out to dinner?"

"Would I like!"

"Go and change, and call for me in half an hour. We can go somewhere where we are not likely to be seen," she said, softly. "I must cover myself up in my cloak. Whatever will Perkins say? Please remember that I have no hat."

He held her hands and looked into her eyes.

"Don't go for one moment," he pleaded. "I want to realize it. I want to feel sure of you."

The gravity of his manner was for a moment reflected in her tone.

"I think," she said, "that you may feel sure. There are things which we may have to say to one another—presently—but—"

He stooped and kissed her fingers.

# CHAPTER VI

## THE CONSCIENCE OF A STATESMAN

He was shown into her own little boudoir by a smiling maid-servant, who seemed already to treat him with an especial consideration. The wonder of this thing was still lying like a thrall upon him, and yet he knew that the joy of life was burning once more in his veins. He caught sight of himself in a mirror, and he was amazed. The careworn look had gone from his eyes, the sallowness from his complexion. His step was elastic, he felt the firm, quick beat of his heart, even his pulses seem to throb to a new and a wonderful tune. These moments whilst he waited for her were a joy to him. The atmosphere was fragrant with the perfume of her favourite roses, a book lay upon the little inlaid table face downwards as she had left it. There was a delicately engraved etching upon the wall, which he recognized as her work; the watercolours, all of a French school which he had often praised, were of her choosing. Perfect though the room was in colouring and detail, there was yet a habitable, almost a homely, air about it. Mannering moved about amidst her treasures like a man in a dream, only it was a dream of loneliness gone forever, of a grey life suddenly coloured and transformed. It was wonderful.

Then the soft swish of a skirt, and she came in. She had

changed her gown. She wore white lace, with a string of pearls about her neck. He looked eagerly into her face, and a great relief took the place of that single instant of haunting fear. The change was still there. It was not the great lady who swept in, but the woman who has found an answer to the one question of life, a little tremulous still, a little less self-assured. She looked at him almost appealingly. A delicate tinge of colour lingered in her cheeks. He moved quickly forward to meet her.

"Dear!" she murmured.

He raised her hand to his lips. He was satisfied.

"You see what my new-born vanity has led to," she declared, smilingly. "I have had to keep you waiting whilst I changed my gown. I hope you like me in white."

"You are adorable," he declared.

She laughed.

"I wonder," she said, "would you mind dining here alone with me? It will be quite a scratch meal, but I thought that it would be cosier than a restaurant, and afterwards—we could come in here and talk."

"I should like it better than anything in the world," he declared, truthfully.

"You may take me in, then," she said. "I hope that you are as hungry as I am. No, not that way. I have ordered dinner to be served in the little room where I dine when I am alone."

To Mannering there seemed something almost unreal about the chaste perfection of the meal and its wonderful service.

They dined at a small round table, so small that more than once their fingers touched upon the tablecloth. A single servant waited upon them, swiftly and perfectly. The butler appeared only with the wine, which he served, and quietly withdrew. Across the tangled mass of flowers, only a few feet away all the time, sat the woman who had suddenly made the world so beautiful to him. A murmur of conversation continually flowed between them, but he was never very sure what they were talking about. He wanted to sit still, to feast his eyes, all his senses, upon her, to strive to realize this new thing, that from henceforth she was his! And then suddenly she broke the spell. She leaned back in her chair and laughed softly.

"I have just remembered," she said, in response to his inquiring look, "why I came to call upon you this evening. What a long time ago it seems."

He smiled.

"And I never thought to ask you," he remarked.

"We must have no secrets now," she said, with a delightful smile. "Leslie Borrowdean came to see me this afternoon, and he was very anxious about you. He declared that you wanted to postpone your great meetings in the North until after you had made some independent investigations in some of the manufacturing centres. Poor Sir Leslie! You had frightened him so completely that he was scarcely coherent."

Mannering smiled a little gravely. It was like coming back to earth.

"Politics with Borrowdean are so much a matter of pounds, shillings and pence that the bare idea of his finding himself a day further away from office frightens him to death," he said.

"We are all like the pawns, to be moved about the chessboard of his life."

Berenice smiled.

"He is certainly a very self-centred person," she remarked; "but do you know, I am really a little curious to know how you succeeded in frightening him so thoroughly."

"I had a fright myself," Mannering said. "I was made to feel for an hour or so like a Rip van Winkle with the cobwebs hanging about me—Rip van Winkle looking out upon a new world!"

"You a Rip van Winkle!" she laughed. "What was it that man who wrote in the *Nineteenth Century* called you last week? 'The most precise and far-seeing of our politicians.'"

"The men who write in reviews," he murmured, "sometimes display the most appalling ignorance. There was also some one in the *Saturday Review* who alluded to me last week as a library politician. My friend quoted that against me. 'A man who essays to govern a people he knows nothing of.' It was one of the labour party who wrote it, I know, but it sticks."

"You are not losing confidence in yourself, surely?" she remarked, smiling.

"My views are unchanged, if that is what you mean," he answered. "I believe I know what is good for the people, and when I am sure of it I shall not be afraid to take up the gauntlet. But I must be quite sure."

"You puzzle me a little," she admitted. "Has any one written more convincingly than you? Arguments which are founded upon logic and statistics must yield truth, and you have set it down in black and white."

"On the other hand," he said, "my unlearned but eloquent friend dismissed all statistics, all the science of argument and deduction, with the wave of a not too scrupulously clean hand. 'Figures,' he said, 'are dead things. They are the playthings of the charlatan politician, who, by a sort of mental sleight of hand, can make them perform the most wonderful antics. If you desire the truth, seek it from live things. If you desire really to call yourself the champion of the people, come and see for yourself how they are faring. Figures will not feed them, nor statistics keep them from the great despair. Come and let me show you the sinews of the country, whether they are sound or rotten. You cannot see them through your library walls. It is only the echo of their voice which you hear so far off. If you would really be the people's man, come and learn something of the people from their own lips.' This is what my friend said to me."

"And who," she asked, "was this prophet who came to you and talked like this?"

"A retired bookmaker," he answered. "I will tell you of our meeting."

She listened gravely. After he had finished there was a short silence. The dessert was on the table, and they were alone. Berenice was looking thoughtful.

"Tell me," he begged, "exactly what that wrinkled forehead means?"

"I was wondering," she said, "whether Sir Leslie was right, when he said that you had too much conscience ever to be a great politician."

"It mirrors Borrowdean's outlook upon politics precisely," he remarked.

She smiled at him with a sudden radiance. She had risen to her feet, and with a quick, graceful movement leaned over him. This new womanliness which he had found so irresistible was alight once more in her face. Her eyes sought his fondly, she touched his lips with hers. The perfume of her clothes, the touch of her hair upon his cheek, were like a drug. He had no more words.

"You may have one peach and one glass of the Prince's Burgundy, and then you must come and look for me," she said. "We have wasted too much time talking of other things. You haven't even told me yet what I have a right to hear, you know. I want to be told that you care for me better than anything else in the world."

He caught her hands. There was a rare passion vibrating in his tone.

"You do not doubt it, Berenice?"

"Perhaps not," she answered, "but I want to be told. I am a middle-aged woman, you know, Lawrence, but I want to be made love to as though I were a silly girl! Isn't that foolish? But you must do it," she whispered, with her lips very close to his.

He drew her into his arms.

"I am not at all sure," he said, "that I have enough courage to make love to a Duchess!"

"Then you can remember only that I am a woman," she whispered, "very, very, very much a woman, and—I'm afraid—a woman shockingly in love!"

She disengaged herself suddenly, and was at the door before he could reach it. She looked back. Her cheeks were flushed. There was even a faint tinge of pink underneath the creamy white of her slender, stately neck.

"Don't dare," she said, "to be more than five minutes!"

Mannering poured himself out a glass of wine, and sat quite still with his head between his hands. He wanted to realize this thing if he could. The grinding of the great wheels fell no more upon his ears. He looked into a new world, so different from the old that he was almost afraid.

And in her room, Berenice waited for him impatiently.

# CHAPTER VII

## A BLOW FOR BORROWDEAN

There was a somewhat unusual alertness in Borrowdean's manner as he passed out from the little house in Sloane Gardens and summoned a passing hansom. He drove to the corner of Hyde Park, and dismissing the cab strolled along the broad walk.

The many acquaintances whom he passed and repassed he greeted with a certain amount of abstraction. All the time he kept his eyes upon the road. He was waiting to catch sight of some familiar liveries. When at last they came he contrived to stop the carriage and hastily threaded his way to the side of the barouche.

Berenice was looking radiantly beautiful. The exquisite simplicity of her white muslin gown and large hat of black feathers, the slight flush with which she received him, as though she carried about with her a secret which she expected every one to read, the extinction of that air of listlessness which had robbed her for some time of a certain share of her good looks—of all these things Borrowdean made quick note. His face grew graver as he accepted her not very enthusiastic invitation and occupied the back seat of the carriage. For the first time he admitted to himself the possibility of failure in his carefully laid plans. He recognized the fact, that there were forces at work against which he had no weapon ready. He had believed that Berenice was attracted by Mannering's personality and genius. He had never seriously considered the question of her feelings becoming more deeply involved. So many men had paid vain court to her. She had a wonderful reputation for inaccessibility. And yet he remembered her manner when he had paid his first unexpected visit to Blakely. It should have been a lesson to him. How far had the mischief gone, he wondered!

"So Mannering has gone North," he remarked, noticing that she avoided the subject.

She nodded. Her parasol drooped a little his way, and he wondered whether it was because she desired her face hidden.

"You saw him?"

"Yes," she answered. "He explained how he felt to me."

"And you could not dissuade him?"

"I did not try," she answered, simply. "Lawrence Mannering is not a man of ordinary disposition, you know. He had come to the conclusion that it was right for him to go, and opposition would only have made him the more determined. I cannot see that there is any harm likely to come of it."

"I am not so sure of that," Borrowdean answered, seriously. "Mannering is *au fond* a man of sentiment. There is no clearer thinker or speaker when his judgment is unbiassed, but on the other hand, the man's nature is sensitive and complex. He has a sort of maudlin self-consciousness which is as dangerous a thing as the nonconformist conscience. Heaven knows into whose hands he may fall up there."

"He is going incognito," she remarked.

"He is not the sort of man to escape notice," Borrowdean answered. "He will be discovered for certain. Of course, if it comes off all right, the whole thing will be a feather in his cap. But when I think how much we are dependent upon him, I don't like the risk."

"You are sure," she remarked, thoughtfully, "that you do not over-rate—"

"Mannering himself, perhaps," Borrowdean interrupted. "There is no man whose personal place cannot be filled. But one thing is very certain. Mannering is the only man who unites both sides of our scattered party, the only man under whom Fergusson and Johns would both serve. You know quite well the curse which has rested upon us. We have become a party of units, and our whole effectiveness is destroyed. We want welding into one entity. A single session, a single year of office, and the thing would be done. We who do the mechanical work would see that there was no breaking away again. But we must have that year, we must have Mannering. That is why I watch him like a child, and I must say that he has given me a good deal of anxiety lately."

"In what way?" she asked.

Borrowdean hesitated. He seemed uncertain how to answer.

"If I explain what I mean," he said, "you will understand that I do not speak to you as a woman and an acquaintance of Mannering's, but simply as one of ourselves. Mannering's private life is, of course, interesting to me only as an index to his political destiny, and my acquaintance with it arises solely from my political interest in him. There are things in connection with it which I feel that I shall never properly be able to understand."

She looked at him steadily. Her cheeks were a little whiter, but her tone was deliberate.

"I do not wish to hear anything about Mr. Mannering's private life," she said. "You will understand that I am not free or disposed to listen when I tell you that I am going to marry him."

This was perhaps the worst blow Borrowdean had ever experienced in the course of his whole life. The possibility of this was a danger which he had recognized might some time have to be reckoned with, but for the present he had felt safe enough. He was taken so completely aback that for a few moments his mind was a blank. He remained silent.

"You do not offer me the conventional wishes," she remarked, presently.

"They go—from me to you—as a matter of course," he answered. "To tell you the truth, I never thought of Mannering, for many reasons, as a marrying man."

"You will have to readjust your views of him," she said, quietly, "for I think that we shall be married very soon."

Borrowdean was a little white, and his teeth had come together. Whatever happened, he told himself, fiercely, this must never be. He felt his breast-pocket mechanically. Yes, the letter was there. Dare he risk it? She was a proud woman, she would be unforgiving if once she believed. But supposing she found him out? He temporized.

"Thank you for telling me," he said. "Do you mind putting me down here?"

"Why? You seemed in no hurry a few minutes ago."

"The world," he said, "was a different place then."

She looked at him searchingly.

"You had better tell me all about it," she remarked. "You have something on your mind, something which you are half disposed to tell me, a little more than half, I think. Go on."

He looked at her as one might look at the magician who has achieved the apparently impossible.

"You are wonderful," he said. "Yes, I will tell you my dilemma, if you like. I have just come from Sloane Gardens!"

Her face changed instantly. It was as though a mask had been dropped over it. Her eyes were fixed, her features expressionless.

"Well?" she said, simply.

He drew a letter from his pocket.

"You may as well see it yourself," he remarked. "For reasons which you may doubtless understand, I have always kept on good terms with Mrs. Phillimore, and she was to have dined with me and some other friends to-morrow night. Here is a note which I had from her yesterday. Will you read it?"

Berenice held it between her finger tips. There were only a few lines, and she read them at a glance.

Sloane Gardens,
*Tuesday.*

My dear Sir Leslie,

I am so sorry, but I must scratch for to-morrow night. L. is going North on some mysterious expedition, and I am afraid that he will want me to go with him. In fact, he has already said so. Ask me again some time, won't you?

Yours ever,
Blanche Phillimore.

Berenice folded up the letter and returned it.

"It is a little extraordinary," she remarked. "I am much obliged to you for showing me this. If you do not mind, we will talk of something else. Look, there is Clara Mannering alone under the trees. Go and talk to her."

Berenice touched the checkstring, and Borrowdean was forced to depart. She smiled upon him graciously enough, but she spoke not another word about Mannering. Borrowdean was obliged to leave her without knowing whether he had lost or gained the trick.

Clara Mannering received him not altogether graciously. As a matter of fact, she was looking for some one else. They strolled along, talking almost in monosyllables. Borrowdean found time to notice the change which even these few months in London had wrought in her. She was still graceful in her movements, but a smart dressmaker had contrived to make her a perfect reproduction of the recognized type of the moment. She had lost her delicate colouring. There was a certain hardness in her young face, a certain pallor and listlessness in her movements which Borrowdean did not fail to note. He tried to lead the conversation into more personal channels.

"We seem to have met very little during the last month," he said. "I have scarcely had an opportunity to ask you whether you find the life here as pleasant as you hoped, whether it has realized your expectations."

"Does anything ever do that?" she asked, a little flippantly. "It is different, of course. I do not think that I should be willing to go back to Blakely, at any rate."

"You have made a great many friends," he remarked. "I hear of you continually."

"A host of acquaintances," she remarked. "I do not think that I have materially increased the circle of my friends. I hear of you too, Sir Leslie, very often. It seems that people give you a good deal of credit for inducing my uncle to come back into politics."

"I certainly did my best to persuade him," Sir Leslie answered, smoothly. "If I had known how much anxiety he was going to cause us I might perhaps have been a little less keen."

"Anxiety!" she repeated.

"Yes! Do you know where he is now?"

"I have no idea," Clara answered. "All that I do know is that he has gone away for three weeks, and that I am going to stay with the Duchess till he comes back. It is very nice of her, and all that, of course, but I feel rather as though I were going into prison. The Duchess isn't exactly the modern sort of chaperon."

Borrowdean nodded sympathetically.

"And consider my anxiety," he remarked. "Your uncle has gone North to consider the true position of the labouring classes. Now Mr. Mannering is a brilliant politician and a sound thinker, but he is also a man of sentiment. They will drug him with it up there. He will probably come back with half a dozen new schemes, and we don't want them, you know. He ought to be speaking at Glasgow and Leeds this week. He simply ignores his responsibilities. He yields to a sudden whim and leaves us *plantes la*."

She seemed scarcely to have heard the conclusion of his sentence. Her attention was fixed upon a group of men who were talking near.

"Do you know—isn't that Major Bristow?" she asked Borrowdean, abruptly.

Borrowdean put up his glass.

"Looks like him," he admitted.

"I should be so much obliged," she said, "if you would tell him that I wish to see him. I have a message for his sister," she concluded, a little lamely.

Borrowdean did as he was asked. He noticed the slight impatience of the man as he delivered his message, and the flush with which she greeted him. Then, with a little shrug of the shoulders, he pursued his way.

# CHAPTER VIII

## A PAGE FROM THE PAST

She swept into the room, humming a light opera tune, bringing with her the usual flood of perfumes, suggestion of cosmetics, a vivid apparition of the artificial. Her skirts rustled aggressively, her voice was just one degree too loud. Mannering rose to his feet a little wearily.

She looked at him with raised eyebrows.

"Heavens!" she exclaimed. "What have you been doing with yourself, Lawrence? You look like a ghost!"

"I am quite well," he answered, calmly.

"Then you don't look it," she answered, bluntly. "Where have you been for the last few weeks?"

"Up in the North," he answered. "It was very hot, and I had a great deal to do. I suppose I am suffering, like the rest of us, from a little overwork."

She spread herself out in a chair opposite to him.

"Don't stand," she said; "you fidget me. I have something to say to you."

"So I gathered from your note," he remarked.

"You haven't hurried."

"I only got back to London last night," he answered. "I could scarcely come sooner, could I?"

"I suppose not," she admitted.

Then for a moment or two she was silent. She was watching him a little curiously.

"Is this true?" she asked, "this rumour?"

"Won't you be a little more explicit?" he begged.

"They say that you are going to marry the Duchess of Lenchester!"

"It is true," he answered.

She leaned forward. Her clasped hands rested upon her knee. She seemed to be examining the tip of her patent shoe. Suddenly she looked up at him.

"You ought to have come and told me yourself!" she said.

"I had no opportunity," he reminded her. "I left London the morning after—it happened—and I returned last night."

"Political business?" she asked.

"Entirely."

"Lawrence," she said, "I don't like it."

"Why not?" he asked. "Has mine been such a successful life, do you think, that you need grudge me a little happiness towards its close?"

"Bosh!" she answered. "You are only forty-six. You are a young man still."

"I had forgotten my years," he declared. "I only know that I am tired."

"You look it," she remarked. "I must say that there is very little of the triumphant suitor about you. You work too hard, Lawrence."

"If I do," he asked, with a note of fierceness in his tone, "whose fault is it? I was almost happy at Blakely. I had almost learned to forget. It was you who dragged me out again. You were not satisfied with half of my income; you were always in debt, always wanting more money. Then Borrowdean made use of you. He wanted me back into politics, you wanted more money for your follies and extravagances. Back I had to come into harness. Blanche, I've tried to do my duty to you, but there is a limit. I owed you a comfortable place in life, and I have tried to see that you have it. I have never refused anything you have asked me, I have never mentioned the sacrifices which I have been forced to make. But there is a limit. I draw it here. I will not suffer any interference between the Duchess of Lenchester and myself!"

Blanche Phillimore rose slowly to her feet. He was used to her fits of passion, but there was no sign of anything of the sort in her face. She was agitated, but in some new way. Her words were an attack, but her manner suggested rather an appeal. Her large, fine eyes, her one perfectly natural feature, were soft and luminous. They seemed somehow to transfigure her face. To him it seemed like the foolish, handsome woman of fifteen years ago who had suddenly come to life again.

"You owed me—a comfortable place in life, Lawrence! Thank—you. You have paid the debt very well. You owed me—a respectable guardianship; you paid that, too. Thank you again. Now tell me, do you owe me nothing else?"

"I owed you one debt," he said, gravely, "which neither I nor any other man who incurs it can ever discharge."

"I am glad you realize it," she answered. "But have you ever tried to discharge it? You have given me a home and money to throw away on any folly which could kill thought. What about the rest?"

"Blanche," he said, gravely, "the rest was impossible! You know that as well as I do."

"It is fifteen years ago, Lawrence," she said, "and all that time we have fenced with our words. Now I am going to speak a little more plainly. You robbed me of my husband. The fault may not have been wholly yours, but the fact remains. You struck him, and he died. I was left alone!"

Mannering's face was ashen. The whole horrible scene was rising up again before him. He covered his face with his hands. It was more distinct than ever. He saw the man's flushed face, heard his stream of abuse, felt the sting of his blow, the hot anger with which he had struck back. Then those few awful moments of suspense, the moment afterwards when they had looked at one another. He shivered! Why had she let loose this flood of memories? She was speaking to him again.

"I was left alone," she repeated, quietly, "and I have been alone ever since. You don't know much about women, Lawrence. You never did! Try and realize, though, what that must mean to a woman like myself, not strong, not clever, with very few resources—just a woman. I cared for my husband, I suppose, in an average sort of way. At any rate he loved me. Then—there was you. Oh, you never made love to me, of course. You were not the sort of man to make love to another man's wife. But you used to show that you liked to be with me, Lawrence. Your voice and your eyes and your whole manner used to tell me that. Then there came—that hideous day! I lost you both. What have I had since, Lawrence?"

"Very little, I am afraid, worth having."

"'Very little—worth having'!" She flung the words from her with passionate scorn. "I had your alms, your cold, hurried visits, when you seemed to shiver if our fingers touched. It would have seemed to you, I suppose, a terrible sin to have touched the lips of the woman whom you had helped to rob of her husband, to have spoken kindly to her, to have given her at least a little affection to warm her heart. Poor me! What a hell you made of my days, with your selfish model life, your panderings to conscience. I didn't want much, you know, Lawrence," she said, with a sudden choking in her voice. "I would never have robbed you of your peace of mind. All I wanted was kindness. And I think, Lawrence, that it was a debt, but you never paid it."

Mannering had a moment of self-revelation, a terrible, lurid moment. Every word that she had said was true.

"You have never spoken to me like this before," he reminded

her, desperately. "I never knew that you cared."

"Don't lie!" she answered, calmly. "You turned your head away that you might not see. In your heart you knew very well. What else, do you think, made me, a very ordinary, nervous sort of woman, get you out of the house that day, tell my story, the story that shielded you, without faltering, put even the words into your own mouth? It was because I was fool enough to care! And oh, my God, how you have tortured me since! You would sit there, coldly censorious, and reason with me about my friends, my manner of life. I knew what you thought. You didn't hide it very well. Lawrence, I wonder I didn't kill you!"

"I wish that you had," he said, bitterly.

She nodded.

"Oh, I know how you are feeling just now," she said. "Truth strikes home, you know, and it hurts just a little, doesn't it? In a few days your admirable common sense will prevail. You will say to yourself: 'She was that sort of woman, she had that sort of disposition, she was bound to go to the dogs, anyway!' So you are going to marry the Duchess of Lenchester, Lawrence!"

He stood up.

"Blanche," he said, "that was all a mistake. I didn't understand. Let us forget that day altogether. Marry me now, and I will try to make up for these past years."

She stared at him blankly. The colour in her cheek was like a lurid patch under the pallor of her skin. She gave a little gasp, and her hand went to her side. Then she laughed hardly, almost offensively.

"What a man of sentiment," she declared. "After fifteen years, too, and only just engaged to another woman! No, thank you, my dear Lawrence. I've lived my life, such as it has been. I'm not so very old, but I look fifty, and I've vices enough to blacken an entire neighbourhood. Fancy, if people saw me, and heard that you might have married the Duchess of Lenchester. They'd hint at an asylum."

"Never mind about other people," he said. "Give me a chance, Blanche, to show that I'm not such an absolute brute."

"Rubbish," she interrupted. "Fifteen years ago I would have married you. In fact, I expected to. The reason why I found the courage to shield you from any unpleasantness that awful day was because I knew if trouble came and there was any scandal you would feel yourself obliged to marry me, and I wanted you to marry me—because you wanted to. What an idiot I was! Now, please go away, Lawrence. Marry the Duchess, if you like, but don't worry me with your re-awakened conscience. I'm going my own way for the rest of my few years, and the less I see of you the better I shall be pleased. You will forgive me—but I have an engagement—down the river! I really must hurry you off."

Her teeth were set close together, the sobs seemed tangled in her throat. It seemed to her that all the longing in her life was concentrated in that one passionate desire, that he should seize her in his arms now, hold her there—tell her that it had all been a mistake, that the ugly times were dreams, that after all he had cared—a little! The room swam round with her, but she pointed smilingly to the door, which her trim parlour-maid was holding open. And Mannering went.

# CHAPTER IX

## THE FALTERING OF MANNERING

Mannering left by the afternoon train for Hampshire, where he was to be the guest for a few days of the leader of his party. He arrived without sending word of his coming, to find the whole of the house party absent at a cricket match. The short respite was altogether welcome to him. He changed his clothes and wandered off into the gardens. Here an hour or so later Berenice's maid found him.

"Her Grace would like to see you, sir, if you would come to her sitting-room," the girl said, with a demure smile.

Mannering, with something of an inward groan, followed her. Berenice, very slim and stately in her simple white muslin gown, rose from the couch as he entered, and held out her hands.

"At last," she murmured. "You provoking man, to stay away so long. And what have you been doing with yourself?"

Her sentence concluded with a little note of dismay. Mannering was positively haggard in the clear afternoon light. There were lines underneath his eyes, and his face had a tense, drawn appearance. He did not kiss her, as she had

E. Phillips Oppenheim

more than half expected. He held her hands for a moment, and then sank down upon the couch by her side.

"It was not exactly easy work—up there," he said.

She noticed the repression.

"Tell me all about it," she begged.

His thoughts surged back to those three weeks of tragedy. His personal misery became for the moment a shadowy thing. The sorrows of one man, what were they to the breaking hearts of millions? He thought of the children, and he shuddered.

"It isn't so much to tell," he said. "I have been to a dozen or so of the largest towns in the North, and have taken the manufacturers one by one. I have taken their wage sheets and compared them with past years. The result was always the same. Less money distributed amongst more people. Afterwards we went amongst the people themselves—to see how they lived. It was like a chapter from the inferno—an epic of loathsome tragedy. I have seen the children, Berenice, and God help the next generation."

"You must not forget, Lawrence," she said, "that character is an essential factor in poverty. Poverty there must always be, because of the idle and shiftless."

"Individual poverty, yes," he answered. "Not wholesale poverty, not streets of it, towns of it. I don't talk about starving people, although I saw them too. Our vicious charitable system may keep their cry from our ears, but my sympathies go out to the man who ought to be earning two pounds a week, and who is earning fifteen shillings; the man who used to have his bit of garden, and smoke, and Sunday clothes, and a day or so's holiday now and then. He was a contented, decent, God-fearing citizen, the backbone of the whole nation, and he has been blotted away from the face of the earth. They work now passively, like dumb brutes, to resist starvation, and human character isn't strong enough for such a strain. The public houses thrive, and the pawnshops are full. But the children haven't enough to eat. They are growing up lank, white, prematurely aged, the spectres to dance us statesmen down into hell."

"You are overwrought, dear," she said, gently. "You have been in the hands of a man whose object it was to show you only one side of all this."

"I have sought for the truth," Mannering answered, "and I have seen it. I have learned more in three weeks than all the Commissions and statistics and Board-of-Trade figures have taught me in five years."

"And yet," she said, thoughtfully, "you hesitated about that last Navy vote. Don't you see that the imperialism which you are a little disposed to shrug your shoulders at is the most logical and complete cure for all this? We must extend and maintain our colonies, and people them with our surplus population."

He shook his head.

"That is not a policy which would ever appeal to me," he answered. "It is like an external operation to remove a malady which is of internal origin. Either our social laws or our political systems are at fault when our trade leaves us, and our labouring classes are unable to earn a fair wage. That is the position we are in to-day."

She rose to her feet, and walked restlessly up and down the

room. Mannering had the look of a crushed man. She watched him critically. Writers in magazines and reviews had often made a study of his character. She remembered a brilliant contributor to a recent review, who had dwelt upon a certain lack of cohesion in his constitution, an inability to relegate sentiment to its proper place in dealing with the great workaday problems of the world. Conscientious, but never to be trusted, was the last anomalous but luminous criticism. Was this frame of mind of his a sign of it, she wondered? His place in politics was fixed and sure. What right had he, as a man of principle, with a great following, to run even the risk of being led away by false prophets? A certain hardness stole into her face as she watched him. She tried to steel herself against the sight of his suffering, and though she was not wholly successful, there was a distinct change in her tone and attitude towards him as she resumed her seat.

"Tell me," she asked, "what this means from a practical point of view? How will it effect your plans?"

"I must give up my public meetings," he answered, slowly. "I have written to Manningham to tell him that he must get some one else to lead the campaign."

Berenice was very pale. So many of these wonderful dreams of hers seemed vanishing into thin air.

"This is a terrible blow," she said. "It is the worst thing which has happened to us for years. Are you going over to the other side, Lawrence?"

He shook his head.

"I can't do that altogether," he said. "The position is simply this: I am still, so far as my judgment and research go, opposed to tariff reform. On the other hand, I dare not take any leading part in fighting any scheme which has the barest chance of bringing better times to the working classes. I simply stand apart for the moment on this question."

She laughed a little bitterly.

"There is no other question," she said. "You will never be allowed to remain neutral. You appear to me to be in a very singular position. You are divided between sentiment and conviction, and you prefer to yield to the former. Lawrence, do not be hasty! Think of all that depends upon your judgment in this matter. From the very first you have been the bitterest and most formidable opponent of this absurd scheme. If you turn round you will unsettle public opinion throughout the country. Remember, the power of the states-man is almost a sacred charge."

"I am remembering," he murmured, "those children. I am bound to think this matter out, Berenice. I am going to meet Graham and Mellors next week. I shall not rest until I have made some effort to put my hand upon the weak spot. Some-where there is a rotten place. I want to reach it."

"Do you mean to give up your seat?" she asked.

"Not unless I am asked to," he answered. "I may need to work from there."

She sighed.

"I suppose your mind is quite made up," she said.

"Absolutely," he answered.

Her maid came in just then, and Mannering offered to

E. Phillips Oppenheim

withdraw. She made no effort to detain him, and he went at once in search of his host and hostess. He found every one assembled in the hall below. Lord Redford, Borrowdean, and the chief whip of his party were talking together in a corner, and from their significant look at his approach, he felt sure that he himself had been the subject of their conversation. The situation was more than a little awkward. Lord Redford stepped forward and welcomed him cordially.

"I'm afraid you've been knocking yourself up, Mannering," he said. "I've just been proposing to Culthorpe here that we bar politics completely for twenty-four hours. We'll leave the dinner table with the ladies, and you and I will play golf to-morrow. I've had Taylor down here, and I can assure you that my links are worth playing over now. Then on Thursday we'll have a conference."

"I was scarcely sure," Mannering said, with a slight smile, "whether I should be expected to stay until then. Sir Leslie has told you of my telegrams?"

"Yes, yes," Lord Redford said, quickly. "We've postponed the meetings for the present. We'll talk that all out later on. You've had some tea, I hope? No? Well, Eleanor, you are a nice hostess," he added, turning to his wife. "Give Mr. Mannering some tea at once, and feed him up with hot cakes. Come into the billiard-room afterwards, Mannering, will you? I've got a new table in the winter-garden, and we're going to have a pool before dinner."

Berenice came in and laid her hand upon her host's arm.

"You need not worry about Mr. Mannering," she declared. "He is going to have tea with me at that little table, and I am going to take him for a walk in the park afterwards."

"So long as you feed him well," Lord Redford declared, with a little laugh, "and turn up in good time for dinner, you may do what you like. If you take my advice, Berenice, you will join our league. We have pledged ourselves not to utter a word of shop for twenty-four hours."

"I submit willingly," Berenice answered. "Mr. Mannering and I will find something else to talk about."

# CHAPTER X

## THE END OF A DREAM

"You can guess why I brought you here, perhaps," Berenice said, gently, as she motioned him to sit down by her side. "This place, more than any other I know, certainly more than any other at Bayleigh, seems to me to be completely restful. There are the trees, you see, and the water, and the swans, that are certainly the laziest creatures I know. You look to me as though you needed rest, Lawrence."

"I suppose I do," he answered, slowly. "I am not sure, though, whether I deserve it."

"You are rather a self-distrustful mortal," she remarked, leaning back in her corner and looking at him from under her parasol. "You have worked hard all the session, and now you have finished up by three weeks of, I should think, herculean labour. If you do not deserve rest who does?"

"The rest which I deserve," Mannering answered, bitterly, "is the rest of those whose bones are bleaching amongst the caves and corals of the sea there! That is Matapan Point, isn't it, where the hidden rocks are?"

She nodded.

"Really, you are developing into a very gloomy person," she said. "Lawrence, don't let us fence with one another any longer. What you may decide to do politically may be ruinous to your career, to your chance of usefulness in the world, and to my hopes. But I want you to understand this. It can make no difference to me. I have had dreams perhaps of a great future, of being the wife of a Prime Minister who would lead his country into a new era of prosperity, who would put the last rivets into the bonds of a great imperial empire. But one never realizes all one's hopes, Lawrence. I love politics. I love being behind the scenes, and helping to move the pawns across the board. But I am a woman, too, Lawrence, and I love you. Put everything connected with your public life on one side. Let me ask you this. You are changed. Has anything come between us as man and woman?"

"Yes," he answered, "something has come between us."

She sat quite still for several minutes. She prayed that he too might keep silence, and he seemed to know her thoughts. Over the little sheet of ornamental water, down the glade of beech and elm trees narrowing towards the cliffs, her eyes travelled seawards. It was to her a terrible moment. Mannering had represented so much to her, and her standard was a high one. If there was a man living whom she would have reckoned above the weaknesses of the herd, it was he. In those days at Blakely she had almost idealized him. The simple purity of his life there, his delicate and carefully chosen pleasures, combined with his almost passionate love of the open places of the earth, had led her to regard him as something different from any other man whom she had ever known. All Borrowdean's hints and open statements had gone for very little. She had listened and retained her trust. And now she had a horrible fear. Something had gone out of the man, something which went for strength, something

E. Phillips Oppenheim

without which he seemed to lack that splendid militant vitality which had always seemed to her so admirable. Perhaps he was going to make a confession, one of those crude, clumsy confessions of a stained life, which have drawn the colour and the joy from so many beautiful dreams. She shivered a little, but she inclined her head to listen.

"Well," she said, "what is it?"

"I have asked another woman to marry me only a few hours ago," he said, quietly.

Berenice was a proud woman, and for the moment she felt her love for this man a dried-up and shrivelled thing. She was white to the lips, but she commanded her voice, and her eyes met his coldly.

"May I inquire into the circumstances—of this—somewhat remarkable proceeding?" she inquired.

"There is a woman," he said, "whose life I helped to wreck— not in the orthodox way," he added, with a note of scorn in his tone, "but none the less effectually. The one recompense I never thought of offering her was marriage. I have seen that, despite all my efforts to aid her, her life has been a failure. Her friends have been the wrong sort of friends, her life the wrong sort of life. What it was that was dragging her downwards I never guessed, for she, too, in her way, was a proud woman. To-day she sent for me. What passed between us is her secret as much as mine. I can only tell you that before I left I had asked her to marry me."

"I think," she said, calmly, "that you need tell me no more."

"There is very little more that I can tell you," he answered. "I have no affection for her, and she has refused to marry me.

But she remains—between us—irrevocably!"

"You are lucidity itself," she replied. "Will you forgive me if I leave you? I am scarcely used to this sort of situation, and I should like to be alone."

"Go by all means, Berenice," he answered. "You and I are better apart. But there is one thing which I must say to you, and you must hear. What has passed between you and me is the epitome of the love-making of my life. You are the only woman whom I have desired to make my wife. You are the only woman whom I have loved, and shall love until I die. I can make you no reparation, none is possible! Yet these things are my justification."

Berenice had turned away. The passionate ring of truth in his tone arrested her footsteps. She paused. Her heart was beating very fast, her coldness was all assumed. It was so much happiness to throw away, if indeed there was a chance. She turned and faced him, nervous, gaunt, hollow-eyed, the wreck of his former self. Pity triumphed in spite of herself. What was this leaven of weakness in the man, she wondered, which had so suddenly broken him down? He had only to hold on his way and he would be Prime Minister in a year. And at the moment of trial he had crumpled up like a piece of false metal. A wave of false sentiment, a maniacal hyper-conscientiousness, had been sufficient to sap the very strength from his bones. And then—there was this other woman. Was she to let him go without an effort? He might recover his sanity. It was perhaps a mere nervous break-down, which had made him the prey of strange fancies. She spoke to him differently. She spoke once more as the woman who loved him.

"Lawrence," she said, "you are telling me too much, and not enough. If you want to send me away I must go. But tell me this first. What claim has this woman upon you?"

"It is not my secret," he groaned. "I cannot tell you."

"Leslie Borrowdean knows it," she said. "I could have heard it, but I refused to listen. Remember, whatever you may owe to other people you owe me something, too."

"It is true," he answered. "Well, listen. I killed her husband!"

"You! You—killed her husband!" she repeated vaguely.

"Yes! She shielded me. There was an inquest, and they found that he had heart disease. No one knew that I had even seen him that day, no one save she and a servant, who is dead. But the truth lives. He had reason to be angry with me—over a money affair. He came home furious, and found me alone with his wife. He called me—well, it was a lie—and he struck me. I threw him on one side—and he fell. When we picked him up he was dead."

"It was terrible!" she said, "but you should have braved it out. They could have done very little to you."

"I know it," he answered. "But I was young, and my career was just beginning. The thing stunned me. She insisted upon secrecy. It would reflect upon her, she thought, if the truth came out, so I acquiesced, I left the house unseen. All these days I have had to carry the burden of this thing with me. To-day—seemed to be the climax. For the first time I understood."

"She can never marry you," Berenice said. "It would be horrible."

"She refused to marry me to-day," he answered, "but she laid her life bare, and I cannot marry any one else."

Berenice was trembling. She was no longer ashamed to show her agitation.

"I am very sorry for you, Lawrence," she said. "I am very sorry for myself. Good-bye!"

She left him, and Mannering sank back upon the seat.

# CHAPTER XI

## BORROWDEAN SHOWS HIS "HAND"

"To be plain with you," Borrowdean remarked, "Mannering's defection would be irremediable. He alone unites Redford, myself, and—well, to put it crudely, let us say the Imperialistic Liberal Party with Manningham and the old-fashioned Whigs who prefer the ruts. There is no other leader possible. Redford and I talked till daylight this morning. Now, can nothing be done with Mannering?"

"To be plain with you, too, then, Sir Leslie," Berenice answered, "I do not think that anything can be done with him. In his present frame of mind I should say that he is better left alone. He has worked himself up into a thoroughly sentimental and nervous state. For the moment he has lost his sense of balance."

Borrowdean nodded.

"Desperate necessity," he said, "sometimes justifies desperate measures. We need Mannering, the country and our cause need him. If argument will not prevail there is one last alternative left to us. It may not be such an alternative as we should choose, but beggars must not be choosers. I think that you will know what I mean."

"I have no idea," Berenice answered.

"You are aware," he continued, "that there is in Mannering's past history an episode, the publication of which would entail somewhat serious consequences to him."

"Well?"

It was a most eloquent monosyllable, but Borrowdean had gone too far to retreat.

"I propose that we make use of it," he said. "Mannering's attitude is rankly foolish, or I would not suggest such a thing. But I hold that we are entitled, under the circumstances, to make use of any means whatever to bring him to his senses."

Berenice smiled. They were standing together upon a small hillock in the park, watching the golf.

"Charlatanism in politics does not appeal to me," she said, drily. "Any party that adopted such means would completely alienate my sympathies. No, my dear Sir Leslie, don't stoop to such low-down means. Mannering is honest, but infatuated. Win him back by fair means, if you can, but don't attempt anything of the sort you are suggesting. I, too, know his history, from his own lips. Any one who tried to use it against him, would forfeit my friendship!"

"Success then would be bought too dearly," Borrowdean answered, with a gallantry which it cost him a good deal to assume. "May I pass on, Duchess, in connexion with this matter, to ask you a somewhat more personal question?"

"I think," Berenice said, calmly, "that I can spare you the necessity. You were going to speak, I believe, of the engagement between Lawrence Mannering and myself."

"I was," Borrowdean admitted.

"It does not exist any longer," Berenice said, "I should be glad if you would inform any one who has heard the rumour that it is without any foundation."

Borrowdean looked thoughtfully at the woman by his side.

"I am very glad to hear it," he declared. "I am glad for many reasons, and I am glad personally."

She raised her eyebrows.

"Indeed! I cannot imagine how it should affect you personally."

"I perhaps said more than I meant to," he replied, calmly. "I am a poor, struggling politician myself, whose capital consists of brains and a capacity for work, and whose hopes are coloured with perhaps too daring ambitions. Amongst them—"

"Mr. Mannering has holed out from off the green," she interrupted. "Positively immoral, I call it."

"Amongst them," Borrowdean continued, calmly, "is one which some day or other I must tell you, for indeed you are concerned in it."

"I can assure you, Sir Leslie," she said, looking at him steadily, "that I am not at all a sympathetic person. My strong advice to you would be—not to tell me. I do not think that you would gain anything by it."

Borrowdean met his fate with a bow and a shrug of the shoulders.

"It only remains," he said, "for me to beg you to pardon what might seem like presumption. Shall we meet them on the last green?"

Mannering would have avoided Berenice, but she gave him no option. She laid her hand upon his arm, and volunteered to show him a new way home.

"You must be on your guard, Lawrence," she said. "Lord Redford is very fond of concealing his plans to the last moment, but he is a very clever man. And Sir Leslie Borrowdean would give his little finger to catch you tripping. All this avoidance of politics is part of a scheme. They will spring something upon you quite suddenly. Don't give any hasty pledges."

"Thank you for your warning," he said. "I will be careful."

"Tell me," she said, "as a friend, what are your plans? Forget that I am interested in politics altogether. I simply want to know how you are spending your time for the next few months."

"It depends upon them," he answered, looking downwards into the valley, where Lord Redford and Borrowdean were walking side by side. "If they ask me to resign my seat I shall go North again, and it is just possible that I might come back into the House as a labour member. On the other hand, if they are content with such support as I can give them, and to have me on the fence at present so far as the tariff question is concerned, why, I shall go back and do the best I can for them."

"You are not quite won over to the other side yet, then," she remarked, smiling.

"Not yet," he answered. "If ever there was an honest doubter, I am one. If I had never left my study, England could not have contained a more rabid opponent of any change in our fiscal policy than I. I am like a small boy who is absolutely sure that he has worked out his sum correctly, but finds the answer is not the one which his examiner expects. There is something wrong somewhere. I want, if I can, to discover it. I only want the truth! I don't see why it should be so hard to find, why figures and common sense should clash entirely and horribly with existing facts."

"You wore dun-coloured spectacles when you took your walks abroad," she said, smiling. "No one else seems to have discovered so distressing a state of affairs as you have spoken of."

"Because they never looked beneath the surface," he answered. "I myself might have failed to understand if I had not been shown. Remember that our workingman of the better class does not go marching through the streets with an unemployed banner and a tin cup when he is in want. He takes his half wages and closes the door upon his sufferings. God help him!"

"Adieu, politics," she declared, with a shrug of the shoulders. "Isn't that Clara playing croquet with Major Bristow? I wish I didn't dislike that man so much. I hate to see the child with him."

Mannering sighed.

"Poor Clara!" he said. "I am afraid I have left her a good deal to herself lately."

"I am afraid you have," she agreed, a little gravely. "May I give you a word of advice?"

"You know that I should be grateful for it," he declared.

"Be sure that she never goes to the Bristows again, and ask her whether she has any other card debts. It may be my fancy, but I don't like the way that man hangs about her, and looks at her. I am sure that she does not like him, and yet she never seems to have the courage to snub him."

"I am very much obliged to you," he said. "I will speak to her to-day."

"I don't know where I am going, or what I shall do for the autumn," she continued, with a little sigh, "but if you like to trust Clara with me I will look after her. I think that she needs a woman. Yes, I thought so. Redford and Sir Leslie are waiting for you. Go and have it out with them, my friend."

"You are too kind to me," he said; "kinder than I deserve!"

"Oh, I don't know," she answered. "I am afraid that my kindness is only another form of selfishness. I am rather a lonely person, you know. Lord Redford is beckoning to you. I am going to break up that croquet party."

Mannering joined the other two men. Berenice strolled on to the lawn. Major Bristow eyed her coming with some disfavour. He was one of the men whom she always ignored. Clara, on the other hand, seemed proportionately relieved.

"I want you to come to my room as soon as you possibly can, child," Berenice said. "Shall I wait while you finish your game?"

"Oh, I will come at once," Clara exclaimed, laying down her mallet. "Major Bristow will not mind, I am sure."

Major Bristow looked as though he did mind very much, but lacked the nerve to say so. Berenice calmly took Clara by the arm and led her away.

"You are not engaged to Major Bristow by any chance, are you?" she asked, calmly.

"Engaged to Major Bristow? Heavens, no!" Clara answered. "I don't think he is in the least a marrying man."

"So much the better for our sex," Berenice answered. "I wouldn't spend so much time with him, my dear, if I were you. I have known people with nicer reputations."

Clara turned a shade paler.

"I can never get away from him," she said. "He follows me— everywhere, and—"

"You do not by any chance, I suppose, owe him money?" Berenice asked. "They tell me that he has a somewhat objectionable habit of winning money from girls, more than they can afford to pay, and then suggesting that it stand over for a time."

Clara turned towards her with terrified eyes.

"I—I do owe Major Bristow a little still," she admitted. "I seem to have been so unlucky. He told me that any time would do, that I should win it back again, and I had no idea what stakes we were playing. I don't touch a card now at all, but this was at Ellingham House. They insisted on my making a fourth at bridge."

Berenice tightened her grasp upon the girl's arm.

"Don't say anything about this to your uncle just now," she insisted. "I am going to take you up to my room and write you a cheque for the amount, whatever it may be. Afterwards I will have a talk with Major Bristow. Nonsense, child, don't cry! The money is nothing to me, and I always promised your uncle that I would look after you a little."

"I have been such a fool!" the girl sobbed.

Berenice for a moment was also sad. Her lips quivered, her eyes were wistful.

"We all think that sometimes, child," she said, quietly. "We all have our foolish moments and our hours of repentance, even the wisest of us!"

# CHAPTER XII

## SIR LESLIE BORROWDEAN INCURS
## A HEAVY DEBT

"I suppose," Lord Redford remarked, thoughtfully, "politics represents a different thing to all of us, according to our temperament. To me, I must confess, it is a plain, practical business, the business of law-making. To you, Mannering, I fancy that it appeals a little differently. Now, let us understand one another. Are you prepared to undertake this campaign which we planned out a few months ago?"

"If I did undertake it," Mannering said, "it would be to leave unsaid the things which you would naturally expect from me, and to say things of which you could not possibly approve. I am very sorry. You can command my resignation at any moment, if you will. But my views, though in the main they have not changed, are very much modified."

Lord Redford nodded.

"That," he said, "is our misfortune, but it certainly is not your fault. As for your resignation, if you crossed the floor of the House to-morrow we should not require it of you. You are responsible to your constituents only. We dragged you back into public life—you see I admit it freely—and we are willing to take our risk. Whether you are with us or against us, we recognize you as one of those whose place is amongst the rulers of the people."

"You are very generous, Lord Redford," Mannering answered.

"Not at all. It is no use being peevish. You are a great disappointment to us, but we have not given up hope. If you are not altogether with us to-day, there is to-morrow. I tell you frankly, Mannering, that I look upon you as a man temporarily led astray by a wave of sentimentality. So long as the world lasts there will be rich men and poor, but you must always remember in considering this that it is character as well as circumstances which is at the root of the acquisition of wealth. Generations have gone to the formation of our social fabric. It is the slow evolution of the human laws of necessity. The socialist and the sentimentalist and the philanthropist, dropping gold through his fingers, have each had their fling at it, but their cry is like the cry from the wilderness—a long, lone thing! And then to come to the real point, Mannering. Grant for a moment all that you have told Borrowdean and myself about the condition of the labour classes in the great towns and the universal depression of trade. How can you possibly imagine that the imposition of tariff duties is the sovereign, or even a possible, remedy? Why, you yourself have been one of the most brilliant pamphleteers against anything of the sort. You have been called the Cobden of the day. You cannot throw principles away like an old garment."

"Let us leave for one moment," Mannering answered, "the personal side of the matter. I have seen in the majority of our large cities terrible and convincing proof of the decline of our manufacturing industries. I have seen the outcome of this in hundreds of ruined homes, in a whole generation coming

E. Phillips Oppenheim

into the world half starved, half clothed—God help those children. I have always maintained that the labouring classes should be the happiest race of people in this country. I find them without leisure or recreation, fighting fate with both hands for food. Redford, the whole world has never shown us a greater tragedy than the one which we others deliberately and persistently close our eyes to—I mean the struggle for life which is being waged in every one of our great cities."

"We have statistics," Borrowdean began.

"Damn statistics!" Mannering interrupted. "I have juggled with figures myself in the old days, and I know how easy it is. So do you, and so does Redford. This is what I want to put to you. The tragedy is there. Perhaps those who have faced it and come back again to tell of their experiences have been a little hysterical—the horror of it has carried them away. They may not have adopted the most effectual means of making the world understand, but it is there. I have seen it. A thousandth part of this misery in a country with which we had nothing to do, and no business to interfere, and we should be having mass meetings at Exeter Hall, and making general asses of ourselves all over the country, shrieking for intervention, wasting a whole dictionary of rhetoric, and probably getting well snubbed for our pains. And because the murders are by slow poison instead of with steel, because they are in our own cities and amongst our own people, we accept them with a sort of placid satisfaction. You, Lord Redford, speak of character and enunciate social laws, and Borrowdean will argue that after all the trade of the country is not so bad as it might be, and will make an epigram on the importation of sentimentality into politics. In plain words, Lord Redford, we, as a party, are asleep to what is going on. One statesman has recognized it, and proposed a startling and drastic remedy. We attack the remedy tooth and nail, but we place forward no counter proposition. It is as though a dying man were attended by two doctors, one of whom has prepared a remedy which the other declines to administer without suggesting one of his own. It is not a logical position. The medicine may not cure, but let the man have his chance of life."

"Your simile," Lord Redford said, "assumes that the man is dying."

"I have seen the mark of death upon his face," Mannering answered. "The men who are traitors to their country to-day are those who, healthy enough themselves, talk causeless and shallow optimism which is fed alone by their own prosperity. The doctrine of Christ is the care of others. If you do not believe, the sick-room is open also to you; go there unprejudiced, and with an open mind, and you will come away as I have come away."

"Must we take it, then, Mannering," Lord Redford said, gravely, "that you are prepared to support the administering of the medicine you spoke of?"

Mannering was silent for a moment.

"At least," he said, "I am not going to be amongst those who cry out against it and offer nothing themselves. I am going to analyze that medicine, and if I see a chance of life in it I shall say, let us run a little risk, rather than stand by inactive, to look upon the face of death. In other words, I become for the moment a passive figure in politics so far as this question is concerned."

Lord Redford held out his hand.

"Let it go at that, Mannering," he said. "I believe that you will come back to us. We shall be always glad of your support, but of course you will understand that the position from to-day is changed. If you had carried the standard, as we had hoped, the reward also was to have been yours. We must elect one of ourselves to take your place. To put it plainly, your defection now releases us from all pledges."

"I understand," Mannering answered. "It was scarcely ambition which brought me back into politics, and I must work for the cause in which I believe. If I am forced to take any definite action, I shall, of course, resign my seat."

The door closed behind him. Borrowdean struck a match, and Lord Redford looked thoughtfully out of the window across the park.

"I was always afraid of this," Borrowdean said, gloomily. "There is a leaven of madness in the man."

Lord Redford shrugged his shoulders.

"Genius or madness," he remarked. "We may yet see him a modern Rienzi carried into power on the shoulders of the people. Such a man might become anything. As a matter of fact, I think that he will go back into his study. He has the brain to fashion wonderful thoughts, and the lips to fire them into life. But I doubt his adaptability. I cannot imagine him ever becoming a real and effective force."

Borrowdean, who was bitterly disappointed, smoked furiously.

"We shall see," he said. "If Mannering is not for us, I think that I can at least promise that he does no harm on the other side."

Lord Redford turned away from the window. He eyed Borrowdean curiously.

"It was you," he remarked, "who brought Mannering back into public life. You had a certain reward for it, and you would have had a much greater one if things had gone our way. But I want you to remember this. Mannering is best left alone—now, for the present. You understand me?"

Borrowdean shrugged his shoulders. There was a good deal too much sentiment in politics.

* * * * *

Mannering and Berenice came together for a few moments on the terrace after dinner. He was not so completely engrossed in his own affairs as to fail to notice her lack of colour and a certain weariness of manner, which had kept her more silent than usual during the whole evening.

"Well?" she said.

"There is nothing definite," he answered. "You see, the question of tariff reform is not before the House at present, and Redford does not require me to resign my seat. But of course it will come to that sooner or later."

She leaned over the grey balustrade. With her it was a moment of weakness. She was suddenly conscious of the fact that she was no longer a young woman. The time when she might hope to find in life the actual flavour and joy of passionate living was nearing the end. And a little while ago they had seemed so near! The pity of it stirred up a certain sense of rebellion in her heart. She was still a beautiful woman. She knew very well the arts by which men are enslaved. Why should she not try them upon him—this man

E. Phillips Oppenheim

who loved her, who seemed willing to sacrifice both their lives to a piece of senseless quixoticism? Her fingers touched his, and held them softly. Thrilled through all his senses, he turned towards her wonderingly.

"Are we wise, Lawrence," she whispered, "if indeed you love me? Life is so short, and I am not a young woman any more. I have been lonely so long. I want a little happiness before I go."

"Don't!" he cried, hoarsely. "You know—what comes between us."

She was a little indignant, but still tender.

"This woman does not want you, Lawrence," she cried. "I do! Oh, Lawrence!"

He faltered. She laid her fingers upon his arm.

"Come down the steps," she murmured, "and I will show you Lady Redford's rose-garden."

Her touch was compelling. He could not have resisted it. And about his heart lay the joy of her near presence. Side by side they moved along the terrace—it seemed to him that they passed towards their destiny. The gentle rustling of her clothes, their slight, mysterious perfume, was like music to him. A sudden wave of passion carried him away. The primitive virility of the man, awake at last, demanded its birthright.

And then upon the lower step they met Borrowdean, and he placed himself squarely in their way.

"I am sorry to interrupt you," he said, gravely, "but Lord

Redford has sent me out to look for you and to send you at once into the library. Something rather serious has happened."

Mannering came down to earth.

"The evening papers have come," Borrowdean said. "The *Pall Mall* has the whole story. You were seen at the working-men's club in Glasgow!"

Mannering turned towards the house. His nerves were all tingling with excitement, but the thread had suddenly been snapped. He was no longer in danger of yielding to that flood of delicious sensations. His voice had been almost steady as he had begged Berenice to excuse him. Berenice stood quite still. Her hand was pressed to her side, her dark eyes were lit with passion. She leaned forward towards Borrowdean, and seemed about to strike him.

"You will find yourself—repaid for this, Sir Leslie," she murmured.

Then she turned abruptly away. For an hour or more she walked alone amongst the trellised walks of Lady Redford's rose-garden. But Mannering did not return.

# CHAPTER XIII

## THE WOMAN AND—THE OTHER WOMAN

"You see, Mannering," Lord Redford said, tapping the outspread evening paper with his forefinger, "the situation now presents a different aspect. I have no wish to force your hand—a few hours ago I think I proved this. But if you are to remain even nominally with us some sort of pronouncement must come from you in reply to these statements."

"Yes," Mannering said, "that is quite reasonable."

"The postponement of your campaign has been hinted at before," Lord Redford continued, "but we have never used the word abandonment. Now, to speak bluntly, the whole fat is in the fire. Your place on the fence is no longer possible. You must make your own declaration, and it must be for one of three things. You must remain with us, abandon public life for a time, or go over to the other side. And you must make promptly an announcement of your intentions."

"I have no alternative in the matter," Mannering said. "In fact, I think that this has happened opportunely. My presence with you was sure to prove something of an embarrassment to all of us. I shall apply for the Chiltern Hundreds to-morrow, and I shall not seek to re-enter the present

Parliament. The few months' respite will be useful to me. I can only express to you, Lord Redford, my sincere gratitude for all your consideration, and my regret for this disarrangement of your plans."

Lord Redford sighed. Why were men born, he wondered, with such a prodigious capacity for playing the fool?

"My chief regret, Mannering," he said, "is for you. The Fates so controlled circumstances that you seemed certain to achieve as a young man what is the crowning triumph of us veterans in the political world. I respect the honest scruples of every man, but it seems to me that you are throwing away an unparalleled opportunity in a fit of what a practical man like myself can only call sentimentality. I have no more to say. Forgive me if I have said too much. For the rest, give us the pleasure of your company here for as long as you find it convenient. We will abjure politics, and you shall give me my revenge at golf."

Mannering shook his head.

"I am very much obliged to you," he said, "but there is only one course open to me. I must go back and make my plans. If I could have a carriage for the nine-forty!"

Lord Redford made no effort to induce him to change his mind, though he remained courteous to the last.

"I was really glad to have him go," he told Borrowdean afterwards. "His very presence—the thought that there could be such colossal fools in the world—irritated me beyond measure. You can write his epitaph, Leslie, if your humorous vein is working, for the man is politically dead."

"One never knows," Berenice said, quietly. "There must be

something great about a man capable of such prodigious self-sacrifice. For at heart Lawrence Mannering is an ambitious man."

Lord Redford shrugged his shoulders.

"Perhaps," he said, "but I am very sure of this. There is nothing so great about the man as his folly."

Berenice smiled.

"We shall see," she said. "Personally, I believe that Sir Leslie would find his epitaph a little previous. I saw a great deal of Lawrence Mannering in the country, and I think that I understand him as well as either of you. I believe that his day will come."

"Well, all I can say is," Lord Redford pronounced, "that I very much wish you had left him down at his country home. Between you you have created a very serious situation. I must go up to town to-morrow and see Manningham. In the meantime, Leslie, I shall leave those reports severely alone. We must ignore Mannering altogether."

Berenice turned away with a smile at her lips. She had a very little opinion of Lord Redford and his following. Already she saw the man whose career they counted finished, at the head of a new and greater party. There were plenty of clever men of the coming generation, plenty of room for compromises, for the formation of a great national party out of the scattered units of a disunited opposition. She believed Mannering strong enough to do this. She saw in it greater possibilities than might have been forthcoming even if he had been chosen to lead the somewhat ragged party represented by Lord Redford and his followers. For the rest, she had been very near the success she so desired. Only an accident had robbed her of victory. If once they had reached the rose-garden she knew that she would have triumphed.

As her maid took off her jewellery that night she smiled at herself in the glass. She was thinking of that moment on the terrace. The glow had not wholly faded from her face—she saw herself with her long, slender neck and smooth, unwrinkled complexion, still beautiful, still a woman to be loved. Her maid ventured to whisper a word of respectful compliment. Truly Madame La Duchesse was growing younger!

\*　\*　\*　\*　\*

What strange whim, or evil fate, had turned his feet in that direction? Mannering often tried to trace backwards the workings of his mind that night, but he never wholly succeeded. He reached London about eleven, and sent his man home with his luggage, intending merely to call in at the club for letters. But afterwards he remembered only that he had strolled aimlessly along homewards, thinking deeply, and not particularly careful as to his direction. Even then he would have passed the house in Sloane Gardens without looking up, but for the civil "Good-night, sir," of a coachman sitting on the box of a small brougham drawn up against the kerb. He raised his head to return the salute, and realized at once where he was. Almost at the same moment the front door opened, and behind a glow of light in the hall he saw a familiar figure in the act of passing out to her carriage. The street was well lit, and he was almost opposite a lamp-post. She recognized him at once.

"Lawrence," she exclaimed, incredulously. "You—were you coming in?"

She was wrapped from head to foot in a long white opera

cloak, but the jewels in her hair and at her throat glistened in the flashing light. She moved slowly forward to his side. Her maid, who had been coming out to open the carriage door, lingered behind.

"I—upon my word, I scarcely know how I came here," he answered, a little bewildered. "I was walking home—it is scarcely out of my way—and thinking. You are going out?"

She nodded. Looking at her now more closely he saw the shadows under her eyes, only imperfectly concealed. The little gesture with which she answered him savoured of weariness.

"Yes, I was going out. I have sat alone with my thoughts all day, and I don't want to end my life in a lunatic asylum. I want a little change, that is all. If you will come in and talk to me instead, that will do as well. Any sort of distraction, you see," she added, with a hard little laugh, "just to keep me from—"

She did not finish her sentence. He looked at her gravely, and from her to the waiting carriage. He suddenly realized how the altered condition of affairs must affect her.

"I shall have to come and see you in a day or two," he said. "But now—" he hesitated.

"Why not now, then?" she asked.

"You have an engagement," he said.

She shook her head.

"I was only going somewhere to supper. I was going to call for Eva Fanesborough, and I suppose we should have had some bridge afterwards. Come in instead, Lawrence. I can telephone to her."

Already a presage of evil seemed to be forming itself in his mind. He would have given anything to have thought of some valid excuse.

"Your carriage—"

"Pooh!" she answered. "John, I shall not want you to-night," she said to the coachman. "Come!"

She led the way, and Mannering followed. As the maid closed the door behind them Mannering felt his breath quicken—his sense of depression grew stronger. He seemed threatened by some new and intangible danger. He stood on the hearthrug while she bent over the switch and turned on the electric light in the sitting-room. Then she threw off her cloak and looked at him curiously for a moment. Her face softened.

"My dear Lawrence," she said, "has politics done this, or are you ill?"

"I am quite well," he answered. "A little tired, perhaps. I have had rather a trying day."

She rang the bell, and ordered sandwiches and wine.

"You look like a corpse," she said, and stood over him while he ate and drank. And all the time that indefinable fear within him grew. She made him smoke. Then she leaned back in an easy-chair and looked across at him.

"You had something to say to me. What was it?"

"Nothing good," he answered. "I have quarrelled with my party, and I have to resign my seat in the House."

"Already?"

"Already! I am sorry, as of course in a few months' time I should have been in office, and drawing a considerable salary. As it is—" he hesitated.

"Oh, I understand!" she said. "Well, it doesn't matter much. I only have the house for six months furnished, and that's paid for in advance. John must go, and the horses can be sold."

He looked at her in amazement. Only a few months ago she had talked very differently.

"I—I am not sure whether all that will be necessary," he said. "I can find a tenant for Blakely, and I daresay I can manage another hundred a year or so. Only, of course, the large increase we had thought of will not be possible now."

"No, I suppose not," she answered, idly.

He moved in his chair uncomfortably. He found her wholly incomprehensible.

"What a beast I must have seemed to you always," she exclaimed, suddenly.

"Why?" he asked, pointlessly.

"I've sponged on you all my life, and you're not a rich man, are you, Lawrence? Then I dragged you into politics to supply me with the means to spend more money. My claim on you was one of sentiment only, but—I've made you pay. No wonder you hate me!"

"Your claim on me, even to every penny I possess," Mannering answered, "was a perfectly just one. I have never denied it, and I have done my best. And as to hating you, you know quite well it is not true!"

"Ah!" She rose suddenly to her feet, and before he had realized her intention she was on her knees by his side. She caught at his hand and kept her face hidden from him.

"Lawrence," she cried, "I was mad the other day. It was all the pent-up bitterness of years which seemed to escape me so suddenly. I said so much that I did not mean to—I was mad, dear. Oh, Lawrence, I am so lonely!"

Then the fear in his heart became a live thing. He was dumb. He could not have spoken had he tried.

"It was your coldness all these years," she murmured. "You were different once. You know that. At first, when the horror of what happened was young, I thought I understood. I thought, as it wore off, that you would be different. The horror has gone now, Lawrence. We know that it was an accident, it might as well have been another as you. But you have not changed. I have given up hoping. I have tried everything else, and I am a very miserable woman. Now I am going to pray to you, Lawrence. You do not care for me more. Pretend that you do! You cannot give me your love. Give me the best you can. Don't despise me too utterly, Lawrence! Pity me, if you will. Heaven knows I need it. And—you will be a little kind!"

Her hands were clasped about his neck. He disengaged himself gently.

"Blanche!" he cried, hoarsely, "I love another woman!"

E. Phillips Oppenheim

"Are you engaged to her?"

"No! Not now!"

"Then what does it matter? What does it matter, anyhow? It is not the real thing I am asking you for, Lawrence—only the make-belief! Keep the rest for her, if you must, but give me lies, false looks, hollow caresses, anything! You see what depths I have fallen to."

He held her hands tightly. A great pity for her filled his heart—pity for her, and for himself.

"Blanche," he said, "there is one way only. It is for you to decide. Will you marry me? I will do my best to make you a good husband!"

"Marry you?" she gasped. "Lawrence, I dare not!"

"I cannot alter the past," he said, sadly. "It never seemed to me possible that you could care for my—after what happened. But—"

"Oh, it is not that," she interrupted. "There is—the other woman, and, Lawrence, I should be afraid. I am not good enough!"

"Whatever you are, Blanche," he said, gravely, "remember that it is I who am responsible for your having been left alone to face the world. Your follies belong to me. I am quite free to share their burden with you."

"But the other woman?" she faltered.

"I must love her always," he said, quietly, "but I cannot marry her."

"And you would kiss me sometimes, Lawrence?" she whispered.

He took her quietly into his arms and kissed her forehead.

"I will do my best, Blanche," he said. "I dare not promise any more."

# BOOK III

## CHAPTER I

### MATRIMONY AND AN AWKWARD MEETING

"How delightfully Continental!" Blanche exclaimed, as the head-waiter showed them to their table. "Hester, did you ever see anything more quaint?"

"It is perfect," the girl answered, leaning back in her chair, and looking around with quiet content.

Mannering took up the menu and ordered dinner. Then he lit a cigarette and looked around.

"It certainly is quaint," he said. "One dines out of doors often enough, especially over here, but I have never seen a courtyard made such excellent use of before. The place is really old, too."

They had found their way to a small seaside resort, in the north of France, which Mannering had heard highly praised by some casual acquaintance. The courtyard of the small hotel was set out with round dining tables, and the illumination was afforded by Japanese lanterns hung from every available spot. A small band played from a wooden balcony. Monsieur, the proprietor, walked anxiously from table to table, all smiles and bows. Through the roofed way, which led from the street, one caught a distant glimpse of the sea.

Mannering, to the surprise of his friends, and to his own secret amazement, had survived the crisis which had seemed at one time likely enough to wreck his life. Politically he was no longer a great power, for the party whose cause he had half espoused had met with a distinct reverse, and he himself was without a seat in Parliament, but amongst the masses his was still a name to conjure with. Socially his marriage with Blanche Phillimore had scarcely proved the disaster which every one had anticipated. Her old ways and manner of life lay in the background. She had aged a little, perhaps, and grown thinner, but she had shown from the first an almost pathetic desire to adapt her life to his, to assume an altogether unobtrusive position, and if she could not in any way influence his destiny, at least she did not hamper it. She had made no demands upon him which he was not able to grant. She had lived where he had suggested, she had never embarrassed him with too vehement an affection. As for Mannering himself, he had found solace in work. Defeated at the polls, he had declined a safe seat, and remained the chosen independent candidate of a great Northern consti-tuency. He addressed public meetings occasionally, and he contributed to the reviews. Without having ever finally committed himself to a definite scheme of tariff reform, he preached everywhere the doctrine of consideration. In a modified way he was reckoned now as one of its possible supporters.

They were almost halfway through their dinner when some commotion was heard in the narrow street outside. Then with much tooting of horns and the shrill shouting of directions from the bystanders, two heavily laden touring cars turned

E. Phillips Oppenheim

slowly into the cobbled courtyard, and drew up within a few feet of the semicircular line of tables. Mannering's little party watched the arrivals with an interest shared by every one in the place. Muffled up in cloaks and veils, they were at first unrecognized. It was Mannering himself who first realized who they were.

"Clara!" he exclaimed to the young lady who was standing almost by his side. "Welcome to Bonestre!"

She turned towards him with a little start.

"Uncle!" she exclaimed. "How extraordinary! Why, how long have you been here?"

"We arrived this afternoon," he answered. "You remember Hester, don't you? And this is Mrs. Mannering."

Clara shook hands with both. She declared afterwards that she was surprised into it, but she would certainly never have recognized in the quiet, rather weary-looking, woman who sat at her uncle's side the Blanche Phillimore whom she had more than once passionately declared that she would sooner die than speak to. She murmured a few mechanical words, and then, suddenly realizing the situation, she glanced a little anxiously over her shoulder.

"You know who I am with, uncle?" she whispered.

But Mannering was already face to face with Berenice. She held out her hand without hesitation. If she felt any emotion she concealed it perfectly. Her voice was steady and cordial, if her cheeks were pale. The dust lay thickly upon them all. Mannering, tall and grave in his plain dinner clothes and black tie, stood almost like a statue before her, until her extended hand invited his movement.

"What an extraordinary meeting," she said, quietly. "I am very glad to see you again, Mr. Mannering. We have had such a ride, all the way from Havre along roads an inch thick in dust. This is your wife, is it not? I am very glad to know you, Mrs. Mannering."

All that might have been embarrassing in the encounter seemed dissolved by the utterly conventional tone of her greeting. Sir Leslie Borrowdean came up and joined them, and Lord and Lady Redford. Then the little party, escorted by the landlord, disappeared into the hotel. Mannering resumed his seat and continued his dinner. He leaned over and addressed his wife. His tone was kinder than usual.

"When we have had our coffee," he said, "I hope that you will feel like a walk. The moon is coming up over the sea."

She shook her head.

"Take Hester," she said. "She loves that sort of thing. I have a headache, and I should like to go upstairs as soon as possible."

So Hester walked with Mannering out to the rocks where pools of water, left by the tide, shone like silver in the moonlight. They talked very little at first, but as they leaned over the rail and looked out seawards Hester broke the silence, and spoke of the things which they both had in their minds.

"I am sorry they came," she said. "I am afraid it will upset mother, and it is not pleasant for you, is it?"

"For me it is nothing, Hester," he answered, "and I hope that your mother will not worry about it. They all behaved very nicely, and we need not see much of them."

E. Phillips Oppenheim

She passed her arm through his.

"Tell me how you feel about it," she begged. "It must seem to you like a glimpse of the life you left when—when you—married!"

"Hester," he said, earnestly, "don't make any mistake about this. Don't let your mother make any mistake. It was my political change of views which separated me from all my former friends—that entirely. To them I am an apostate, and a very bad sort of one. I deserted them just when they needed me. I did it from convictions which are stronger to-day than ever. But none the less I threw them over. I always said that they very much exaggerated my importance as a factor in the situation, and my words are proved. They carried the elections without any difficulty, and they have formed a strong Government. They can afford to be magnanimous to me. If I had stayed with them I should have been in office. As it was, I lost even my seat."

"You did what you thought was right," she said, softly. "No one can do any more!"

Mannering thought over her words as they walked home-wards over the sand-dunes. Yes, he had done that! Was he satisfied with the result? He had become a minor power in politics. Men spoke of him as a weakling—as one who had shrunk from the burden of great responsibility, and left the friends who had trusted him in the lurch. And then—there was the other thing. He had paid a great price for this woman's salvation. Had he succeeded? She had given up all her old ways. She dressed, she lived, she carried herself through life even with a furtive, almost a pathetic, attempt to reach his standard. Often he caught her watching him as though fearful lest some word or action of hers had been displeasing to him. And yet—he wondered—was this what she had hoped for? Had he given her what she had the right to expect? Had he indeed received value for the price he had paid? He asked Hester a sudden question:

"Hester, is your mother happy?"

Hester started a little.

"If she is not," she answered, gravely, "she must be a very ungrateful woman."

He left it at that, and together they retraced their steps to the hotel. Hester slipped up to her room by a side entrance, but Mannering was obliged to pass the table where the new arrivals were lingering over their coffee. Clara and Lord Redford both called to him.

"Come and have a smoke with us, Mannering, and tell us all about this place," the latter said. "The Duchess and your niece are charmed with it, and they want to stay for a few days. Are there any golf links?"

"Come and sit next me, uncle," Clara cried, "and tell me how you like being guardian to an heiress. How I have blessed that dear departed aunt of mine every day of my life."

Mannering accepted a cigarette, and sat down.

"The golf links are excellent," he said. "As for your aunt, Clara, she was a very sensible woman. Her money was so well invested that I have practically nothing to do. I expect my duties will commence when the young men come!"

"Miss Mannering," Sir Leslie said, gravely, "is not at all attracted by young men. She prefers something more staid. I have serious hopes that before our little tour is over I shall have persuaded her to marry me!"

"You dear man!" Clara exclaimed. "I only wish you'd give me the chance."

"There's a brazen child to have to chaperon," the Duchess said. "Positively asking for a proposal."

"And not in vain," Sir Leslie declared. "Walk down to the sea with me, Miss Clara, and I'll propose to you in my most approved fashion. I think you said that the investments were sound, Mannering?"

"The investments are all right," Mannering answered, "but I shall have nothing to do with fortune-hunters."

"And I a Cabinet Minister!" Sir Leslie declared. "Miss Clara, let us have that walk."

"To-morrow night," she promised. "When I get up it will be to go to bed. Even your love-making, Sir Leslie, could not keep me awake to-night."

The Duchess rose. The dust was gone, but she was pale, and looked tired.

"Let us leave these men to make plans for us," she said. "I hope we shall see something of you to-morrow, Mr. Mannering. Good-night, everybody."

Mannering rose and bowed with the others. For a moment their eyes met. Not a muscle of her face changed, and yet Mannering was conscious of a sudden wave of emotion. He understood that she had not forgotten!

## CHAPTER II

## THE SNUB FOR BORROWDEAN

Berenice sat at one of the small round tables in the courtyard, finishing her morning coffee. Sir Leslie sat upon the steps by her side. It was one of those brilliant mornings in early September, when the sunlight seems to find its way everywhere. Even here, surrounded by the pile of worn grey stone buildings, which threw shadows everywhere, it had penetrated. A long shaft of soft, warm light stretched across the cobbles to their feet. Berenice, slim and elegant, fresh as the morning itself, glanced up at her companion with a smile.

"Clara," she remarked, "does not like to be kept waiting."

"She is not down yet," he answered, "and there is something I want to say to you."

Her delicate eyebrows were a trifle uplifted.

"Do you think that you had better?" she asked.

"I am a man," he said, "and things are known to me which a woman would scarcely discover. Do you think that it is quite fair to send Lady Redford out motoring with Mrs. Mannering?"

"Why not?"

"Lady Redford is, of course, ignorant of Mrs. Mannering's antecedents. What you may do yourself concerns no one. You make your own social laws, and you have a right to. But I do not think that even you have a right to pass Blanche Phillimore on to your friends, even under the shelter of Mannering's name."

Berenice looked at him for several seconds without speaking. Borrowdean bit his lip.

"If we were not acquaintances of long standing, Sir Leslie," she said, calmly, "I should consider your remarks impertinent. As it is, I choose to look upon them as a regrettable mistake. The person, whoever she may be, whom the Duchess of Lenchester chooses to receive is usually acceptable to her friends. I beg that you will not refer to the subject again."

Sir Leslie bowed.

"I have no more to say," he declared. "Knowing naturally a good deal more than you concerning the lady in question, I considered it my duty to say what I have said."

"It is the sort of duty," Berenice murmured, "which the whole world seems to accept always with a relish. One does not expect it so much from your sex. Mrs. Mannering was born one of us, and she has had an unhappy life. If she has been indiscreet she has her excuses. I choose to whitewash her. Do you understand? I pay dearly enough for my social position, and I certainly claim its privileges. I recognize Mrs. Mannering, and I require my friends to do so."

Sir Leslie rose up.

"You are, if you will forgive my saying so," he remarked, drily, "more generous than wise."

"That," she answered, "is my affair. Here comes Clara. Before you start, find Mr. Mannering. He is in the hotel somewhere writing letters, and tell him that when he has finished I wish to speak to him."

Sir Leslie only bowed. He felt himself opposed by a will as strong as his own, and he was too seriously annoyed to trust himself to speech. Clara, in her cool white linen dress, came strolling up.

"What have you been doing to Sir Leslie?" she asked, laughing. "He has just gone into the hotel with a face like a thunder-cloud."

"I have been giving him a lesson in Christian charity," Berenice answered. "He needs it."

Clara nodded. She understood.

"I think you are awfully kind," she said.

Berenice smiled.

"I hate all narrowness," she said, "and if there is a man on God's earth who deserves to have people kind to him it is your uncle."

Sir Leslie returned, and he and Clara departed for the golf links. Berenice was left alone in the little grey courtyard, fragrant with the perfume of scented shrubs and blossoming plants, filled too, with the warm sunlight, which seemed to find its way into every corner. She sat at her little table, paler than a few moments ago, her teeth clenched, her white fingers clasped together. Underneath her muslin blouse her heart had suddenly commenced to beat fiercely—a sense of excitement, long absent, was stealing through her veins. The bonds which a year's studied self-repression had forged were snapped apart. She knew now what it meant, the great inexpressible thing, the one eternal emotion which has come throbbing down the world from the days when poets sung their first song and painters flung truth on to canvas. She was a woman like the others, and she loved. Her unique position in society, her carefully studied life, her lofty ambitions, were like vain things crumbling into dust before her eyes. A year of cold misery seemed atoned for by the simple fact that within a few yards of her he sat writing—that within a few minutes he would be by her side. Of the future she scarcely thought. Hers was the woman's love, content with small things. Its passion was of the soul, and its song was self-sacrifice. But if she had known—if she had only known!

He came out to her soon. His manner was quiet and a little grave. Self-control came easier to him because the truth had been with him longer. Nevertheless, he was not wholly at his ease.

"You know what has happened?" she asked, smiling. "The Redfords have taken Mrs. Mannering and her daughter motoring, and Sir Leslie and Clara have gone to the golf links. You and I are left to entertain one another."

"What would you like to do?" he asked, simply.

"I should like to walk," she answered, "down by the sea somewhere. I am ready now."

They made their way through the little town, along the promenade and on to the sands beyond. Then a climb, and they found themselves in a thick wood stretching back inland from the sea. She pointed to a fallen trunk.

"Let us sit down," she said. "There are so many things I want to ask you."

On the way they had spoken only of indifferent matters, yet from the first Mannering had felt the presence of a subtle something in her deportment towards him, for which he could find no explanation. He himself was feeling the tension of this meeting. He had expected to find her so different. Gracious, perhaps, because she was a great lady, but certainly without any of these suggestions of something kept back, which continually, without any sort of direct expression, made themselves felt. And when they sat down she said nothing. He had the feeling that it was because she dared not trust herself to speak. Surprise and agitation kept him, too, silent.

At last she spoke. Her voice was not very steady, and she avoided looking at him.

"I should like," she said, "to have you tell me about yourself —about your life—and your work."

"It is told in a few words," he answered. "Somewhere, somehow, I have failed! I could not adopt the Birmingham programme, I could not oppose it. You know what isolation means politically?—abuse from one side and contempt from the other. That is what I am experiencing. The working classes have some faith in me, I believe. My work, such as it is, is solely for them. I suppose the papers tell the truth when they say that mine is a ruined career—only, you see, I am trying to do the best I can with the pieces."

"Yes," she said, softly, "that is something. To do the best one can with the pieces. We all might try to do that."

He smiled.

"You, at least, have no need to consider such a thing," he said. "So far as any woman can be preeminent in politics you have succeeded in becoming so. I saw that a lady's paper a few weeks ago said that your influence outside the Cabinet was more powerful than any one man's within it."

"Yes," she said, calmly, "the papers talk like that. It gives their readers something to laugh at! I wonder what you would say, my friend, if I told you that I, too, am engaged in that same thankless task. I, too, am striving to do the best I can with the pieces."

"You are not serious!" he protested.

"I am very serious indeed," she declared. "Shall I tell you more? Shall I tell you when I made my mistake?"

"No!" he cried, hoarsely.

"But I shall," she continued, suddenly gripping his arm. "I meant to tell you. I brought you here to tell you. I made my mistake when I let Leslie Borrowdean take you back to Lord Redford just as we were entering the rose-garden at Bayleigh. Do you remember? I made my mistake when I suffered anything in this great world to come between me and a woman's only chance of happiness! I made my mistake when I was too proud to tell you that I loved you, and that nothing else in the world mattered. There! You tried me hard! You know that! But my mistake was none the less fatal. I ought to have held fast by you, and I let you go. And I shall suffer for it all my days."

"You cared like that?" he cried.

"Worse!" she answered, turning her flushed face towards him. "I care now. Kiss me, Lawrence!"

He held her in his arms. Time stood still until she stole away with an odd little laugh.

"There," she said, "I have vindicated myself. No one can ever call me a proud woman again. And you know the truth! I might have had you all to myself and I let you go. Now I am going to do the best I can with the pieces. The half of you I want belongs to your wife. I must be content with the other half. I suppose I may have that?"

"But your friends—"

"Bosh! My friends and your wife must make the best of it. I shan't rob her again as I did just now. You can blot that out—antedate it. It belonged to the past. But I am not going through life as I have gone through this last year, longing for a sight of you, longing to hear you speak, and denying myself just because you are married. Live with your wife, Lawrence, and make her as happy as you can, but remember that you owe me a great deal, too, and you must do your best to pay it. Don't look at me as though I were talking nonsense."

He held her hand. She placed it in his unresistingly. All the lines in his face seemed smoothed out. The fire of youth was in his eyes.

"Do you wonder that I am surprised?" he asked. "All this year you have made no sign. All the time I have been schooling myself to forget you."

"Don't dare to tell me that you have succeeded!" she exclaimed.

"Not an iota!" he answered. "It was the most miserable failure of my life."

She smiled upon him delightfully, and gently withdrew her hand.

"Lawrence," she said, "I am going to talk to you seriously for one minute. You are too conscientious for a politician. Don't let the same vice spoil our friendship! Certain things you owe to your wife. Mind, I admit that, though from some points of view even that might be disputed. But you also owe me certain things—and I mean to be paid. I won't be avoided, mind. I want to be treated as a very close—and dear—companion—and—kiss me once more, Lawrence, and then we'll begin," she wound up, with a little sob in her throat.

An hour later the whole party had *dejeuner* together in the courtyard of the little hotel. The Duchess was noticeably kind to Mrs. Mannering, and she snubbed Sir Leslie. Clara looked on a little gravely. The situation contained many elements of interest.

# CHAPTER III

## CLOUDS—AND A CALL TO ARMS

The first cloud appeared towards the end of the third day at Bonestre. Blanche and Sir Leslie were left alone, and he hastened to improve the opportunity.

"The Duchess and your husband," he remarked, "appear very easily to have picked up again the threads of their old friendship."

"The Duchess," she answered, "is a very charming woman. I am sure that you find her so, don't you?"

"We are very old friends," he answered, "but I was never admitted to exactly the same privileges as your husband enjoys."

"The Duchess," she answered, calmly, "is a woman of taste!"

Sir Leslie muttered something under his breath. Blanche made a movement as though to take up again the book which she had been reading in a sheltered corner of the hotel garden.

"Don't you think," he said, "that we should make better

E. Phillips Oppenheim

friends than enemies?"

"I am not at all sure," she answered, calmly. "To tell you the truth, I don't fancy you particularly in either capacity."

He laughed unpleasantly.

"You are scarcely complimentary," he remarked.

"I did not mean to be," she answered. "Why should I?"

"You are content, then, to let your husband drift back into his old relations with the Duchess? I presume that you know what they were?"

"Whether I am or not," she answered, "what business is it of yours?"

"I will tell you, if you like," he answered. "In fact, I think it would be better. It has been the one desire of my life to marry the Duchess of Lenchester myself."

She smiled at him scornfully.

"Come," she said, "let me give you a little advice. Give up the idea. They say that lookers-on see most of the game, and so far as I am concerned I'm certainly the looker-on of this party. The Duchess doesn't care a row of pins about you!"

"There are other marriages, besides marriages of affection," Sir Leslie said, stiffly. "The Duchess is ambitious."

"But she is also a woman," Blanche declared. "And she is in love."

"With whom?"

"With my husband! I presume that is clear enough to most people!"

Sir Leslie was a little staggered.

"You take it very coolly," he remarked.

"Why not? The Duchess is too proud a woman to give herself away, and my husband—belongs to me!"

"You haven't any idea of taking poison, or anything of that sort, I suppose, have you?" he inquired. "The other woman nearly always does that."

"Not in real life," Blanche answered, composedly. "Besides, I'm not the other woman—I'm the one. The Duchess is the other!"

"But your husband—"

"Do you know, I should prefer not to discuss my husband—with you," Blanche said, calmly, taking up her book. "He is not the sort of man you would be at all likely to understand. If you want a rich wife why don't you propose to Clara Mannering? I suppose you knew that some unheard-of aunt had left her fifty thousand pounds?"

Sir Leslie rose to his feet.

"I don't fancy that you and I are very sympathetic this afternoon," he remarked. "I will go and see if any one has returned."

"Do," she answered. "I shall miss you, of course, but my book is positively absorbing, and I am dying to go on with it."

Sir Leslie left the garden without another word. Blanche held her book before her face until he had disappeared. Then it slipped from her fingers. She looked hard into a cluster of roses, and she saw only two figures—always the same figures. Her eyes were set, her face was wan and old.

"The other woman!" she murmured to herself. "That is what I am. And I can't live up to it. I ought to take poison, or get run over or something, and I know very well I shan't. Bother the man! Why couldn't he leave me alone?"

After dinner that evening she accepted her husband's nightly invitation and walked with him for a little while. The others followed.

"How much longer can you stay away from England, Lawrence?" she asked him.

"Oh—a fortnight, I should think," he answered. "I am not tied to any particular date. You like it here, I hope?"

"Immensely! Are—our friends going to remain?"

"I haven't heard them say anything about moving on yet," he answered.

"Are you in love with the Duchess still, Lawrence?"

"Am I—Blanche!"

"Don't be angry! You made a mistake once, you know. Don't make another. I'm not a jealous woman, and I don't ask much from you, but I'm your wife. That's all!"

She turned and called to Hester. The little party rearranged itself. Mannering found himself with Berenice.

"What was your wife saying to you?" she asked.

He shrugged his shoulders.

"It was the beginning," he remarked.

Berenice sighed.

"It is a strange thing," she said, "but in this world no one can ever be happy except at some one else's expense. It is a most unnatural law of compensation. Shall we move on to-morrow?"

"The day after," he pleaded. "To-morrow we are going to Berneval."

She nodded.

"We are queer people, I think," she said. "I have been perfectly satisfied this week simply to be with you. When it comes to an end I should like it to come suddenly."

He thought of her words an hour later, when on his return to the hotel they handed him a telegram. He passed it on at once to Lord Redford, and glanced at his watch.

"Poor Cunningham," he said, "it was a short triumph for him. I must go back to-night, or the first train to-morrow morning. The sitting member for my division of Leeds died suddenly last night, Blanche," he said to his wife. "I must be on the spot at once."

She rose to her feet.

"I will go and pack," she said.

Lady Redford followed her very soon. Clara and Sir Leslie had not yet returned from their stroll. Lord Redford remained alone with them.

"I scarcely know what sort of fortune to wish you, Mannering," he said. "Perhaps your first speech will tell us."

Berenice leaned back in her chair.

"I can't imagine you as a labour member in the least," she remarked.

"Doesn't this force your hand a little, Mannering?" Lord Redford said. "I understand that you were anxious to avoid a direct pronouncement upon the fiscal policy for the present."

Mannering nodded gravely.

"It is quite time I made up my mind," he said. "I shall do so now."

"May we find ourselves in the same lobby!" Lord Redford said. "I will go and find my man. He may as well take you to the station in the car."

Berenice smiled at Mannering luminously through the shadowy lights.

"Dear friend," she said, "I am delighted that you are going. Our little time here has been delightful, but we had reached its limit. I like to think that you are going back into the thick of it. Don't be faint-hearted, Lawrence. Don't lose faith in yourself. You have chosen a terribly lonely path; if any man can find his way to the top, you can. And don't dare to forget me, sir!"

He caught her cheerful tone.

"You are inspiring," he declared. "Thank heaven, I have a twelve hours' journey before me. I need time for thought, if ever a man did."

"Don't worry about it," she answered, lightly. "The truth is somewhere in your brain, I suppose, and when the time comes you will find it. Much better think about your sandwiches."

The car backed into the yard. Blanche reappeared, and behind her Mannering's bag.

"I do hope that Hester and I have packed everything," she said. "We could come over to-morrow, if there's anything you want us for. If not we shall stay here for another week. Good-bye!"

She calmly held up her lips, and Mannering kissed them after a moment's hesitation. She remained by his side even when he turned to say farewell to Berenice.

"I am sure you ought to be going," she said calmly. "I will send on your letters if there are any to-morrow. Wire your address as soon as you arrive. Good luck!"

The car glided away. They all stood in a group to see him go, and waved indiscriminate farewells. Blanche moved a little apart as the car disappeared, and Berenice watched her curiously. She was rubbing her lips with her handkerchief.

"A sting!" she remarked, becoming suddenly aware of the other's scrutiny. "Nothing that hurts very much!"

# CHAPTER IV

## DISASTER

Mannering, in his sitting-room at last, locked the door and drew a long breath of relief. Upon his ear-drums there throbbed still the yells of his enthusiastic but noisy adherents—the truculent cries of those who had heard his great speech with satisfaction, of those who saw pass from amongst themselves to a newer school of thought one whom they had regarded as their natural leader. It was over at last. He had made his pronouncement. To some it might seem a compromise. To himself it was the only logical outcome of his long period of thought. He spoke for the workingman. He demanded inquiry, consideration, experiment. He demanded them in a way of his own, at once novel and convincing. Many of the most brilliant articles which had ever come from his pen he abjured. He drew a sharp line between the province of the student and the duty of the politician.

And now he was alone at last, free to think and dream, free to think of Bonestre, to wonder what reports of his meeting would reach the little French watering-place, and how they would be received. He could see Berenice reading the morning paper in the little grey courtyard, with the pigeons flying above her head and the sunlight streaming across the flags. He could hear Borrowdean's sneer, could see Lord

Redford's shrug of the shoulders. There is little sympathy in the world for the man who dares to change his mind.

There was a knock at the door, and his servant entered with a tray.

"I have brought the whiskey and soda, sandwiches and cigarettes, sir," he announced. "I am sorry to say that there is a person outside whom I cannot get rid of. His name is Fardell, and he insists upon it that his business is of importance."

Mannering smiled.

"You can show him up at once," he ordered; "now, and whenever he calls."

Fardell appeared almost directly. Mannering had seen him before during the day, but noticed at once a change in him. He was pale, and looked like a man who had received some sort of a shock.

"Come in, Fardell, and sit down," Mannering said. "You look tired. Have a drink."

Fardell walked straight to the tray and helped himself to some neat whiskey.

"Thank you, sir," he said. "I—I've had rather a knockout blow."

He emptied the tumbler and set it down.

"Mr. Mannering, sir," he said, "I've just heard a man bet twenty to one in crisp five-pound bank-notes that you never sit for West Leeds."

"Was he drunk or sober?" Mannering asked.

"Sober as a judge!"

Mannering smiled.

"How often did you take him?" he asked.

"Not once! I didn't dare!"

Mannering, who had been in the act of helping himself to a whiskey and soda, looked around with the decanter in his hand.

"I don't understand you," he said, bewildered. "You know very well that the chances, so far as they can be reckoned up, are slightly in my favour."

"They were!" Fardell answered. "Heaven knows what they are now."

Mannering was a little annoyed. It seemed to him that Fardell must have been drinking.

"Do you mind explaining yourself?" he asked.

"I can do so," Fardell answered. "I must do so. But while I am about it I want you to put on your hat and come with me."

Mannering laughed shortly.

"What, to-night?" he exclaimed. "No, thank you. Be reasonable, Fardell. I've had my day's work, and I think I've earned a little rest. To be frank with you, I don't like mysteries. If you've anything to say, out with it."

"Right!" Richard Fardell answered. "I am going to ask you a question, Mr. Mannering. Go back a good many years, as many years as you like. Is there anything in your life as a younger man, say when you first entered Parliament, which—if it were brought up against you now—might be—embarrassing?"

Mannering did not answer for several moments. He was already pale and tired, but he felt what little colour remained leave his face. Least of all he had expected this. Even now—what could the man mean? What could be known?

"I am not sure that I understand you," he said. "There is nothing that could be known! I am sure of that."

"There is a person," Fardell said, slowly, "who has made extraordinary statements. Our opponents have got hold of him. The substance of them is this: He says that many years ago you were the lover of a married woman, that you sold her husband worthless shares and ruined him, and that finally—in a quarrel—he declares that he was an eye-witness of this—that you killed him."

Mannering slowly subsided into his chair. His cheeks were blanched. Richard Fardell watched him with feverish anxiety.

"It is a lie," Mannering declared. "There is no man living who can say this."

"The man says," Fardell continued, stonily, "that his name is Parkins, and that he was butler to Mr. Stephen Phillimore eleven years ago."

"Parkins is dead!" Mannering said, hoarsely. "He has been dead for many years."

"He is living in Leeds to-day," Fardell answered. "A journalist from the *Yorkshire Herald* was with him for two hours this afternoon."

"Blanche—I was told that he was dead," Mannering said.

"Then the story is true?" Fardell asked.

"Not as you have told it," Mannering answered.

"There is truth in it?"

"Yes."

Richard Fardell was silent for several moments. He paced up and down the room, his hands behind his back, his eyebrows contracted into a heavy frown. For him it was a bitter moment. He was only a half-educated, illiterate man, possessed of sturdy common sense and a wonderful tenacity of purpose. He had permitted himself to indulge in a little silent but none the less absolute hero-worship, and Mannering had been the hero.

"You must come with me at once and see this man," he said at last. "He has not yet signed his statement. We must do what we can to keep him quiet."

Mannering took up his coat and hat without a word. They left the hotel, and Fardell summoned a cab.

"It is a long way," he explained. "We will drive part of the distance and walk the rest. We may be watched already."

Mannering nodded. The last blow was so unexpected that he felt in a sense numbed. His speech only a few hours ago had made large inroads upon his powers of endurance. His partial recantation had cost him many hours of torture, from which he was still suffering. And now, without the slightest warning, he found himself face to face with a crisis far graver, far more acute. Never in his most gloomy moments had he felt any real fear of a resurrection of the past such as that with which he was now threatened. It was a thunderbolt from a clear sky. Even now he found it hard to persuade himself that he was not dreaming.

They were in the cab for nearly half an hour before Fardell stopped and dismissed it. Then they walked up and down and across streets of small houses, pitiless in their monotony, squalid and depressing in their ugliness.

Finally Fardell stopped, and without hesitation knocked at the door of one of them. It was opened by a man in shirt-sleeves, holding a tallow candle in his hand.

"What yer want?" he inquired, suspiciously.

"Your lodger," Fardell answered, pushing past him and drawing Mannering into the room. "Where is he?"

The man jerked his thumb upwards.

"Where he won't be long," he answered, shortly. "The likes of 'im having visitors, and one a toff, too. Say, are yer going to pay his rent?"

"We may do that," Fardell answered. "Is he upstairs?"

"Ay!" the man answered, shuffling away. "Pay 'is rent, and yer can chuck 'im out of the winder, if yer like!"

They climbed the crazy staircase. Fardell opened the door of the room above without even the formality of knocking. An old man sat there, bending over a table, half dressed. Before him were several sheets of paper.

"I believe we're in time," Fardell muttered, half to himself. "Parkins, is that you?" he asked, in a louder tone.

The old man looked up and blinked at them. He shaded his eyes with one hand. The other he laid flat upon the papers before him. He was old, blear-eyed, unkempt.

"Is that Master Ronaldson?" he asked, in a thin, quavering tone. "I've signed 'em, sir. Have yer brought the money? I'm a poor old man, and I need a drop of something now and then to keep the life in me. If yer'll just hand over a trifle I'll send out for—eh—eh, my landlord, he's a kindly man—he'll fetch it. Eh? Two of yer! I don't see so well as I did. Is that you, Mr. Ronaldson, sir?"

Fardell threw some silver coins upon the table. The old man snatched them up eagerly.

"It's not Mr. Ronaldson," he said, "but I daresay we shall do as well. We want to talk to you about those papers there."

The old man nodded. He was gazing at the silver in his hand.

"I've writ it all out," he muttered. "I told 'un I would. A pound a week for ten years. That's what I 'ad! And then it stopped! Did she mean me to starve, eh? Not I! John Parkins knows better nor that. I've writ it all out, and there's my signature. It's gospel truth, too."

"We are going to buy the truth from you," Fardell said. "We have more money than Ronaldson. Don't be afraid. We have gold to spare where Ronaldson had silver."

The old man lifted the candle with shaking fingers. Then it dropped with a crash to the ground, and lay there for a moment spluttering. He shrank back.

"It's 'im!" he muttered. "Don't kill me, sir. I mean you no harm. It's Mr. Mannering!"

E. Phillips Oppenheim

# CHAPTER V

## THE JOURNALIST INTERVENES

The old man had sunk into a seat. His face and hands were twitching with fear. His eyes, as though fascinated, remained fixed upon Mannering's. All the while he mumbled to himself. Fardell drew Mannering a little on one side.

"What can we do with him?" he asked. "We might tear up those sheets, give him money, keep him soddened with drink. And even then he'd give the whole show away the moment any one got at him. It isn't so bad as he makes out, I suppose?"

"It is not so bad as that," Mannering answered, "but it is bad enough."

"What became of the woman?" Fardell asked. "Parkins's mistress, I mean?"

"She is my wife," Mannering answered.

Fardell threw out his hands with a little gesture of despair.

"We must get him away from here," he said. "If Polden gets hold of him you might as well resign at once. It is dangerous for you to stay. He was evidently expecting that fellow Ronaldson to-night."

Mannering nodded.

"What shall you do with him?" he asked.

"Hide him if I can," Fardell answered, grimly. "If I can get him out of this place, it ought not to be impossible. The most important thing at present is for you to get away without being recognized."

Mannering took up his hat.

"I will go," he said. "I shall leave the cab for you. I can find my way back to the hotel."

Fardell nodded.

"It would be better," he said. "Turn your coat-collar up and draw your hat down over your eyes. You mustn't be recognized down here. It's a pretty low part."

Nevertheless, Mannering had not reached the corner of the street before he heard hasty footsteps behind him, and felt a light touch upon his shoulder. He turned sharply round.

"Well, sir!" he exclaimed, "what do you want with me?"

The newcomer was a tall, thin young man, wearing glasses, and although he was a complete stranger to Mannering, he knew at once who he was.

"Mr. Mannering, I believe?" he said, quickly.

"What has my name to do with you, sir?" Mannering

answered, coldly.

"Mine is Ronaldson," the young man answered. "I am a reporter."

Mannering regarded him steadily for a moment.

"You are the young man, then," he said, "who has discovered the mare's nest of my iniquity."

"If it is a mare's nest," the young man answered, briskly, "I shall be quite as much relieved as disappointed. But your being down here doesn't look very much like that, does it?"

"No man," Mannering answered, "hears that a bomb is going to be thrown at him without a certain amount of curiosity as to its nature. I have been down to examine the bomb. Frankly, I don't think much of it."

"You are prepared, then, to deny this man Parkins's story?" the reporter asked.

"I am prepared to have a shot at your paper for libel, anyhow, if you use it," Mannering answered.

"Do you know the substance of his communication?"

"I can make a pretty good guess at it," Mannering answered.

"You really mean to deny it, then?" the reporter asked.

"Assuredly, for it is not true," Mannering answered. "Pray don't let me detain you any longer!"

He turned on his heel and walked away, but the reporter kept pace with him.

"You will pardon me, but this is a very serious affair, Mr. Mannering," he said. "Serious for both of us. Do you mind discussing it with me?"

"Not in the least," Mannering answered, "so long as you permit me to continue my way homewards."

"I will walk with you, sir, if you don't mind," the reporter said. "It is a very serious matter indeed, this! My people are as keen as possible to make use of it. If they do, and it turns out a true story, you, of course, will never sit for Leeds. And if on the other hand it is false, I shall get the sack!"

"Well, it is false," Mannering said.

"Some parts of it, perhaps," the young man answered, smoothly. "Not all, Mr. Mannering."

"Old men are garrulous," Mannering remarked. "I expect you will find that your friend has been letting his tongue run away with him."

"He has committed his statements to paper," Ronaldson remarked.

"And signed them?"

"He is willing to do so," the reporter answered. "I was to have fetched them away to-night."

"You may be a little late," Mannering remarked.

The *double entente* in his tone did not escape Ronaldson's notice. He stopped short on the pavement.

"So you have bought him," he remarked.

Mannering glanced at him superciliously.

"Will you pardon me," he said, "if I remark that this conversation has no particular interest for me? Don't let me bring you any further out of your way."

Ronaldson took off his hat.

"Very good, sir," he remarked. "I will wish you good-night!"

Mannering pursued his way homeward with the briefest of farewells. The young reporter retraced his steps. Arrived at Parkins's lodgings he mounted the stairs, and found the room empty. He returned and interviewed the landlord. From him he only learned that Parkins had departed with one of two gentlemen who had come to see him that evening, and that they had paid his rent for him. The reporter was obliged to depart with no more satisfactory information. But next morning, before nine o'clock, he was waiting to see Mannering, and would not be denied. He was accompanied, too, by a person of no less importance than the editor of the *Yorkshire Herald* himself.

Mannering kept them waiting an hour, and then received them coolly.

"I am glad to see you, Mr. Polden," he said, glancing at the editor's card. "I have already had some conversation with our young friend there," he added, glancing towards the reporter. "What can I have the pleasure of doing for you?"

Mr. Polden produced a sheet of proofs from his pocket. He passed them over to Mannering.

"I should like you to examine these, sir," he said.

"In type already!" Mannering remarked, calmly.

"In proof for our evening's issue," Polden answered.

Mannering read them through.

"It will cost you several thousand pounds!" he said.

"Then the money will be well spent," Polden answered. "No one has a higher regard for you politically than I have, Mr. Mannering, but we don't want you as member for West Leeds. That's all!"

"It happens," Mannering said, "that I am particularly anxious to sit for West Leeds."

"You will go on—in the face of this?" the editor asked Mannering.

"Yes, and with the suit for libel which will follow," Mannering answered.

The editor shrugged his shoulders.

"Do me the favour to believe, Mr. Mannering," he said, "that we have not gone into this matter blindfold. We had a preliminary intimation as to this affair from a person whose word carries considerable weight, and our investigations have been searching. I will admit that the disappearance of the man Parkins is a little awkward for us, but we have ample justification in publishing his story."

"I trust for your sakes that the law courts will support your views," Mannering said, coldly. "I scarcely think it likely."

"Mr. Mannering," Polden said, "I quite appreciate your

attitude, but do you really think it is a wise one? I very much regret that it should have been our duty to unearth this unsavoury story, and having unearthed it, to use it. But you must remember that the issue on hand is a great one. I belong to the Liberal party and the absolute Free Traders, and I consider that for this city to be represented by any one who shows the least indication of being unsafe upon this question would be a national disaster and a local disgrace. I want you to understand, therefore, that I am not playing a game of bluff. The proofs you hold in your hand have been set and corrected. Within a few hours the story will stand out in black and white. Are you prepared for this?"

Mannering shrugged his shoulders.

"I am not prepared to resign my candidature, if that is what you mean," he said. "I presume that nothing short of that will satisfy you?"

"Nothing," the editor answered, firmly.

"Then there remains nothing more," Mannering remarked, coldly, "than for me to wish you a very good-morning."

"I am sorry," Mr. Polden said. "I trust you will believe, Mr. Mannering, that I find this a very unpleasant duty."

Mannering made no answer save a slight bow. He held open the door, and Mr. Polden and his satellite passed out. Afterwards he strolled to the window and looked down idly upon the crowd.

"If I act in accordance with the conventions," he murmured to himself, "I suppose I ought to take, a glass of poison, or blow my brains out. Instead of which—"

He shrugged his shoulders, and rang for his hat and coat. He was due at one of the great foundries in half an hour to speak to the men during their luncheon interval.

"Instead of which," he muttered, as he lit a cigarette, "I shall go on to the end."

E. Phillips Oppenheim

# CHAPTER VI

## TREACHERY AND A TELEGRAM

The sunlight streamed down into the little grey courtyard of the *Leon D'or* at Bonestre. Sir Leslie Borrowdean, in an immaculate grey suit, and with a carefully chosen pink carnation in his button-hole, sat alone at a small table having his morning coffee. His attention was divided between a copy of the *Figaro* and a little pile of letters and telegrams on the other side of his plate. More than once he glanced at the topmost of the latter and smiled.

Mrs. Mannering and Hester came down the grey stone steps and crossed towards their own table. The former lingered for a moment as she passed Sir Leslie, who rose to greet the two women.

"Another glorious day!" he remarked. "What news from Leeds?"

"None," she said. "My husband seldom writes."

Sir Leslie smiled reflectively, and glanced towards the pile of papers at his side.

"Perhaps," she remarked, "you know better than I do how

things are going there."

He shook his head.

"I have no correspondents in Leeds," he answered.

At that moment a puff of wind disturbed the papers by his side. A telegram would have fluttered away, but Blanche Mannering caught it at the edge of the table. She was handing it back, when a curious expression on Borrowdean's face inspired her with a sudden idea. She deliberately looked at the telegram, and her fingers stiffened upon it. His forward movement was checked. She stood just out of his reach.

"No correspondents in Leeds," she repeated. "Then what about this telegram?"

"You will permit me to remind you," he said, stretching out his hand for it, "that it is addressed to me."

Her hands were behind her. She leaned over towards him.

"It can be addressed to you a thousand times over," she answered, "but before I part with it I want to know what it means."

Borrowdean was thinking quickly. He wanted to gain time.

"I do not even know which document you have—purloined," he said.

"It is from Leeds," she answered, "and it is signed Polden. 'Parkins found, has made statement, appears to-night.' Can you explain what this means, Sir Leslie Borrowdean?"

Her voice was scarcely raised above a whisper, but there was a dangerous glitter in her eyes. There were few traces left of the woman whom once before he had found so easy a tool.

"I cannot tell you," he answered. "It is not an affair for you to concern yourself with at all."

"Not an affair for me to concern myself about!" she repeated, leaning a little over towards him. "Isn't it my husband against whom you are scheming? Don't I know what low tricks you are capable of? Isn't this another proof of it? Not an affair for me to concern myself about, indeed! Didn't you worm the whole miserable story out of me?"

"My dear Mrs. Mannering!"

She checked a torrent of words. Her bosom was heaving underneath her lace blouse. She was pale almost to the lips. The sudden and complete disuse of all manner of cosmetics had to a certain extent blanched her face. There was room there now for the writing of tragedy. Borrowdean, still outwardly suave, was inwardly cursing the unlucky chance which had blown the telegram her way.

"Might I suggest," he said, in a low tone, "that we postpone our conversation till after breakfast time? The waiters seem to be favouring us with a great deal of attention, and several of them understand English."

She did not even turn her head. Thinner a good deal since her marriage, she seemed to him to have grown taller, to have gained in dignity and presence, as she stood there before him, her angry eyes fixed upon his face. She was no longer a person to be ignored.

"You must tell me about this—or—"

"Or?" he repeated, stonily.

"Or I will make a public statement," she answered. "If you ruin my husband's career, I can at least do the same with yours. Politics is supposed to be a game for honourable men to play with honourable weapons. I wonder if Lord Redford would approve of your methods?"

"You can go and ask him, my dear madam," he answered. "I am perfectly ready to defend myself."

"Defend! You have no defence," she answered. "Can you deny that you are plotting to keep my husband out of Parliament now, just as a few months ago you plotted to bring him back? You are making use of a personal secret, a forgotten chapter of his life, to move him about like a puppet to do your will."

"I work for the good of a cause and a great party," he answered. "You do not understand these things."

"I understand you so far as this," she answered. "You are one of those to whom life is a chessboard, and your one aim is to make the pieces work for you, and at your bidding, till you sit in the place you covet. There isn't much of the patriot about you, Sir Leslie Borrowdean."

He glanced down at his unfinished breakfast. He had the air of one who is a little bored.

"My dear lady," he said, "is this discussion really worth while?"

"No," she answered, bluntly, "it isn't. You are quite right. We are wandering from the subject."

"Let us talk," he suggested, "after breakfast. Give me back that telegram now, and I will explain it, say, in the garden in half an hour. I detest cold coffee."

"You can do like me, order some fresh," she said. "If I let you out of my sight I know very well how much I shall see of you for the rest of the day. Explain now if you can. What does that telegram mean?"

"Surely it is obvious enough," he answered. "The man Parkins, whom you told me was dead, is alive and in Leeds. He has seen Mannering's name about, has been talking, and the press have got hold of his story. I am sorry, but there was always this possibility, wasn't there?"

"And this telegram?" she asked.

"I know Polden, the editor of the paper, and he referred to me to know if there could be any truth in it."

"These are lies!" she declared. "You were the instigator. You set them on the track."

"I have nothing more to say," Borrowdean declared, coldly.

"I have," she said. "I shall take this telegram to Lord Redford. I shall tell him everything!"

A faint smile flickered upon Borrowdean's lips.

"Lord Redford would, I am sure, be charmed to hear your story," he remarked. "Unfortunately he started for Dieppe this morning before eight o'clock, and will not be back until to-morrow."

"And to-morrow will be too late," she added, rapidly

pursuing his train of thought. "Then I will try the Duchess!"

He started very slightly, but she saw it.

"Sit down for a moment, Mrs. Mannering," he said.

She accepted the chair he placed for her. There was a distinct change in his manner. He realized that this woman held a trump card against him. Even in her hands it might mean disaster.

"Blanche—" he began.

"Thank you," she interrupted, "I prefer 'Mrs. Mannering.'"

He bit his lips in annoyance.

"Mrs. Mannering, then," he continued, "we have been allies before, and I think that you will admit that I have always kept faith with you. I don't see any reason why we should play at being enemies. You have a price, I suppose, for that telegram and your silence. Name it."

She nodded.

"Yes, I have a price," she admitted.

"Remember that, after all, this is not a great issue," he said. "If your husband does not get in for Leeds he will probably find a seat somewhere else."

"That is false," she answered, "If your man Polden publishes Parkins's story my husband's political career is over, and you know it. Do keep as near to the truth as you can."

"I will give you," he said, "five hundred pounds for that

telegram and your silence."

She rose slowly to her feet. A dull flush of colour mounted almost to her eyes. Borrowdean watched her anxiously. Then for a moment came an interruption. The Duchess was descending the grey stone steps from the hotel.

She had addressed some word of greeting to them. They both turned towards her. She wore a white serge dress, and she carried a white lace parasol over her bare head. She moved towards them with her usual languid grace, followed by her maid carrying a tiny Maltese dog and a budget of letters. The loiterrers in the courtyard stared at her with admiration. It was impossible to mistake her for anything but a great lady.

"You have the air of conspirators, you two!" she said, as she approached them. "Is it an expedition for the day that you are planning?"

Blanche Mannering turned her back upon Borrowdean.

"Sir Leslie," she said, "has just offered me five hundred pounds for a telegram which I have here and for my silence concerning its contents. I was wondering whether he had bid high enough."

The Duchess looked from one to the other. She almost permitted herself to be astonished. Borrowdean's face was dark with anger. Blanche Mannering's apparent calmness was obviously of the surface only.

"Are you serious?" she asked.

"Miserably so!" Blanche answered. "Sir Leslie has strange ideas of honour, I find. He is making use of a story which I told him once concerning my husband, to drive him out of political life. Duchess, will you do me the favour to let me talk with you for five minutes, and to make Sir Leslie Borrowdean promise not to leave this hotel till you have seen him again?"

"I have no intention of leaving the hotel," Sir Leslie said, stiffly.

Berenice pointed to her table.

"Come and take your coffee with me, Mrs. Mannering," she said.

\* \* \* \* \*

Mannering passed through the day like a man in a nightmare. He addressed two meetings of working-men, and interviewed half a dozen of his workers. At mid-day the afternoon edition of the *Yorkshire Herald* was being sold in the streets. He bought a copy and glanced it feverishly through. Nothing! He lunched and went on with his work. At three o'clock a second edition was out. Again he purchased a copy, and again there was nothing. The suspense was getting worse even than the disaster itself. Between four and five they brought him in a telegram. He tore it open, and found that it was from Bonestre. The words seemed to stare up at him from the pink form. It was incredible:

"Polden muzzled. Go in and win."

The form fluttered from his fingers on to the floor of his sitting-room. He stood looking at it, dazed. Outside, a mob of people, standing round his carriage, were shouting his name.

# CHAPTER VII

## MR. MANNERING, M.P.

Mannering threw up his window with a sigh of immense relief. The air was cold and fresh. The land, as yet unwarmed by the slowly rising sun, was hung with a faint autumn mist. Traces of an early frost lay in the brown hedgerows inland; the sea was like a sheet of polished glass. Gone the smoke-stained rows of shapeless houses, the atmosphere polluted by a thousand chimneys belching smuts and black vapour, the clanging of electric cars, the rattle of all manner of vehicles over the cobbled streets. Gone the hoarse excitement of the shouting mobs, the poisonous atmosphere of close rooms, all the turmoil and racket and anxiety of those fighting days. He was back again in Bonestre. Below in the courtyard the white cockatoo was screaming. The waiters in their linen coats were preparing the tables for the few remaining guests. And the other things were of yesterday!

Mannering had arrived in the middle of the night unex-pectedly, and his appearance was a surprise to every one. He had knocked at his wife's door on his way downstairs, but Blanche had taken to early rising, and was already down. He found them all breakfasting together in a sheltered corner of the courtyard.

Berenice, after the usual greetings and explanations, smiled at him thoughtfully.

"I am not sure," she said, "whether I ought to congratulate you or not. Sir Leslie here thinks that you mean mischief!"

"Only on the principle," Borrowdean said, "that whoever is not with us is against us."

"We are all agreed upon one thing," Berenice said. "It was your last speech, the one the night before the election, which carried you in. A national party indeed! A legislator, not a politician! You talked to those canny Yorkshiremen with your head in the clouds, and yet they listened."

Mannering smiled as he poured out his coffee.

"I talked common sense to them," he remarked, "and Yorkshiremen like that. We have been slaves to the old-fashioned idea of party Government long enough. It's an absurd thing when you come to think of it. Fancy a great business being carried on by a board of partners of divergent views, and unable to make a purchase or a sale or effect any change whatever without talking the whole thing threadbare, and then voting upon it. The business would go down, of course!"

"Party Government," Borrowdean declared, "is the natural evolution of any republican form of administration. A nation that chooses its own representatives must select them from its varying standpoint."

"Their views may differ slightly upon some matters," Mannering said, "but their first duty should be to come into accord with one another. It is a matter for compromises, of course. The real differences between intelligent men of either party are very slight. The trouble is that under the present system everything is done to increase them instead of bridging them over."

"If you had to form a Government, then," Berenice asked, "you would not choose the members from one party?"

"Certainly not," Mannering answered. "Supposing I were the owner of Redford's car there, and wanted a driver. I should simply try to get the best man I could, and I should certainly not worry as to whether he were, say, a churchman or a dissenter. The best man for the post is what the country has a right to expect, whatever he may call himself, and the country doesn't get it. The people pay the piper, and I consider that they get shocking bad value for their money. The Boer War, for instance, would have cost us less than half as much if we had had the right men to direct the commercial side of it. That money would have been useful in the country just now."

"An absolute monarchy," Hester said, smiling, "would be really the most logical form of Government, then? But would it answer?"

"Why not?" Borrowdean asked. "If the monarch were incapable he would of course be shot!"

"A dictator—" Berenice began, but Mannering held out his hands, laughing.

"Think of my last few days, and spare me!" he begged. "I have thirty-six hours' holiday. How do you people spend your time here?"

Berenice took him away with her as a matter of course. Blanche watched them depart with a curious tightening of the lips. She was standing alone in the gateway of the hotel, and she watched them until they were out of sight. Borrowdean, sauntering out to buy some papers, paused for a moment as he passed.

"Your husband, Mrs. Mannering," he said, drily, "is a very fortunate man."

She made no reply, and Borrowdean passed on. Hester came out with a message from Lady Redford—would Mrs. Mannering care to motor over to Berneval for luncheon? Blanche shook her head. She scarcely heard the invitation. She was still watching the two figures disappearing in the distance. Hester understood, but she spoke lightly.

"I believe," she said, "that the Duchess still has hopes of Mr. Mannering."

"She is a persistent woman," Blanche answered. "They say that she generally succeeds. Let us go in."

\* \* \* \* \*

Berenice was listening to Mannering's account of his last few days' electioneering.

"The whole affair came upon me like a thunderclap," he told her. "Richard Fardell found it out somehow, and he took me to see Parkins. But it was too late. Polden had hold of the story and meant to use it. I never imagined but that Parkins had been talking and this journalist had got hold of him by accident. Now I understand that it was Borrowdean who was pulling the strings."

She nodded.

"He traced Parkins out some time ago, and knew exactly where he was to be found."

"I think," Mannering said, "that it is time Borrowdean and I came to some understanding. I haven't said anything about it yet. I don't exactly know what to say now. You are a very generous woman."

She sighed.

"No," she said, "I don't think that. Sir Leslie is a schemer of the class I detest. I listened to him once, and I have regretted it ever since. Yet you must remember this! If it had not been for him you would have been at Blakely to-day."

His thoughts carried him backwards with a rush. Once more the thrall of that quiet life of passionless sweetness held him. He looked back upon it curiously, as a man who has passed into another country. Days of physical exaltation, alone with the sun and the wind and all the murmuring voices of Nature, God's life he had called it then. And now! The stress of battle was hard upon him. He was fighting in the front ranks, a somewhat cheerless battle, fighting for great causes with inefficient weapons. But he could not go back. Life had become a more strenuous, a more vital, a less beautiful thing! He felt himself ageing. All the inevitable sadness of the man in touch with the world's great problems was in his heart. But he could not go back.

"Yes," he said, quietly, "I owe that much to Borrowdean."

"There is a question," she said, "which I have wanted to ask you. Do you regret, or are you glad to have been forced out once more upon the world's stage?"

He smiled.

"How can I answer you?" he asked. "At Blakely I was as happy as I knew how to be, and until you came I was content! But to-day, well, there are different things. How can I answer your question, indeed? Tell me what happiness means! Tell me whether it is an ignoble or a praiseworthy state!"

Berenice was silent. Into her face there had come a sudden gravity. Mannering, glancing towards her, was at once conscious of the change. He saw the weariness so often and zealously repressed, the ageing of her face, the sudden triumph of the despair which in the quiet moments chilled her heart. It seemed to him that for that moment they had come into some closer communion. He bent over towards her.

"Ah!" he murmured, "you, too, are beginning to understand. Happiness is only for the ignorant. For you and for me knowledge has eaten its way too far into our lives. We climb all the while, but the flowers in the meadows are the fairest."

She shook her head.

"The little white flower which grows in the mountains is what we must always seek," she answered. "The meadows are for the others."

"We are accursed with this knowledge, and the desire for it," he declared, fiercely. "The suffering is for us, and the joy for the beasts of the field. Why not throw down the cards? We are the devil's puppets in this game of life."

"There is no place for us down there," she answered, sadly. "There is joy enough for them, because the finger has never touched their eyes. But for us—no, we have to go on! I was a foolish woman, Lawrence. I lost my sense of proportion.

Traditions, you see, were hard to break away from. I did not understand. Let this be the end of all mention of such things between us. We have missed the turning, and we must go on. That is the hardest thing in life. One can never retrace one's steps."

"We go on—apart?"

"We must," she said. "Don't think me prejudiced, Lawrence. I must stand by my party. Theoretically, I think that you are the only logical politician I have ever known. Actually, I think that you are steering your course towards the sand-banks. You will fail, but you will fail magnificently. Well, that is something."

"It is a good deal," he answered, "but if I live long enough, and my strength remains, I shall succeed. I shall place the Government of this country upon an altogether different basis. I shall empty the work-houses and fill the factories. Nothing short of that will content me. Nothing short of that would content any man upon whose shoulders the burden has fallen."

"You have centuries of prejudice to fight," she warned him. "You may not succeed! Yet you have all my good wishes. I shall always watch you."

They turned homeward in silence. All that had passed between them seemed to be already far back in the past. Their retrogression seemed almost symbolical. They spoke of indifferent things.

"Tell me," he asked, "how you came to know what was going on in Leeds."

"It was your wife," she said, "who discovered it!"

"My wife?"

"She saw a telegram on Sir Leslie's table at breakfast, a telegram from the man Polden. She read it and demanded an explanation. Sir Leslie tried all he could to wriggle out of it, but in vain. She appealed to me. Even I had a great deal of difficulty in dealing with him, but eventually he gave way."

"Then the telegram," Mannering asked, "wasn't that from you?"

She shook her head.

"It was from your wife," she said. "I cannot take much credit for myself. It is she whom you must thank for your election. I came out at rather a dramatic moment. Sir Leslie had just offered her money, five hundred pounds, I think, to give him back his telegram and say nothing. She appealed to me at once, and Sir Leslie looked positively foolish."

"I am much obliged to you for telling me," Mannering muttered. He remembered now that he had scarcely spoken a dozen words to his wife since his return.

"Mrs. Mannering appears to have your interests very much at heart," Berenice said, quietly. "She proved herself quite a match for Sir Leslie. I think that he would have left here at once, only we are expecting Clara back."

Mannering smiled scornfully.

"I do not think that even Clara," he said, "is quite fool enough not to recognize in Borrowdean the arrant opportunist. For my part I am glad that all pretence at friendship between us is now at an end. He is one of those men whom I should count more dangerous as a friend than as an enemy."

Berenice did not reply. They were already in the courtyard of the hotel. Blanche was in a wicker chair in a sunny corner, talking to a couple of young Englishmen. Berenice turned towards the steps. They parted without any further words.

# CHAPTER VIII

## PLAYING THE GAME

Mannering for a moment hesitated. One of the two young men who were talking to his wife he recognized as a former acquaintance of hers—one of a genus whom he had little sympathy with and less desire to know. While he stood there Blanche laughed at some remark made by one of her companions, and the laugh, too, seemed somehow to remind him of the old days. He moved slowly forward.

The young men strolled off almost at once. Mannering took a vacant chair by his wife's side.

"I have only just heard," he said, "how much I have to thank you for. I took it for granted somehow that it was the Duchess who had discovered our friend Borrowdean's little scheme and sent that telegram. Why didn't you sign it?"

She shrugged her shoulders.

"It was the Duchess who made him chuck it up," she said. "I could never have made him do that. I was an idiot to let Parkins stay in England at all."

"I always understood," he said, "that he was dead."

"I let you think so," she answered. "I thought you might worry. But seriously, if he told the truth, now, after all these years, would any one take any notice of it?"

"Very likely not," he said, "so far as regards any criminal responsibility. But our political life is fenced about by all the middle-class love of propriety and hatred of all form of scandal. Parkins's story, authenticated or not, would have lost me my seat for Leeds."

"Then I am very glad," she said, "that I happened to see the telegram. Do you know where Parkins is now?"

"One of my supporters," he said, "a queer little man named Richard Fardell, has him in tow. He is bringing him up to London, I think."

She nodded.

"What are you doing this afternoon?" he asked.

She looked at him curiously.

"Mr. Englehall has asked me to go out in his car," she said. "I am rather tired of motoring, but I think I shall go."

Mannering lit a cigarette which he had just taken from his case.

"I don't think I should," he remarked.

She turned her head slowly, and looked at him.

"Why not?" she asked. "How can it concern you? Your plans for the afternoon are, I presume, already made!"

"It may not concern me directly," he answered, "but I have an idea that Mr. Englehall is not exactly the sort of person I care to have you driving about with."

She laughed hardly.

"I am most flattered by your interest in me," she declared. "Pray consider Mr. Englehall disposed of. You have some other plans, perhaps?"

"If you care to," he said, "we will walk down to the club for lunch and come home by the sea."

"Alone?"

"Certainly! Unless you choose to bring Hester."

She rose slowly to her feet.

"No," she said. "Let us go alone. It will be almost the first time since we were married, I think. I am curious to see how much I can bore you! Will you wait here while I find a hat?"

She disappeared inside the hotel. Mannering watched her absently. In a vague sort of way he was wondering what it was that had made their married life so completely a failure. He had imagined her as asking very little from him, content with the shelter of his name and home, content at any rate without those things of which he had made no mention when he had spoken to her of marriage. And he was becoming gradually aware that it was not so. She expected, had hoped for more. The terms which he had zealously striven to cultivate with her were terms of which she clearly did not approve. The signs of revolt were already apparent.

Mannering became absorbed in thought. He remembered

clearly the feelings with which he had gone to her and made his offer. He went over it all again. Surely he had made himself understood? But then there was her confession to him, the confession of her love. He had ignored that, but it was unforgetable. Had he not tacitly accepted the whole situation? If so, was he doing his duty? The shelter of his name and home, what were those to a warm-hearted woman, if she loved him? He had married her, loving another woman. She must have known this, but did she understand that he was not prepared to make any effort to accept the inevitable? He was still deep in thought when Berenice came out.

"What are you doing there all by yourself?" she asked. "Where is your wife?"

"She has gone to get a hat," he answered. "We thought of going to the club for *dejeuner*."

She nodded.

"A delightful idea," she said. "Do invite me, and I will take you in the car. Mrs. Mannering likes motoring, I know."

"Of course!" he said. "We shall be delighted!"

She beckoned to her chauffer, who was in the courtyard. Just then Blanche came out. She had changed her gown for one of plain white serge, and she wore a hat of tuscan straw which Mannering had once admired.

"You won't mind motoring, Mrs. Mannering?" Berenice said, as she approached. "I have invited myself to luncheon with you, and I am going to take you round to the club in the car."

Blanche stood quite still for a moment. The sun was in her

eyes, and she lowered her parasol for a moment.

"It will be very pleasant," she said, quietly, "only I think that I will go in and change my hat. I thought that we were going to walk."

She retraced her steps, walking a little wearily. Berenice came and sat down by Mannering's side.

"I hope Mrs. Mannering does not object to my coming," she said. "It occurred to me that she was not particularly cordial."

"It is only her manner," he answered. "It is very good of you to take us."

"Your wife doesn't like me," Berenice said. "I wonder why. I thought that I had been rather decent to her."

"Blanche is a little odd," Mannering answered. "I am afraid that it is my fault. Here are the Redfords. I wonder if they would join us."

"Three," she murmured, "is certainly an awkward number."

In the end the party became rather a large one, for Lord Redford met some old friends at the club who insisted upon their joining tables. In the interval, whilst they waited for luncheon, Mannering contrived to have a word alone with his wife.

"I am not responsible," he said, "for this enlargement of our party. The Duchess invited herself."

"It does not matter," she declared, listlessly. "What are you doing afterwards?"

"Playing golf, I fancy," he answered. "You heard what Redford said about a foursome."

"And you are returning—when?"

"I must leave here at six to-morrow morning."

They were leaning over the white palings of the pavilion, looking out upon the last green. She seemed to be watching the approach of two players who were just coming in.

"It is a long way to come," she remarked, "for so short a time."

He shrugged his shoulders.

"The aftermath of a contested election is a thing to escape from," he said. "I felt that I wanted to get as far away as possible, and then again I wanted to find out who it was who had sent that telegram."

They sat apart at luncheon, and Blanche was much quieter than usual. The others were all old friends. It seemed to her more than ordinarily apparent that she was present on sufferance, accepted as Mannering's wife, as an evil to be endured, and, so far as possible, ignored. Mannering himself spoke to her now and then across the table. Lord Redford, always good-natured, made a few efforts to draw her into the conversation. But it seemed to her that she had lost her confidence. The freemasonry of old acquaintance which existed between all of them left her outside an invisible but very real circle. Words came to her with difficulty. She felt stupid, almost shy. When she made an effort to break through it she was acutely conscious of her failure. Her laugh was too hard, it lacked sincerity or restraint. The cigarette which she smoked out of bravado with her coffee, seemed somehow out of place. When at last luncheon was over Mannering left his place and came over to her.

"The Duchess and I," he said, "are going to play Lord Redford and Mrs. Arbuthnot. Won't you walk round with us? The links are really very pretty."

"Thanks, I hate watching golf," she answered, rising and shaking out her skirt. "Hester and I will walk home."

"Do take the car, Mrs. Mannering," Berenice said. "It will simply be waiting here doing nothing."

"Thank you," Blanche answered. "I shall enjoy the walk."

The foursome was played in very leisurely fashion. There was plenty of time for conversation.

"I don't quite understand your wife," Berenice said to Mannering. "Her dislike of me is a little too obvious. What does it mean? Do you know?"

He shook his head. He was looking very pale and tired.

"I am not sure that I know anything about it at all," he said. "I am beginning to distrust my own judgment."

"Your marriage—" she began, thoughtfully.

"Don't let us talk about it," he interrupted. "I tried to pay a debt. It seems to me that I have only incurred a fresh one."

They were silent for some time. Then their opponents lost a ball and displayed no particular diligence in attempting to find it. Berenice sat down upon a plank seat.

"Your marriage," she said, "seemed always to me a piece of quixotism. I never altogether understood it."

"It was an affair of impulse," he said, slowly. "Life from a personal point of view had lost all interest to me. I did not dream after my—shall we call it apostacy?—that I could rely upon even a modicum of your friendship. I looked upon myself as an outcast commencing life afresh. Then chance intervened. I thought I saw my way to making some atonement to a woman whose life I had certainly helped to ruin. That was where the serious part of the mistake came. I thought what I had to offer would be sufficient. I am beginning now to doubt it."

"And what are you going to do?" she asked, looking steadily away from him.

"Heaven knows," he answered, bitterly. "I cannot give what I do not possess."

Was it his fancy, or was there a gleam of satisfaction about her still, pale face? He went on.

"I don't want to play the hypocrite. On the other hand I don't want all that I have done to go for nothing. Can you advise me?"

"No, nor any one else," she answered, softly.

"Yet I can perhaps correct a little your point of view. I think that you overestimate your indebtedness to the woman whom you have made your wife. Her husband was a weak, dissipated creature and he was a doomed man long before that unfortunate day. It is even very questionable whether that scene in which you figured had anything whatever to do in hastening his death. That is a good many years ago, and ever since then you seem to have impoverished yourself to find her the means to live in luxury. I consider that you paid your debt over and over again, and that your final act of self-abnegation was entirely uncalled for. What more she wants from you I do not know. Perhaps I can imagine."

There was a moment's silence. She turned her head and looked at him—looked him in the eyes unshamed, yet with her secret shining there for him to see.

"There may be others, Lawrence," she said, "to whom you owe something. A woman cannot take back what she has given. There may be sufferers in the world whom you ought also to consider. And a woman loves to think that what she may not have herself is at least kept sacred—to her memory."

"Fore!" cried Lord Redford, who had found his ball. "Awfully decent of you people to wait so long. We were afraid you meant to claim the hole!"

Mannering rose to play his shot.

"The Duchess and I, Lord Redford," he said, lightly, "scorn to take small advantages. We mean to play the game!"

# CHAPTER IX

## THE TRAGEDY OF A KEY

Blanche, in a plain black net gown, sat on Lord Redford's right hand at the hastily improvised dinner party that evening. Berenice, more subtly and more magnificently dressed, was opposite, by Mannering's side. The conversation seemed mostly to circle about them.

"A very charming place," Lord Redford declared. "I have enjoyed my stay here thoroughly. Let us hope that we may all meet here again next year," he added, raising his glass. "Mannering, you will drink to that, I hope?"

"With all my heart," Mannering answered. "And you, Blanche?"

She raised her almost untasted glass and touched it with her lips. She set it down with a faint smile. Berenice moved her head towards him.

"Your wife is not very enthusiastic," she remarked.

"She neither plays golf nor bathes," Mannering said. "It is possible that she finds it a little dull."

"Both are habits which it is possible to acquire," Berenice answered. "I am telling your husband, Mrs. Mannering," she continued, "that you ought to learn to play golf."

"Lawrence has offered to teach me more than once," Blanche answered, calmly. "I am afraid that games do not attract me. Besides, I am too old to learn!"

"My dear Mrs. Mannering!" Lord Redford protested.

"I am forty-two," Blanche replied, "and at that age a woman thinks twice before she begins anything new in the shape of vigorous exercise. Besides, I find plenty to amuse me here."

"Might one ask in what direction?" Berenice murmured. "I have found in the place many things that are delightful, but not amusing."

"I find amusement often in watching my neighbours," Blanche said. "I like to ask myself what it is they want, and to study their way of attaining it. You generally find that every one is fairly transparent when once you have found the key—and everybody is trying for something which they don't care for other people to know about."

The Duchess looked at Blanche steadily. There was a certain insolence, the insolence of her aristocratic birth and assured position in the level stare of her clear brown eyes. But Blanche did not flinch.

"I had no idea, Mrs. Mannering, that you had tastes of that sort," Berenice said, languidly. "Suppose you give us a few examples."

"Not for the world," Blanche answered, fervently. "Did you say that we were to have coffee outside, Lord Redford? How

E. Phillips Oppenheim

delightful! I wonder if Lady Redford is ready."

They all trooped out in a minute or two. Berenice laid her hand upon Mannering's arm.

"Your wife," she said, quietly, "is going a little too far. She is getting positively rude to me!"

Mannering muttered some evasive reply. He, too, had marked the note of battle in Blanche's tone. He had noticed, too, the unusual restraint of her manner. She had drunk little or no wine at dinner time, and she had talked quietly and sensibly. Directly they reached the courtyard she seated herself on a settee for two, and made room for him by her side.

"Come and tell me about the golf match," she said. "Who won?"

Mannering had no alternative but to obey. Lady Redford, however, drew her chair up close to theirs, and the conversation was always general. Berenice in a few minutes rose to her feet.

"Listen to the sea," she exclaimed. "Don't some of you want to come down to the rocks and watch it?"

Blanche rose up at once.

"Do come, Lawrence, if you are not too tired!" she said.

The whole party trooped out on to the promenade. Blanche passed her arm through her husband's, and calmly appropriated him.

"You can walk with whom you please presently, Lawrence,"

she said, "but I want you for a few minutes. I suppose you will admit that I have some claim?"

"Certainly," Mannering answered. "I have never denied it."

"I am your wife," Blanche said, "though heaven knows why you ever married me. The Duchess is, I suppose, the woman whom you would have married if you hadn't got into a mess with your politics. She is a very attractive woman, and you married me, of course, out of pity, or some such maudlin reason. But all the same I am here, and—I don't care what you do when I can't see you, but I won't have her make love to you before my face."

"The Duchess is not that sort of woman, Blanche," Mannering said, gravely.

"Isn't she?" Blanche remarked, unconvinced. "Well, I've watched her, and in my opinion she isn't very different from any other sort of woman. Do you wish you were free very much? I know she does!"

"Is there any object to be gained by this conversation?" Mannering asked. "Frankly, I don't like it. I made you no absurd promises when I married you. I think that you understood the position very well. So far as I know I have given you no cause to complain."

They had reached the end of the promenade. Blanche leaned over the rail. Her eyes seemed fixed upon a light flashing and disappearing across the sea. Mannering stood uncomfortably by her side.

"No cause to complain!" she repeated, as though to herself. "No, I suppose not. And yet, how much the better off do you think I am, Lawrence? I had friends before of some sort or another. Some of them pretended to like me, even if they didn't. I did as I chose. I lived as I liked. I was my own mistress. And now—well, there is no one! I enjoy the respectability of your name, the privilege of knowing your friends, the ability to pay my bills, but I should go stark mad if it wasn't for Hester. I gave myself away to you, I know. You married me for pity, I know. But what in God's name do I get out of it?"

A note of real passion quivered in her tone. Mannering looked down at her helplessly, taken wholly aback, without the power for a moment to formulate his thoughts. There was a touch of colour in her pale cheeks, her eyes were lit with an unusual fire. The faint moonlight was kind to her. Her features, thinner than they had been, seemed to have gained a certain refinement. She reminded him more than ever before of the Blanche of many years ago. He answered her kindly, almost tenderly.

"I am very sorry," he said, "if I have caused you any suffering. What I did I did for the best. I don't think that I quite understood, and I thought that you knew—what had come into my life."

"I knew that you cared for her, of course," she answered, with a little sob, "but I did not know that you meant to nurse it—that feeling. I thought that when we were married you would try to care for me—a little. I—Here are the others!"

Lord Redford, who had failed to amuse Berenice, and who had a secret preference for the woman who generally amused him, broke up their *tete-a-tete*. He led Blanche away, and Mannering followed with Berenice.

"What does this change in your wife mean?" she asked, abruptly.

"Change?" he repeated.

"Yes! She watches us! If it were not too absurd, one would believe her jealous. Of course, it is not my business to ask you on what terms you are with your wife, but—"

"You know what terms," he interrupted.

Her manner softened. She looked at him for a moment and then her eyes dropped.

"I am rather a hateful woman!" she said, slowly. "I wish I had not said that. I don't think we have managed things very cleverly, Lawrence. Still, I suppose life is made up of these sorts of idiotic blunders."

"Mine," he said, "has been always distinguished by them."

"And mine," she said, "only since I came to Blakely, and learnt to talk nonsense in your rose-garden! But come," she added, more briskly, "we are breaking our compact. We agreed to be friends, you know, and abjure sentiment."

He nodded.

"It seemed quite easy then," he remarked.

"And it is easy now! It must be," she added. "I have scarcely congratulated you upon your election. What it all means, and with which party you are going to vote, I scarcely know even now. But I can at least congratulate you personally."

"You are generous," he said, "for I suppose I am a deserter. As to where I shall sit, it is very hard to tell. I fancy myself that we are on the eve of a complete readjustment of parties. Wherever I may find myself, however, it will scarcely be with your friends."

She nodded.

"I realize that, and I am sorry," she said. "All that we need is
a leader, and you might have been he. As it is, I suppose we
shall muddle along somehow until some one comes out of
the ruck strong enough to pull us together.... Come and see
me in London, Lawrence. Who knows but that you may be
able to convert me!"

"You are too staunch," he answered, "and you have not seen
what I have seen."

She sighed.

"Didn't you once tell me at Blakely that politics for a woman
was a mischosen profession—that we were at once too
obstinate and too sentimental? Perhaps you were right. We
don't come into touch with the same forces that you meet
with, and we come into touch with others which make the
world seem curiously upside-down. Good-night, Lawrence! I
am going to my room quietly. Lady Redford wants to play
bridge, and I don't feel like it! *Bon voyage!*"

Mannering stood alone in the little courtyard, lit now with
hanging lights, and crowded with stray visitors who had
strolled in from the streets. The rest of the party had gone
into the salon beyond, and Mannering felt curiously
disinclined to join them. Suddenly there was a touch upon
his arm. He turned round. Blanche was standing there
looking up at him. Something in her face puzzled him. Her
eyes fell before his. She was pale, yet as he looked at her a
flood of colour rushed into her cheeks. His momentary
impression of her eyes was that they were very soft and very
bright. She had thrown off her wrap, and with her left hand

was holding up her white skirt. Her right hand was clenched as though holding something, and extended timidly towards him.

"I wanted to say good-night to you—and—there was something else—this!"

Something passed from her hand to his, something cold and hard. He looked at her in amazement, but she was already on her way up the grey stone steps which led from the courtyard into the hotel, and she did not turn back. He opened his hand and stared at what he found there. It was a key—number forty-four, *Premier etage.*

# CHAPTER X

## BLANCHE FINDS A WAY OUT

Mannering was conscious of an overpowering desire to be alone. He made his way out of the courtyard and back to the promenade. Some of the lights were already extinguished, and a slight drizzling rain was falling. He walked at once to the further wall, and stood leaning over, looking into the chaos of darkness. The key, round which his fingers were still tightly clenched, seemed almost to burn his flesh.

What to do? How much more of himself was he bound to surrender? Through a confusion of thoughts some things came to him then very clearly. Amongst others the grim, pitiless selfishness of his life. How much must she have suffered before she had dared to do this thing! He had taken up a burden and adjusted the weight to suit himself. He had had no thought for her, no care save that the seemliness of his own absorbed life might not be disturbed. And behind it all the other reason. What a pigmy of a man he was, after all.

A clock from the town struck eleven. He must decide! A vision of her rose up before him. He understood now her weakness and her strength. She was an ordinary woman, seeking the affection her sex demanded from its legitimate source. He understood the coming and going of the colour in her cheeks, her strained attempts to please, her barely controlled jealousy. In that mad moment when he had planned for her salvation he had imagined that she would have understood. What folly! Why should she? The complex workings of his innermost nature were scarcely likely to have been patent to her. What right had he to build upon that? What right, as an honest man, to contract a debt he never meant to pay? If he had not at the moment realized his responsibilities that was his own fault. From her point of view they were obvious enough, and it was from her point of view as well as his own that they must be considered.

He turned back to the hotel, walking a little unsteadily. All the time he was not sure that this was not a dream. And then on the wet pavement he came face to face with two cloaked figures, one of whom stopped short and called him by name. It was Berenice!

"You!" he exclaimed, more than ever sure that he was not properly awake.

"Is it so wonderful?" she answered. "To tell you the truth, I was not sleepy, and I felt like a little walk. You can go back now, Bryan," she said, turning to her maid. "Mr. Mannering will see me home."

As though by mutual consent they crossed to the sea-wall.

"What made you come out again?" she asked. "No, don't answer me! I think that I know."

"Impossible," he murmured.

"I was going up to my room," she said, "and as I passed the landing window which looks into the courtyard I saw you talking to your wife. I—I am afraid that I watched. I saw her leave you."

"Yes!"

"What was it that she gave you? What is it that you have in your hand?"

He opened his fingers. She turned her head away. It seemed to him an eternity that she stood there. When she spoke her voice was scarcely more than a whisper.

"Lawrence," she said, "we have been very selfish, you and I! There have been no words between us, but I think the compact has been there all the same. It seemed to me somehow that it was a compensation, that it was part of the natural order of things, that as our own folly had kept us apart, you should still belong to me—in my thoughts. And I have no right to this, or any share of you, Lawrence."

He drew a little nearer to her. She moved instantly away.

"I am glad," she said, "that our party breaks up to-morrow. When we meet again, Lawrence, it must be differently. I am parting with a great deal that has been precious to me, but it must be. It is quite clear."

"I made no promise!" he cried, hoarsely. "I did not mean—"

She stopped him with a swift glance.

"Never mind that. You and I are not of the race of people who shrink from their duty, or fear to do what is right. Your wife's face taught me mine. Your conscience will tell you yours."

"You mean?" he exclaimed.

"You know what I mean. We shall meet again, of course, but this is none the less our farewell. No, don't touch me! Not even my hand, Lawrence. Don't make it any harder. Let us go in."

But he did not move. The place where they stood was deserted. From below the white spray came leaping up almost to their faces as the waves beat against the wall. Behind them the town was black and deserted, save where a few lights gleamed out from the hotel. She shivered a little, and drew her cloak around her.

"Come," she said, "I am getting cold and cramped."

He walked by her side to the hotel. At the foot of the steps she left him.

"We shall meet again in London," she said, quietly. "Don't be too hard upon your old friends when you take your seat. Remember that you were once one of us."

She looked round and waved her hand as she disappeared. He caught a glimpse of her face as she passed underneath the hanging lamp—the face of a tired woman suddenly grown old. With a little groan he made his way into the hotel, and slowly ascended the stairs.

Early the next morning Mannering left Bonestre, and in twenty-four hours he was back again, summoned by a telegram which had met him in London. It seemed to him that everybody at the station and about the hotel regarded him with shocked and respectful sympathy. Hester, looking like a ghost, took him at once to her room. He was haggard and weary with rapid travelling, and he sank into a chair.

"Tell me—the worst!" he said.

"She started with Mr. Englehall about mid-day," Hester said. "They had luggage, but I explained that he was going to Paris, she was coming back by train. At two o'clock we were rung up on the telephone. Their brake had snapped going down the hill by St. Entuiel, and the chauffeur—he is mad now—but they think he lost his nerve. They were dashed into a tree, and—they were both dead—when they were got out from the wreck."

"God in Heaven!" Mannering murmured, white to the lips.

There was a silence between them. Mannering had covered his head with his hands. Hester tried once or twice to speak, but the tears were streaming from her eyes. She had the air of having more to say. The white horror of tragedy was still in her face.

"There is a letter," she said at last. "She left a letter for you."

Mannering rose slowly to his feet and moved to the lamp. Directly he had broken the seal he understood. He read the first line and looked up. His eyes met Hester's.

"Who knows—this?" he asked, hoarsely.

"No one! They had not been gone two hours. I explained everything."

Then Mannering read on.

"My dear Husband:

"I call you that for the last time, for I am going off with Englehall to Paris. Don't be too shocked, and don't despise me too much. I am just a very ordinary woman, and I'm afraid I've bad blood in my veins. Anyhow, I can't go on living under a glass case any longer. The old life was rotten enough, but this is insupportable. I'm going to have a fling, and after that I don't care what becomes of me.

"Now, Lawrence, I don't want you to blame yourself. I did think perhaps that when we were married I might have got you to care for me a little, but I suppose that was just my vanity. It wasn't very possible with a woman like—well, never mind who—about. You did your best. You were very nice and very kind to me last night, but it wasn't the real thing, was it? I knew you hated being where you were. I could almost hear your sigh of relief when I let you go. The fact of it is, our marriage was a mistake. I ought to have been satisfied with your name, I suppose, and the position it gave me, but I'm not that sort of woman. I've been in Bohemia too long. I like cheery friends, even if their names are not in Debrett, and I must have some one to care for me, or to pretend to care for me. You know I've cared for you—only you in a certain way—but I'm not heroic enough to be content with a shadowy love. I'm not an idealist. Imagination doesn't content me in the least. I'd rather have an inferior substance than ideal perfection. You see, I'm a very commonplace person at heart, Lawrence—almost vulgar. But these are my last words to you, so I've gone in for plain speaking. Now you're rid of me.

"That's all! From your point of view I suppose, and your friends, I've gone to the devil. Don't be too sure of it. I'm going to have a good time, and when the end comes I'm willing to pay. If you are idiotic enough to come after me, I shall be angry with you for the first time in my life, and it wouldn't be the least bit of use. Englehall's an old friend of mine, and he's a good sort. He's wanted me to do this often enough for years, but I never felt quite like it. I believe he'd marry me after, but he's got a wife shut up somewhere.

"I expect you think this a callous sort of letter. Well, I can't help it. If it disgusts you with me, so much the better. I'm sorry for the scandal, but you will get over that. Good-bye, Lawrence. Forgive me all the bother I've been to you.

"Blanche."

Mannering looked up from the letter, and again his eyes met Hester's. The secret was theirs alone. Very carefully he tore the pages into small pieces. Then he opened the stove and watched them consumed.

"No one will ever know," Hester said. "She said—when she left—that it was a morning's ride—but motors were so uncertain that she took a bag."

Mannering's eyes were filled once more with tears. The intolerable pity of the whole thing, its awful suddenness swept every other thought out of his mind. He remembered how anxiously she had tried to please him on that last night. He loathed himself for the cold brutality of his chilly affection. Hester came and knelt by his side, but she said nothing. So the hours passed.

# BOOK IV

## CHAPTER I

### THE PERSISTENCY OF BORROWDEAN

"And what does Mannering think of it all, I wonder!" Lord Redford remarked, lighting a fresh cigarette. "This may be his opportunity, who can tell!"

"Will he have the nerve to grasp it?" Borrowdean asked. "Mannering has never been proved in a crisis."

"He may have the nerve. I should be more inclined to question the desire," Lord Redford said. "For a man in his position he has always seemed to me singularly unambitious. I don't think that the prospect of being Prime Minister would dazzle him in the least. It is part of the genius of the politician too, to know exactly when and how to seize an opportunity. I can imagine him watching it come, examining it through his eyeglass, and standing on one side with a shrug of the shoulders."

"You do not believe, then," Berenice said, "that he is suffi- ciently in earnest to grasp it?"

"Exactly," Lord Redford said. "I have that feeling about

Mannering, I must admit, especially during the last two years. He seems to have drawn away from all of us, to live altogether too absorbed and self-contained a life for a man who has great ambitions to realize, or who is in downright earnest about his work."

"What you all forget when you discuss Lawrence Mannering is this," Berenice said. "He holds his position almost as a sacred charge. He is absolutely conscientious. He wants certain things for the sake of the people, and he will work steadily on until he gets them. I believe it is the truth that he has no personal ambition, but if the cause he has at heart is to be furthered at all it must be by his taking office. Therefore I think that when the time comes he will take it."

"That sounds reasonable enough," Lord Redford admitted. "By the bye, did you notice that he is included in the house party at Sandringham again this week?"

Anstruther, the youngest Cabinet Minister, and Lord Redford's nephew, joined in the conversation.

"I can tell you something for a fact," he said. "My cousin is Lady-in-Waiting, and she's been up in town for a few days, and she asked me about Mannering. A Certain Personage thinks very highly of him indeed. Told some one that Mr. Mannering was the most statesman-like politician in the service of his country. I believe he'd sooner see Mannering Prime Minister than any one."

"But he has no following," Borrowdean objected.

"I think," Berenice said, slowly, "that he keeps as far aloof as possible for one reason, and one reason only. He avoids friendship, but he makes no enemies. He cultivates a neutral position whenever he can. What he is looking forward to, I am sure, is to found a coalition Government."

"It is very possible," Lord Redford remarked. "I wonder if he will ask me to join."

"Always selfish," Berenice laughed. "You men are all alike!"

"On the contrary," Lord Redford answered, "my interest was purely patriotic. I cannot imagine the affairs of the country flourishing deprived of my valuable services. Let us go and wander through the crowd. Members of a Government in extremes like ours ought not to whisper together in corners. It gives rise to comment."

Anstruther came hurrying up. He drew Redford on one side.

"Mannering is here," he said, quietly. "Just arrived from Sandringham. He is looking for you."

Almost as he spoke Mannering appeared. He did not at first see Berenice, and from the corner where she stood she watched him closely.

It was two years since those few weeks at Bonestre, and during all that time they had scarcely met. Berenice knew that he had avoided her. For twelve months he had declined all social engagements, and since then he had pleaded the stress of political affairs as an excuse for leading the life almost of a recluse. Unseen herself, she studied him closely. He was much thinner, and every trace of his once healthy colouring had disappeared. His eyes seemed deeper set. There were streaks of grey in his hair. But for all that to her he was unaltered. He was still the one man in the world. She saw him shake hands with Lord Redford and draw him a little on one side.

"Can you spare me five minutes?" he asked. "I have a matter to discuss with you."

"Certainly!" Lord Redford answered. "I am leaving directly, and I might drive you home if you liked. We heard that you were at Sandringham."

"I came up this afternoon," Mannering answered. "I heard that you were likely to be here, and as Lady Herrington had been kind enough to send me a card I came on."

Lord Redford nodded.

"Borrowdean and Anstruther are here too," he remarked. "We all felt in need of diversion. As you know very well, we're in a tight corner."

Berenice came out from her place. At the sound of the rustling of her skirts both men turned their heads. She wore a gown of black velvet and a wonderful rope of pearls hung from her neck. She raised her hand and smiled at Mannering.

"I am glad to see you again," she said, softly. "It is quite an age since we met, isn't it?"

He held her hand for a moment. The touch of his fingers chilled her. He greeted her with quiet courtesy, but there was no answering smile upon his lips.

"I have heard often of your movements from Clara," he said. "You have been very kind to her."

"It has never occurred to me in that light," she said. "Clara needs a chaperon, and I need a companion. We were talking yesterday of going to Cairo for the winter. My only fear is that I am robbing you of your niece."

"Please do not let that trouble you," he said. "Clara would be a most uncomfortable member of my household."

"But are you never at all lonely?" she asked.

"I never have time to think of such a thing," he answered. "Besides, I have Hester. She makes a wonderful secretary, and she seems to enjoy the work."

"I should like to have a talk with you some time," she said. "Won't you come and see me?"

He hesitated.

"It is very kind of you to ask me," he said. "Don't think me churlish, but I go nowhere. I am trying to make up, you see, for my years of idleness."

She looked at him steadfastly, and her heart sank. The change in his outward appearance seemed typical of some deeper and more final alteration in his whole nature. She felt herself powerless against the absolute impenetrability of his tone and manner. She felt that he had fought a battle within himself and conquered; that for some reason or other he had decided to walk no longer in the pleasanter paths of life. She had come to him unexpectedly, but he had shown no sign of emotion. Her influence over him seemed to be wholly a thing of the past. She made one more effort.

"I think," she said, "that as one grows older one parts the less readily with the few friends who count. I hope that you will change your mind."

He bowed gravely, but he made no answer. Berenice took Borrowdean's arm and passed on. There was a little spot of colour in her cheeks. Borrowdean felt nerved to his enterprise.

"Let us go somewhere and sit down for a few minutes," he suggested. "The rooms are so hot this evening."

She assented without words, and he found a solitary couch in one of the further apartments.

"I wonder," he said, after a moment's pause, "whether I might say something to you, whether you would listen to me for a few minutes."

Berenice was absorbed in her own thoughts. She allowed him to proceed.

"For a good many years," he said, lowering his voice a little, "I have worked hard and done all I could to be successful. I wanted to have some sort of a position to offer. I am a Cabinet Minister now, and although I don't suppose we can last much longer this time, I shall have a place whenever we are in again."

The sense of what he was saying began to dawn upon her. She stopped him at once.

"Please do not say any more, Sir Leslie," she begged. "I should have given you credit for sufficient perception to have known beforehand the absolute impossibility of—of anything of the sort."

"You are still a young woman," he said, quietly. "The world expects you to marry again."

"I have no interest in what the world expects of me," she answered, "but I may tell you at once that my refusal has nothing whatever to do with the question of marriage in the abstract. You are a man of perception, Sir Leslie! It will be, I trust, sufficient if I say that I have no feelings whatever towards you which would induce me to consider the subject even for a moment."

She was unchanged, then! This time he recognized the note of finality in her tone. All the time and thought he had given to this matter were wasted. He had failed, and he knew why. He seldom permitted himself the luxury of anger, but he felt all the poison of bitter hatred stirring within him at that moment, and craving for some sort of expression. There was nothing he could do, nothing he could say. But if Mannering had been within reach then he would have struck him. He rose and walked slowly away.

E. Phillips Oppenheim

## CHAPTER II

## HESTER THINKS IT "A GREAT PITY"

"You will understand," Mannering said, as the brougham drove off, "that you and I are speaking together merely as friends. I have nothing official to say to you. It would be presumption on my part to assume that the time is ripe for anything definite while you are still at the head of an unbeaten Government. But one learns to read the signs of the times. I think that you and I both know that you cannot last the session."

"It is a positive luxury at times," Redford answered, "to be able to indulge in absolute candour. We cannot last the session. You pulled us through our last tight corner, but we shall part, I suppose, on the New Tenement Bill, and then we shall come a cropper."

Mannering nodded.

"The Opposition," he said, "are not strong enough to form a Government alone. And I do not think that a one-man Cabinet would be popular. It has been suggested to me that at no time in political history have the conditions been more favourable for a really strong coalition Government, containing men of moderate views on both sides. I am anxious to know whether you would be willing to join such a combination."

"Under whom?" Lord Redford asked.

"Under myself," Mannering answered, gravely. "Don't think me over-presumptuous. The matter has been very carefully thought out. You could not serve under Rushleigh, nor could he serve under you. But you could both be invaluable members of a Cabinet of which I was the nominal head. I do not wish to entrap you into consent, however, without your fully understanding this: a modified, and to a certain extent an experimental, scheme of tariff reform would be part of our programme."

"You wish for a reply," Lord Redford said, "only in general terms?"

"Only in general terms, of course," Mannering assented.

"Then you may take it," Lord Redford said, "that I should be proud to become a member of such a Government. Anything would be better than a fourth-party administration with Imperialism on the brain and rank Protection on their programme. They might do mischief which it would take centuries to undo."

"We understand one another, Lord Redford," Mannering said, simply. "I am very much obliged to you. This is my turning."

Mannering, when he found himself alone in his study, drew a little sigh of relief. He flung himself into an easy-chair, and sat with his hands pressed against his temples. The events of the day, from the morning at Sandringham to his recent conversation with Lord Redford, were certainly of sufficiently exciting a nature to provide him with food for thought. And yet his mind was full of one thing only, this chance meeting with Berenice. It was wonderful to him that she should have changed so little. He himself felt that the last two years were equal to a decade, that events on the other side of that line with which his life was riven were events with which some other person was concerned, certainly not the Lawrence Mannering of to-day. And yet he knew now that the battle which he had fought was far from a final one. Her power over him was unchanged. He was face to face once more with the old problem. His life was sworn to the service of the people. He had crowded his days with thoughts and deeds and plans for them. Almost every personal luxury and pleasure had been abnegated. He had found a sort of fierce delight in the asceticism of his daily life, in the unflinching firmness with which he had barred the gates which might lead him into smoother and happier ways. To-night he was beset with a sudden fear. He rose and looked at himself in the glass. He was pale and wan. His face lacked the robust vitality of a few years ago. He was ageing fast. He was conscious of certain disquieting symptoms in the routine of his daily life. He threw himself back into the chair with a little groan. The mockery of his life of ceaseless toil seemed suddenly to spread itself out before him, a grim and unlovely jest. What if his strength should go? What if all this labour and self-denial should be in vain? He found himself growing giddy at the thought.

He rang the bell and ordered wine. Then he went to the telephone and rang up a doctor who lived near. Very soon, with coat and waistcoat off, he was going through a somewhat prolonged examination. Afterwards the doctor sat down opposite to him and accepted a cigar.

"What made you send for me this evening?" he asked, curiously.

Mannering hesitated.

"An impulse," he said. "To-morrow I should have no time to come to you. I wasn't feeling quite myself, and it is possible that I may be undertaking some very important work before long."

"I shouldn't if I were you," the doctor remarked, quietly.

"The work is of such a nature," Mannering said, "that I could not refuse it. It may not come, but if it does I must go through with it."

"I doubt whether you will succeed," the doctor said. "There is nothing the matter with you except that you have been drawing on your reserve stock of strength to such an extent that you are on the verge of a collapse. The longer you stave it off the more complete it will be."

"You are a Job's comforter," Mannering remarked, with a smile. "Send me some physic, and I will take things as easy as I can."

"I'll send you some," the doctor answered, "but it won't do you much good. What you want is rest and amusement."

Mannering laughed, and showed him out. When he returned to his study Hester was there, just returned from a visit to the theatre with some friends. She threw off her wrap and looked through the letters which had come by the evening's post.

"Did you see this from Richard Fardell?" she asked him. "Parkins is dead at last. Fardell says that he has been quite childish for the last eighteen months! Are you ill?" she broke off, suddenly.

Mannering, who was lying back in his easy-chair, white almost to the lips, roused himself with an effort. He poured out a glass of wine and drank it off.

"I'm not ill," he said, with rather a weak smile, "but I'm a little tired."

"Who was your visitor?" she asked.

"A doctor. I felt a little run down, so I sent for him. Of course he told me the usual story. Rest and a holiday."

She came and sat on the arm of his chair. Every year she grew less and less like her mother. Her hair was smoothly brushed back from her forehead, and her features were distinctly intellectual. She was by far the best secretary Mannering had ever had.

"You need some one to look after you," she said, decisively.

"It seems to me that you do that pretty well," he answered. "I don't want any one else."

"You need some one with more authority than I have," she said. "You ought to marry."

"Marry!" he gasped.

"Yes."

"Any particular person?"

"Of course! You know whom."

Mannering did not reply at once. He was looking steadfastly

into the fire, and the gloom in his face was unlightened.

"Hester," he said, at last, in a very low tone, "I will tell you, if you like, a short, a very short chapter of my life. It lasted a few hours, a day or so, more or less. Yet of course it has made a difference always."

"I should like to hear it," she whispered.

"The two great events of my life," he said, "came together. I was engaged to be married to the Duchess of Lenchester at the same time that I found myself forced to sever my connexion with the Liberal party. You know, of course, that the Duchess has always been a great figure in politics. She has ambitions, and her political creed is almost a part of the religion of her life. She looked upon my apostasy with horror. It came between us at the very moment when I thought that I had found in life the one great and beautiful thing."

"If ever she let it come between you," Hester interrupted, softly, "I believe that she has repented. We women are quick to find out those things, you know," she added, "and I am sure that I am right. She has never married any one else. I do not believe that she ever will."

"It is too late," Mannering said. "A union between us now could only lead to unhappiness. The disintegration of parties is slowly commencing, and I think that the next few years will find me still further apart than I am to-day from my old friends. Berenice"—he slipped so easily into calling her so— "is heart and soul with them."

"At least," Hester said, "I think that for both your sakes you should give her the opportunity of choosing."

"Even that," he said, "would not be wise. We are man and woman still, you see, Hester, and there are moments when sentiment is strong enough to triumph over principle and sweep our minds bare of all the every-day thoughts. But afterwards—there is always the afterwards. The conflict must come. Reason stays with us always, and sentiment might weaken with the years."

She shook her head.

"The Duchess is a woman," she said, "and the hold of all other things grows weak when she loves. Give her the chance."

"Don't!" Mannering exclaimed, almost sharply. "You can't see this matter as I do. I have vowed my life now. I have seen my duty, and I have kept my face turned steadily towards it. Once I was contented with very different things, and I think that I came as near happiness then as a man often does. But those days have gone by. They have left a whole world of delightful memories, but I have locked the doors of the past behind me."

Hester shook her head.

"You are making a mistake," she said. "Two people who love one another, and who are honest in their opinions, find happiness sooner or later if they have the courage to seek for it. Don't you know," she continued, after a moment's pause, "that—she understood? I always like to think what I believe to be the truth. She went away to leave you free."

Mannering rose to his feet and pointed to the clock.

"It is time that you and I were in bed, Hester," he said. "Remember that we have a busy morning."

"It seems a pity," she murmured, as she wished him good-night. "A great pity!"

E. Phillips Oppenheim

# CHAPTER III

## SUMMONED TO WINDSOR

Berenice, who had just returned from making a call, was standing in the hall, glancing through the cards displayed upon a small round table. The major-domo of her household came hurrying out from his office.

"There is a young lady, your Grace," he announced, "who has been waiting to see you for half an hour. Her name is Miss Phillimore."

"Where is she?" Berenice asked.

"In the library, your Grace."

"Show her into my own room," Berenice said, "I will see her at once."

Hester was a little nervous, but Berenice set her immediately at her ease by the graciousness of her manner. They talked for some time of Bonestre. Then there was a moment's pause. Hester summoned up her courage.

"I am afraid," she said, "that you may consider what I am going to say rather a liberty. I've thought it all out, and I decided to come to you. I couldn't see any other way."

Berenice smiled encouragingly.

"I will promise you," she said, "that I will consider it nothing of the sort."

"That is very kind of you," Hester said. "I have come here because Mr. Mannering is the greatest friend I have in the world. He stands to me for all the relatives most girls have, and I am very fond of him indeed. I scarcely remember my father, but Mr. Mannering was always kind to me when I was a child. You know, perhaps, that I am living with him now as his secretary?"

Berenice nodded pleasantly.

"I see him every day," Hester continued, "and I notice things. He has changed a great deal during the last few years. I am getting very anxious about him."

"He is not ill, I hope?" Berenice asked. "I too noticed a change. It grieved me very much."

"He is simply working himself to death," Hester continued, "without relaxation or pleasure of any sort. And all the time he is unhappy. Other men, however hard they work, have their hobbies and their occasional holidays. He has neither. And I think that I know why. He fights all the time to forget."

"To forget what?" Berenice asked, slowly turning her head.

"To forget how near he came once to being very happy," Hester answered, boldly. "To forget—you!"

Then her heart sang a little song of triumph, for she saw the instant change in the still, cold face turned now a little away from her. She saw the proud lips tremble and the unmistakable light leap out from the dark eyes. She saw the colour rush into the cheeks, and she had no more fear. She rose from her chair and dropped on one knee by Berenice's side.

"Make him happy, please," she begged. "You can do it. You only! He loves you!"

Berenice smiled, although her eyes were wet with tears. She laid her long, delicate fingers upon the other's hand.

"But, my dear child," she protested, "what can I do? Mr. Mannering won't come near me. He won't even write to me. I can't take him by storm, can I?"

"He is so foolish," Hester said, also smiling. "He will not understand how unimportant all other things are when two people care for one another. He talks about the difference in your politics, as though that were sufficient to keep you apart!"

Berenice was silent for a moment.

"There was a time," she said, softly, "when I thought so, too."

"Exactly!" Hester declared. "And he doesn't know, of course, that you don't think so now."

Berenice smiled slightly.

"You must remember, dear," she said, "that Mr. Mannering and I are in rather a peculiar position. My great-grandfather, my father and my uncle were all Prime Ministers of England,

and they were all staunch Liberals. My family has always taken its politics very seriously indeed, and so have I. It is not a little thing, this, after all."

"But you will do it!" Hester exclaimed. "I am sure that you will."

Berenice rose to her feet. A sense of excitement was suddenly quivering in her veins, her heart was beating fiercely. After all, this child was wise. She had been drifting into the dull, passionless life of a middle-aged woman. All the joys of youth seemed suddenly to be sweeping up from her heart, mocking the serenity of her days, these stagnant days, sheltered from the great winds of life, where the waves were ripples and the hours changeless. She raised her arms for a moment and dropped them to her side.

"Oh, I do not know!" she cried. "It is such an upheaval. If he were here—if he asked me himself. But he will never come now."

"I believe that he would come to-morrow," Hester said, "if he were sure—"

Berenice laughed softly. There was colour in her cheeks as she turned to Hester.

"Tell him to come and have tea with me to-morrow afternoon," she said. "I shall be quite alone."

\*   \*   \*   \*   \*

Hester felt all her confidence slipping away from her. The echoes of her breathless, passionate words had scarcely died away, and Mannering, to all appearance, was unmoved. His still, cold face showed no signs of agitation, his dark, beringed eyes were full of nothing but an intense weariness.

"Do I understand, Hester," he asked, "that you have been to see the Duchess?—that you have spoken of these things to her?"

Her heart sank. His tone was almost censorious. Nevertheless, she stood her ground.

"Yes! I have told you the truth. And I am glad that I went. You are very clever people, both of you, but you are spoiling your lives for the sake of a little common sense. It was necessary for some one to interfere."

Mannering shook his head slowly.

"You meant kindly, Hester," he said, "but it was a mistake. The time when that might have been possible has gone by. Neither she nor I can call back the hand of time. The last two years have made an old man of me. I have no longer my enthusiasm. I am in the whirlpool, and I must fight my way through to the end."

She sat at his feet. He was still in the easy-chair into which he had sunk on his first coming into the room. He had been speaking in the House late, amidst all the excitement of a political crisis.

"Why fight alone," she murmured, "when she is willing to come to you?"

He shook his head.

"There would be conditions," he said, "and she would not understand. I may be in office in a month with most of her friends in opposition. The situation would be impossible!"

"Rubbish!" Hester declared. "The Duchess is too great a woman to lose so utterly her sense of proportion. Don't you understand—that she loves you?"

Mannering laughed bitterly.

"She must love a shadow, then!" he said, "for the man she knew does not exist any longer. Poor little girl, are you disappointed?" he added, more kindly. "I am sorry!"

"I am disappointed to hear you talking like this," she declared. "I will not believe that it is more than a mood. You are overtired, perhaps!"

"Ay!" he said. "But I have been overtired for a long time. The strength the gods give us lasts a weary while. You must send my excuses to the Duchess, Hester. The fates are leading me another way."

"I won't do it," she sobbed. "You shall be reasonable! I will make you go!"

He shook his head.

"If you could," he murmured, "you might alter the writing on one little page of history. We defeated the Government to-night badly, and I am going to Windsor to-morrow afternoon."

Hester rose to her feet and paced the room restlessly. Mannering had spoken without exultation. His pallid face seemed to her to have grown thin and hard. He saw himself the possible Prime Minister of the morrow without the slightest suggestion of any sort of gratified ambition.

"I don't know whether to say that I am glad or not," Hester

declared, stopping once more by his side. "If you are going to shut yourself off from everything else in life which makes for happiness, to forget that you are a man, and turn yourself into a law-making machine, well, then, I am sorry. I think that your success will be a curse to you. I think that you will live to regret it."

Mannering looked at her for a moment with a gleam of his old self shining out of his eyes. A sudden pathos, a wave of self-pity had softened his face.

"Dear child!" he said, gravely, "I cannot make you understand. I carry a burden from which no one can free me. For good or for evil the powers that be have set my feet in the path of the climbers, and for the sake of those whose sufferings I have seen I must struggle upwards to the end. Berenice and the Duchess of Lenchester are two very different persons. I cannot take one into my life without the other. It is because I love her, Hester, that I let her go. Good-night, child!"

She kissed his hand and went slowly to her room, stumbling upstairs through a mist of tears. There was nothing more that she could do.

# CHAPTER IV

## CHECKMATE TO BORROWDEAN

Mannering's town house, none too large at any time, was transformed into a little hive of industry. Two hurriedly appointed secretaries were at work in the dining-room, and Hester was busy typing in her own little sanctum.

Mannering sat in his study before a table covered with papers, and for the first time during the day was alone for a few moments.

His servant brought in a card. Mannering glanced at it and frowned.

"The gentleman said that he would not keep you for more than a moment, sir," the servant announced quietly, mindful of the half-sovereign which had been slipped into his hand.

Mannering still looked at the card doubtfully.

"You can show him up," he said at last.

"Very good, sir!"

The man withdrew, and reappeared to usher in Sir Leslie

E. Phillips Oppenheim

Borrowdean. Mannering greeted him without offering his hand.

"You wished to see me, Sir Leslie?" he asked.

Borrowdean came slowly into the room. He closed the door behind him.

"I hope," he said, "that you will not consider my presence an intrusion!"

"You have business with me, I presume," Mannering answered, coldly. "Pray sit down."

Borrowdean ignored the chair, towards which Mannering had motioned. He came and stood by the side of the table.

"Unless your memory, Mannering," he said, with a hard little laugh, "is as short as the proverbial politician's, you can scarcely be surprised at my visit."

Mannering raised his eyebrows, and said nothing.

"I must confess," Borrowdean continued, "that I scarcely expected to find it necessary for me to come here and remind you that it was I who am responsible for your reappearance in politics."

"I am not likely," Mannering said, slowly, "to forget your good offices in that respect."

"I felt sure that you would not," Borrowdean answered. "Yet you must not altogether blame me for my coming! I understand that the list of your proposed Cabinet is to be completed to-morrow afternoon, and as yet I have heard nothing from you."

"Your information," Mannering said, "is quite correct. In fact, my list is complete already. If your visit here is one of curiosity, I have no objection to gratify it. Here is a list of the names I have selected."

He handed a sheet of paper to Borrowdean, who glanced it eagerly down. Afterwards he looked up and met Mannering's calm gaze. There was an absolute silence for several seconds.

"My name," Borrowdean said, hoarsely, "is not amongst these!"

"It really never occurred to me for a single second to place it there," Mannering answered.

Borrowdean drew a little breath. He was deathly pale.

"You include Redford," he said. "He is a more violent partizan than I have ever been. I have heard you say a dozen times that you disapprove of turning a man out of office directly he has got into the swing of it. Has any one any fault to find with me? I have done my duty, and done it thoroughly. I don't know what your programme may be, but if Redford can accept it I am sure that I can."

"Possibly," Mannering answered. "I have this peculiarity, though. Call it a whim, if you like. I desire to see my Cabinet composed of honourable men."

Borrowdean started back as though he had received a blow.

"Am I to accept that as a statement of your opinion of me?" he demanded.

"It seems fairly obvious," Mannering answered, "that such

E. Phillips Oppenheim

was my intention."

"You owe your place in public life to me," Borrowdean exclaimed.

"If I do," Mannering answered, "do you imagine that I consider myself your debtor? I tell you that to-day, at this moment, I have no political ambitions. Before you appeared at Blakely and commenced your underhand scheming, I was a contented, almost a happy man. You imagined that my reappearance in political life would be beneficial to you, and with that in view, and that only, you set yourself to get me back. You succeeded! We won't say how! If you are disappointed with the result what concern is that of mine? You have called yourself my friend. I have not for some time considered you as such. I owe you nothing. I have no feeling for you save one of contempt. To me you figure as the modern political adventurer, living on his wits and the credulity of other people. Better see how it will pay you in opposition."

Borrowdean, a cold-blooded and calculating man, knew for the first time in his life what it was to let his passions govern him. Every word which this man had spoken was truth, and therefore all the more bitter to hear. He saw himself beaten and humiliated, outwitted by the man whom he had sought to make his tool. A slow paroxysm of anger held him rigid. He was white to the lips. His nerves and senses were all tingling. There was red fire before his eyes.

"If your business with me is ended," Mannering said, waving his hand towards the door, "you will forgive me if I remind you that I am much occupied."

Borrowdean snatched up the square glass paper cutter from the table, and without a second's warning he struck

Mannering with it full upon the temple.

"Damn you!" he said.

Mannering tried to struggle to his feet, but collapsed, and fell upon the floor. Borrowdean kicked his prostrate body.

"Now go and form your Cabinet," he muttered. "May you wake in hell!"

* * * * *

Borrowdean, who left the study a madman, was a sane person the moment he began to descend the stairs and found himself face to face with a tall, heavily cloaked woman. The flash of familiar jewels in her hair, something, perhaps, in the quiet stateliness of her movements, betrayed her identity to him. His heart gave a quick jump. A sickening fear stole over him. He barred the way.

"Duchess!" he exclaimed.

She waved him aside with an impatient gesture. He could see the frown gathering upon her face.

"Sir Leslie!" she replied. "Please let me pass! I want to see Mr. Mannering before any one else goes up!"

Sir Leslie drew immediately to one side.

"Pray do not let me detain you," he said, coolly. "Between ourselves, I do not think that Mannering is in a fit state to see anybody. I have not been able to get a coherent word out of him. He walks all the time backwards and forwards like a man demented."

Berenice smiled slightly.

"You are annoyed," she declared, "because you will be in opposition once more!"

"If I go into opposition again," Borrowdean answered, "it will be my own choice. Mannering has asked me to join his Cabinet."

Berenice raised her eyebrows. Her surprise was genuine.

"You amaze me!" she declared.

"I was amazed myself," he answered.

She passed on her way, and Borrowdean descending, took a cab quietly home. Berenice, with her hand upon the door, hesitated. Hester had purposely sent her up alone. They had waited until they had heard Borrowdean leave the room. And now at the last moment she hesitated. She was a proud woman. She was departing now, for his sake, from the conventions of a lifetime. He had declined to come to her; no matter, she had come to him instead. Suppose—he should not be glad? Suppose she should fail to see in his face her justification? It was very quiet in the room. She could not even hear the scratching of his pen. Twice her fingers closed upon the knob of the door, and twice she hesitated. If it had not been for facing Hester below she would probably have gone silently away.

And then—she heard a sound. It was not at all the sort of sound for which she had been listening, but it brought her hesitation to a sudden end. She threw open the door, and a little cry of amazement broke from her trembling lips. It was indeed a groan which she had heard. Mannering was stretched upon the floor, his eyes half closed, his face ghastly white. For a moment she stood motionless, a whole torrent of arrested speech upon her quivering lips. Then she dropped on her knees by his side and lifted his cold hand.

"Oh, my love!" she murmured. "My love!"

But he made no sign. Then she stood up, and her cry of horror rang through the house.

E. Phillips Oppenheim

# CHAPTER V

## A BRAZEN PROCEEDING

Mannering opened his eyes lazily. His companion had stopped suddenly in his reading. He appeared to be examining a certain paragraph in the paper with much interest. Mannering stretched out his hand for a match, and relit his cigarette.

"Read it out, Richard," he said. "Don't mind me."

The young man started slightly.

"I am very sorry, sir," he said. "I thought that you were asleep!"

Mannering smiled.

"What about the paragraph?" he asked.

"It is just this," Richard answered, reading. "'The Duchess of Lenchester and Miss Clara Mannering have arrived at Claridge's from the South of Italy.'"

Mannering looked at him keenly.

"I am curious to know which part of that announcement you find so interesting," he said.

"Certainly not the latter part, sir," the young man answered. "I thought perhaps you would have noticed—I meant to speak to you as soon as you were a little stronger—I have asked Hester to be my wife!"

"Then all I can say," Mannering declared, gravely, "is, that you are a remarkably sensible young man. I am quite strong enough to bear a shock of that sort."

"I'm very glad to hear you say so, sir," Richard said. "Of course I shouldn't think of taking her away until you were quite yourself again."

"The cheek of the young man!" Mannering murmured. "She wouldn't go!"

"I don't believe she would," Richard laughed. "Of course we consider that you are very nearly well now."

"You can consider what you like," Mannering answered, "but I shall remain an invalid as long as it pleases me."

Hester appeared on the upper lawn, and Richard rose up at once.

"If you don't mind, sir," he said, "I think that I should like to go and tell Hester that I have spoken to you."

Mannering nodded. He watched the two young people stroll off together towards the rose-garden, talking earnestly. He heard the little iron gate open and close. He watched them disappear behind the hedge of laurels. A puff of breeze brought the faint odour of roses to him, and with it a sudden host of memories. His eyes grew wistful. He felt something tugging at his heartstrings. Only a few years ago life here had seemed so wonderful a thing—only a few years, but with all the passions and struggles of a lifetime crowded into them. The maelstrom was there still, but he himself had crept out of it. What was there left? Peace, haunted with memories, rest, troubled by desire. He heard the sound of their voices in the rose-garden, and he turned away with a pain in his heart of which he was ashamed. These things were for the young! If youth had passed him by, still there were compensations!

Compensations, aye—but he wanted none of them! He picked up the newspaper, and with a little difficulty, for his sight was not yet good, found a certain paragraph. Then the paper slipped again from his fingers, and he heard the sweeping of a woman's dress across the smooth-shaven lawn. He gripped the sides of his chair and set his teeth hard. He struggled to rise, but she moved swiftly up to him with a gesture of remonstrance.

"Please don't move," she exclaimed, as though her coming were the most natural thing in the world. "I am going to sit down with you, if I may!"

He murmured an expression of conventional delight. She wore a dress of some soft white material, and her figure was as wonderful as ever. He recovered himself almost at once and studied her admiringly.

"Paris?" he murmured.

"Paquin!" she answered. "I remembered that you liked me in white."

"But where on earth have you come from?" he asked.

"The Farm," she answered. "I'm going to take it for three months—if you're decent to me!"

"That rascal Richard!" he muttered. "Never told me a word! Pretended to be surprised when he heard you and Clara were back."

She nodded.

"Clara is going to marry that Frenchman next month," she said, "and I shall be looking for another companion. Do you know of one?"

"I haven't another niece," he answered.

"Even if you had," she said, "I have come to the conclusion that I want something different. Will you listen to me patiently for a moment?"

"Yes."

"Will you marry me, please?" she said. "No, don't interrupt. I want there to be no misunderstandings this time. I don't care whether you are an invalid or not. I don't care whether you are going back into politics or not. I don't care whether we live here or in any other corner of the world. You can call yourself anything, from an anarchist to a Tory—or be anything. You can have all your workingmen here to dinner in flannel shirts, if you like, and I'll play bowls with their wives on the lawn. Nothing matters but this one thing, Lawrence. Will you marry me—and try to care a little?"

"This is absolutely," Mannering declared, taking her into his arms, "the most brazen proceeding!"

"It's a good deal better than the bungle we made of it before," she murmured.

## THE END

# ABOUT THE AUTHOR

**Edward Phillips Oppenheim** (1866–1946), self-styled "prince of storytellers," was an English novelist, a major and successful writer of genre fiction including thrillers. He composed during his lifetime more than a hundred novels, mostly of the suspense and international intrigue nature, as well as romances, comedies, and parables of everyday life. The sole biography of Oppenheim is Robert Standish's (pseudonym of Digby George Gerahty) Prince of Storytellers: The Life of E. Phillips Oppenheim; London: Peter Davies 1957.

Oppenheim's work possesses a unique charm all its own, featuring protagonists who delight in Epicurean meals, surroundings of intense luxury, and the relaxed pursuit of criminal practice, on either side of the law.

For most of his life, Oppenheim maintained a regular schedule of work and productivity of an almost monastic nature, despite his fondness for Monte Carlo and his love of good food and wine. Troubled in his last years by intense prostate problems, Oppenheim persevered in the creation of a series of charming, escapist novels which still hold the reader's attention today.

Oppenheim's books, including the four omnibus volumes, total 151; he published published 109 novels, of which 12 have not been published in the United States (unless in pirated editions). Several of his novels appeared under the pseudonym "Anthony Partridge."

E. Phillips Oppenheim

# Choose from Thousands of 1stWorldLibrary Classics By

A. M. Barnard
Ada Leverson
Adolphus William Ward
Aesop
Agatha Christie
Alexander Aaronsohn
Alexander Kielland
Alexandre Dumas
Alfred Gatty
Alfred Ollivant
Alice Duer Miller
Alice Turner Curtis
Alice Dunbar
Allen Chapman
Alleyne Ireland
Ambrose Bierce
Amelia E. Barr
Amory H. Bradford
Andrew Lang
Andrew McFarland Davis
Andy Adams
Angela Brazil
Anna Alice Chapin
Anna Sewell
Annie Besant
Annie Hamilton Donnell
Annie Payson Call
Annie Roe Carr
Annonaymous
Anton Chekhov
Archibald Lee Fletcher
Arnold Bennett
Arthur C. Benson
Arthur Conan Doyle
Arthur M. Winfield
Arthur Ransome
Arthur Schnitzler
Arthur Train
Atticus
B.H. Baden-Powell
B. M. Bower
B. C. Chatterjee
Baroness Emmuska Orczy
Baroness Orczy
Basil King
Bayard Taylor
Ben Macomber
Bertha Muzzy Bower
Bjornstjerne Bjornson

Booth Tarkington
Boyd Cable
Bram Stoker
C. Collodi
C. E. Orr
C. M. Ingleby
Carolyn Wells
Catherine Parr Traill
Charles A. Eastman
Charles Amory Beach
Charles Dickens
Charles Dudley Warner
Charles Farrar Browne
Charles Ives
Charles Kingsley
Charles Klein
Charles Hanson Towne
Charles Lathrop Pack
Charles Romyn Dake
Charles Whibley
Charles Willing Beale
Charlotte M. Braeme
Charlotte M. Yonge
Charlotte Perkins Stetson
Clair W. Hayes
Clarence Day Jr.
Clarence E. Mulford
Clemence Housman
Confucius
Coningsby Dawson
Cornelis DeWitt Wilcox
Cyril Burleigh
D. H. Lawrence
Daniel Defoe
David Garnett
Dinah Craik
Don Carlos Janes
Donald Keyhoe
Dorothy Kilner
Dougan Clark
Douglas Fairbanks
E. Nesbit
E. P. Roe
E. Phillips Oppenheim
E. S. Brooks
Earl Barnes
Edgar Rice Burroughs
Edith Van Dyne
Edith Wharton

Edward Everett Hale
Edward J. O'Biren
Edward S. Ellis
Edwin L. Arnold
Eleanor Atkins
Eleanor Hallowell Abbott
Eliot Gregory
Elizabeth Gaskell
Elizabeth McCracken
Elizabeth Von Arnim
Ellem Key
Emerson Hough
Emilie F. Carlen
Emily Bronte
Emily Dickinson
Enid Bagnold
Enilor Macartney Lane
Erasmus W. Jones
Ernie Howard Pie
Ethel May Dell
Ethel Turner
Ethel Watts Mumford
Eugene Sue
Eugenie Foa
Eugene Wood
Eustace Hale Ball
Evelyn Everett-green
Everard Cotes
F. H. Cheley
F. J. Cross
F. Marion Crawford
Fannie E. Newberry
Federick Austin Ogg
Ferdinand Ossendowski
Fergus Hume
Florence A. Kilpatrick
Fremont B. Deering
Francis Bacon
Francis Darwin
Frances Hodgson Burnett
Frances Parkinson Keyes
Frank Gee Patchin
Frank Harris
Frank Jewett Mather
Frank L. Packard
Frank V. Webster
Frederic Stewart Isham
Frederick Trevor Hill
Frederick Winslow Taylor

Friedrich Kerst
Friedrich Nietzsche
Fyodor Dostoyevsky
G.A. Henty
G.K. Chesterton
Gabrielle E. Jackson
Garrett P. Serviss
Gaston Leroux
George A. Warren
George Ade
Geroge Bernard Shaw
George Cary Eggleston
George Durston
George Ebers
George Eliot
George Gissing
George MacDonald
George Meredith
George Orwell
George Sylvester Viereck
George Tucker
George W. Cable
George Wharton James
Gertrude Atherton
Gordon Casserly
Grace E. King
Grace Gallatin
Grace Greenwood
Grant Allen
Guillermo A. Sherwell
Gulielma Zollinger
Gustav Flaubert
H. A. Cody
H. B. Irving
H.C. Bailey
H. G. Wells
H. H. Munro
H. Irving Hancock
H. R. Naylor
H. Rider Haggard
H. W. C. Davis
Haldeman Julius
Hall Caine
Hamilton Wright Mabie
Hans Christian Andersen
Harold Avery
Harold McGrath
Harriet Beecher Stowe
Harry Castlemon
Harry Coghill
Harry Houidini

Hayden Carruth
Helent Hunt Jackson
Helen Nicolay
Hendrik Conscience
Hendy David Thoreau
Henri Barbusse
Henrik Ibsen
Henry Adams
Henry Ford
Henry Frost
Henry James
Henry Jones Ford
Henry Seton Merriman
Henry W Longfellow
Herbert A. Giles
Herbert Carter
Herbert N. Casson
Herman Hesse
Hildegard G. Frey
Homer
Honore De Balzac
Horace B. Day
Horace Walpole
Horatio Alger Jr.
Howard Pyle
Howard R. Garis
Hugh Lofting
Hugh Walpole
Humphry Ward
Ian Maclaren
Inez Haynes Gillmore
Irving Bacheller
Isabel Cecilia Williams
Isabel Hornibrook
Israel Abrahams
Ivan Turgenev
J.G.Austin
J. Henri Fabre
J. M. Barrie
J. M. Walsh
J. Macdonald Oxley
J. R. Miller
J. S. Fletcher
J. S. Knowles
J. Storer Clouston
J. W. Duffield
Jack London
Jacob Abbott
James Allen
James Andrews
James Baldwin

James Branch Cabell
James DeMille
James Joyce
James Lane Allen
James Lane Allen
James Oliver Curwood
James Oppenheim
James Otis
James R. Driscoll
Jane Abbott
Jane Austen
Jane L. Stewart
Janet Aldridge
Jens Peter Jacobsen
Jerome K. Jerome
Jessie Graham Flower
John Buchan
John Burroughs
John Cournos
John F. Kennedy
John Gay
John Glasworthy
John Habberton
John Joy Bell
John Kendrick Bangs
John Milton
John Philip Sousa
John Taintor Foote
Jonas Lauritz Idemil Lie
Jonathan Swift
Joseph A. Altsheler
Joseph Carey
Joseph Conrad
Joseph E. Badger Jr
Joseph Hergesheimer
Joseph Jacobs
Jules Vernes
Julian Hawthrone
Julie A Lippmann
Justin Huntly McCarthy
Kakuzo Okakura
Karle Wilson Baker
Kate Chopin
Kenneth Grahame
Kenneth McGaffey
Kate Langley Bosher
Kate Langley Bosher
Katherine Cecil Thurston
Katherine Stokes
L. A. Abbot
L. T. Meade

L. Frank Baum
Latta Griswold
Laura Dent Crane
Laura Lee Hope
Laurence Housman
Lawrence Beasley
Leo Tolstoy
Leonid Andreyev
Lewis Carroll
Lewis Sperry Chafer
Lilian Bell
Lloyd Osbourne
Louis Hughes
Louis Joseph Vance
Louis Tracy
Louisa May Alcott
Lucy Fitch Perkins
Lucy Maud Montgomery
Luther Benson
Lydia Miller Middleton
Lyndon Orr
M. Corvus
M. H. Adams
Margaret E. Sangster
Margret Howth
Margaret Vandercook
Margaret W. Hungerford
Margret Penrose
Maria Edgeworth
Maria Thompson Daviess
Mariano Azuela
Marion Polk Angellotti
Mark Overton
Mark Twain
Mary Austin
Mary Catherine Crowley
Mary Cole
Mary Hastings Bradley
Mary Roberts Rinehart
Mary Rowlandson
M. Wollstonecraft Shelley
Maud Lindsay
Max Beerbohm
Myra Kelly
Nathaniel Hawthrone
Nicolo Machiavelli
O. F. Walton
Oscar Wilde

Owen Johnson
P.G. Wodehouse
Paul and Mabel Thorne
Paul G. Tomlinson
Paul Severing
Percy Brebner
Percy Keese Fitzhugh
Peter B. Kyne
Plato
Quincy Allen
R. Derby Holmes
R. L. Stevenson
R. S. Ball
Rabindranath Tagore
Rahul Alvares
Ralph Bonehill
Ralph Henry Barbour
Ralph Victor
Ralph Waldo Emmerson
Rene Descartes
Ray Cummings
Rex Beach
Rex E. Beach
Richard Harding Davis
Richard Jefferies
Richard Le Gallienne
Robert Barr
Robert Frost
Robert Gordon Anderson
Robert L. Drake
Robert Lansing
Robert Lynd
Robert Michael Ballantyne
Robert W. Chambers
Rosa Nouchette Carey
Rudyard Kipling
Saint Augustine
Samuel B. Allison
Samuel Hopkins Adams
Sarah Bernhardt
Sarah C. Hallowell
Selma Lagerlof
Sherwood Anderson
Sigmund Freud
Standish O'Grady
Stanley Weyman
Stella Benson
Stella M. Francis

Stephen Crane
Stewart Edward White
Stijn Streuvels
Swami Abhedananda
Swami Parmananda
T. S. Ackland
T. S. Arthur
The Princess Der Ling
Thomas A. Janvier
Thomas A Kempis
Thomas Anderton
Thomas Bailey Aldrich
Thomas Bulfinch
Thomas De Quincey
Thomas Dixon
Thomas H. Huxley
Thomas Hardy
Thomas More
Thornton W. Burgess
U. S. Grant
Upton Sinclair
Valentine Williams
Various Authors
Vaughan Kester
Victor Appleton
Victor G. Durham
Victoria Cross
Virginia Woolf
Wadsworth Camp
Walter Camp
Walter Scott
Washington Irving
Wilbur Lawton
Wilkie Collins
Willa Cather
Willard F. Baker
William Dean Howells
William le Queux
W. Makepeace Thackeray
William W. Walter
William Shakespeare
Winston Churchill
Yei Theodora Ozaki
Yogi Ramacharaka
Young E. Allison
Zane Grey